# ANOTHER
# MOTHER

Other Books by
Ruthann
Robson

# ANOTHER
# MOTHER

A NOVEL

## RUTHANN
## ROBSON

*St. Martin's Press* ✳ *New York*

Design by Jaye Zimet

Library of Congress Cataloging-in-Publication Data
Robson, Ruthann.
    Another mother  /  Ruthann Robson.
        p.    cm.
    ISBN 0-312-13431-2
    1. Lesbian  mothers—United  States—Fiction.
2.  Women  lawyers—United  States—Fiction.
3. Lesbians—United States—Fiction.
I. Title.
PS3568.O3187A83    1995
813'.54—dc20                          95-31727
                                        CIP

First Edition: October 1995

10 9 8 7 6 5 4 3 2 1

# CONTENTS

# ANOTHER

# MOTHER

OCTOBERS

OCTOBERS

**OCTOBERS**

OCTOBERS

OCTOBERS

"Evangelina?" Claire's voice is raw, childish.

"Hello," Angie says.

"I just called to tell you one thing," Claire announces.

"What?"

"I've just been thinking about how awful you treat me." Claire says this, as if she has never said it before, as if she had not said it yesterday, or last week, or last month, or last year.

"I don't treat you awful." A flat denial.

"Maybe you don't realize you do, but you do."

"Well, I don't think I do."

"That's because you are around people who don't know how to treat other people except awful."

Silence.

"Like your newest girlfriend. That awful woman you live with. Doesn't know how to treat you. Or treat anyone."

Silence.

"And that kid. No respect at all. You pick that girl out of the gutter in Argentina or wherever; her own mother doesn't even want her, and the kid treats you awful."

Silence.

"Of course, you did give her such a stupid name. No wonder she treats you so awful."

More silence.

Then, finally, denial: "No one treats me awful."

"Well, you must have learned somewhere," Claire concludes, "since you treat me so awful."

Silence.

Less silence. Coughing.

Claire continues: "Well, I guess it's just obvious. You love your girlfriend and don't love me. Probably never loved me. It doesn't matter to you that I've worked like a dog for you. I hope the three of you are very happy playing house. I haven't even seen your new house. But so what, do you think I care? I used to know everything about you, until you got that kid. Off the fucking street. Love that kid more than me. And you never even liked kids. But don't think I care. I don't care about who you're sleeping with. Or about you. Just like you don't care about me."

Silence.

"I'm sorry if this sounds harsh, but I just wanted to share my feelings with you."

More silence.

"Well, do you have anything to say?" Claire asks conversationally.

"Do *you*?" Angie asks. She is not startled by Claire's change in tone, but does hope it will last until she gets off the phone.

"Oh, I meant to tell you. There was this program yesterday. About people losing their kids because, because, you know."

Angie does not mention Claire's persistent inability to say the word *lesbian*, but only asks: "Was one of them Sharon Delsarado?"

"Maybe. That sounds like one."

"From North—or South—Dakota, with two kids and a fundamentalist husband?"

"Yeah," Claire agrees.

"That's my client," Angie says.

"Not a bad-looking woman."

"I guess not." Angie does not want to tell Claire she cannot really remember what Sharon Delsarado looks like. And Angie does not tell Claire that she had advised her client against appearing on the TV talk-show segment: *Lesbians Losing Children*. But Sharon had said she wanted someone to hear her side of the story.

"Looked respectable. And you know, no woman should lose her kids."

So at least one person had heard Sharon's side, even if it was through the sparkling if temporary husk of an antidepressant. And at least one person had sided with Sharon and against the fundamentalist former husband, who had also appeared on the show.

"That's why I'm working on her case." Angie agrees. Wondering if maybe Claire is even slightly impressed that little Evangelina has become important enough to be a lawyer for someone important enough to be on TV.

"Well, at least you've learned about blood . . . blood is thicker than water. Isn't that how the expression goes? I wonder if you'd work on the case of that mother whose kid you stole?" Claire laughs. "Would you help her? The kid with the stupid name? Would you help her mother? Help her mother get her kid back from the nuts who stole her? Bought her like she was a dog. Would you help her?"

Silence.

More silence.

"Well, do you have anything to say to me?" Claire asks, again. But this time there is nothing conversational in her tone.

"I don't know what to say."

"Nothing to say to me? Nothing at all? Nothing good happened to you yesterday that you might like to share with me? Nothing you thought about me that you might like to tell me? Nothing to say to me? I bet you have lots to say to your girlfriend. And that brat with the stupid name. But nothing to me. I might as well be dead. I might as well just kill myself and get it over with. Maybe when I'm dead you'll think of something to say to me. But of course, then it will be too late. Just too late. Good-bye."

"Good-bye," she says to Claire. Polite.

She hangs up.

Silence.

She unplugs the phone. Then takes it off the hook. Then replugs it, putting on the answering machine. Then takes it off the hook again.

Silence. A long long river, a lifetime of barely moving water. Her silence. Deep. Deliberate. Defiant. Silence. Her compassion and her guilt and her denial and her loyalty all concentrated into the numb silt of silence.

She puts the receiver back on the hook, waiting for the red light to signal the auto-answer. Claire always hangs up if the answering machine is on.

She wanders around the house she shares with Rachel, her lover, and Skye, their daughter. Looks out each wood-framed window, out at the woods preserved through restrictive zoning and conservation laws. She is surrounded by trees she has learned to name. Elm. Amply leafed, but poised like yellow waves about to crash. Sugar maple. Looking as if only a part of them has turned red in shock at the future, while other parts remain a lulling green. Oak. Heavy branches wound with coral snakes of vines, brilliantly ugly and maybe even poisionous.

It is important to know the right names. It is the difference between *Rhus toxicondendron* and *Parthenocissus quinquefolia,* the difference between poison ivy and Virginia creeper. The wrong name for the wrong plant would confuse Skye. The wrong name for a person could ruin everything. The wrong name on the right pleading would offend the court clerk, who would send it back to Angie.

She picks up a stack of catalogs and goes to the kitchen table, back to her cold coffee, which waits for her like an imaginary forever-faithful former lover. In catalog time, the seasons can be rearranged; it can be approaching spring. She chooses one of her favorites: *HOME,* with a sun for the O. She reads the descriptions. The text is full of promises: Softness. Comfort. Absorbency. She looks at the photographs. An older woman, with lavender-white hair, sits on a bed, reading a letter and smiling. The bathrobe is ballerina length, silk-screened with violets and trimmed in white terry. The bed is brimming with a violet-printed dust ruffle, violet-printed comforter cover, violet-printed pillow cases, breakfast pillows, and neckrolls. Light from a window, through the pouf valance in matching violet-studded print. Towels, solid shades of lilac (or possibly dusty grape), woven of combed cotton, neatly folded, on a chair. The towels, the chair, the curtain, the bedclothes, the bathrobe, all for sale. But not the light, what Angie really needs approaching winter, and not the woman, what she really wants. Another mother. A mother who is not Claire. Or a mother who is only Claire at her best, brushing Angie's hair gently. This mother ordered from a catalog, complete with a guarantee.

She should order something from the catalog, something comforting, something soft and absorbent. She lifts the receiver from the table, achieves a dial tone. Instead of the toll-free number, she pushes the speed-dial. In a moment, her own voice greets her, telling her she is not in her office. She presses her code, retrieving her Voicemail. Seven new messages. She writes them down, comforted by her efficiency and her Book. She loves her appointment Book the way other dykes love their jackets: black leather worn into softness. She loves its tabs and organizers, its graph paper with squares small enough to impose order, its colored paper with hues deep enough to inspire adventure.

She tucks her Book—and the *HOME* catalog—into her briefcase. Flings her briefcase into her cocoon of a car. Shakes her head, free of Claire, free in her phoneless car. Climbs into the bucket seat thinking—as she always does—that the seat seems speckled as red as her lover Rachel's cunt. And then thinking—as she always does—that she makes this comparison every time she gets into her little car. A mental ritual. But perhaps more like a hopeless reiteration of some forgotten originary moment; a moment that keeps its promise that time is irrelevant. A moment, like sex perhaps, that obliterates past and future both. A moment engorged with itself and only itself. A moment her mind pulls toward, rehearsing incessantly even as it is convinced that the moment cannot be recaptured; that the moment has not yet occurred. Still, this longing for a moment that renders the present superfluous. And the past and future irrelevant.

Angie struggles to reorient herself. To time. To place. Today. Car. The passenger seat is shiny, virginal. She runs her thumb across its vinyl. Today. Car. Not then. Not there. Not Claire.

She checks the gas gauge, the oil gauge, the safety-belt signal. Her habits are those of a careful driver, although a driver who is sometimes too tired to recognize roads she passes every day and often wonders if she missed her exit and is on the wrong bridge going the wrong way. She shifts the gears to back out of her driveway, struggling with reverse a bit and keeping her left foot a little too long on the clutch. Her habits are also those of a driver who taught herself to drive, a driver who bought a six-hundred-dollar Volkswagen with a standard shift she could not yet operate, because she wanted to be the kind of person who could.

"Evangelina?" Claire's voice is floating, drifting.

"Yes?" she asks, although she can barely recognize the name Claire calls her.

"Are you all right?"

"Yes, I'm fine. Fine."

"I was so worried when you called last night."

"Sorry. Didn't mean to worry you."

"Do you want me to come get you? Bring you home?"

"No. No. I'm fine. I'm going home tomorrow. Getting out of here."

"Do the doctors know anything else?"

"They think it was an allergic reaction," Angie lies.

"To what?"

"Something I ate. Maybe in the cafeteria."

"You shouldn't eat that terrible stuff. Who knows where it comes from? The cans could have been rusty."

"I guess," Angie says.

"Well, don't eat there again."

"I won't."

"I've got to go now. I just got home from work and my program's coming on. I'll call you later. Or you call me."

"Love you," Angie says.

"I love you too, Evangelina." Claire makes kissing sounds.

The hospital room is cool, like autumn in the mountains. Something yellow-green drips into Angie's arm. On the food tray, the extra plate nests discreetly under its twin. The mashed potatoes had been best. The nurse brings her a Coke. Another blanket. Angie wishes for a quilt, something soft. Angie wishes for a visitor, someone comforting.

But she cannot think of anyone other than the hospital workers who might glide through the wide corridors to her door. She cannot think of anyone she might want to stand next to her narrow metal bed. Not the bankruptcy judge teaching the class she'd been going to go to if she had not collapsed, in his velveteen jacket and men's cologne. Not the law students who ran to get help or the law students who stayed to watch her get whiter and whiter and maybe even convulse, or the law students who looked away.

Not even the other dyke law student, the one who found Angie sprawled on the floor. Especially not her. Not any professor—not even her favorite, the criminal law professor with a beard and accompanying liberal politics, and not even the only woman, the family law professor with a father on the state supreme court and three divorces.

And not the law school dean she works for as a research assistant, and not the lawyer she works for as a law clerk, and not the manager of the nightclub she works for as a bartender. And not the trustees she pours for at scholarship teas. She would tell them it was an allergy, as she told Claire. An allergic reaction.

And she would not tell the law school bursar, Mr. Frame, especially not him. That wonderful flaming faggot who managed to flounce even without the bottom half of the leg he had lost in World War II. That financial official who juggled Angie's scholarships and loans, trying to package her into something like survival. That man who scratched numbers across his desk during her first semester to explain the requirements to keep her scholarship, monitored her grade-point average like a mother hen, and then crowed when Angie made dean's list. She could not tell Mr. Frame; could not tell him that his careful calculations had not included Claire; could not tell him that she sent her government Guaranteed Student Loan check to her mother. Would not tell him.

She would not tell him—tell any of them—about the diagnosis on the chart, clanging at the bottom of her bed. About malnutrition. Exhaustion. Dehydration. She would not risk anyone knowing that. Not in her last year. Not when she is so close to graduation. And she would graduate, she would bet all of them that, all of the ones who are not visitors. All of the ones who must not know she is this frail, this weak, this close to not making it. She is going to make it. What she wants more than almost anything: to graduate from law school and get a job that might let her make a difference.

Angie turns on the television. And then she sleeps.

"Evangelina?" Claire's voice is garbled, but frenzied.

"Yes," she says, not reminding Claire that she is changing her name from Evangelina.

"Have you made up your mind about Christmas?"

"It's only October," she says.

"It's fine with me if you don't come home for Christmas. Have you even told me when you're coming home? Even mentioned to me that you want to see me? Are even glad I'm still alive? But don't expect me to still be alive whenever you get around to getting your ass back home. Don't expect me to keep from dying just so that you can visit me whenever you get damn good and ready. Think you're so smart at that stupid college. You're too young to be in college, I told you. Can't even wait to graduate high school like everybody else. Think you're so smart, but you couldn't even pass Home Ec, could you? The only practical thing they tried to teach you and you failed. Failed 'cause you're too damn smart, or think you are. Ran away to college like you're some genius. Or couldn't you wait to get away from me? And what do they teach you at that college? How to hate your own mother? How stupid I am? How just because I didn't go to college I ain't worth talking to? Well, let me tell you again, Little Miss Smart-ass, I didn't even get through fourth grade. Do you hear that? Fourth grade. So you can tell all your teachers that, then see how smart they think you are."

Angie presses the receiver closer to her ear, hoping the woman in the room cannot hear. Hoping the woman in the room would just disappear. Hoping Claire will wear herself out and hang up. Finally, Claire announces her good-bye.

"Problems?" the woman asks.

"Not really. Just complications." Angie likes to thinks she is vague enough to imply a former lover.

"As you get older, those things get better," the woman promises. Then she kisses Angie on the neck, pulling her toward the bed.

"I can't," she says.

"You can," the woman counters.

"You're right," she says, but then, without getting dressed, leaves the woman alone in the room. The woman she met outside the bar last night. The woman she drove to her apartment in her Volkswagen. The woman she wants.

She is becoming Angie for this woman, and for other women. She is inventing herself from scraps of the counterculture: mimeographed gay liberation, pamphlet feminism, and the swaggering but desperate phrases of a Mick Jagger ballad. Evangelina is becoming Angie ("Ain't it good to be alive?"); a radicalesbian (one word); and a Stonewall commemorator (if not survivor). She has cut to the quick the curls that Claire had coaxed from her head. She has been tattooed in a place she thinks she can hide from Claire. She is hanging out on the fringes— leather bars, women's collectives, Stones concerts—too young to be taken seriously but young enough to be tolerated. From the faggots she is learning how to dance and dish and drink. From the dykes she is learning how to fuck and think and dress. From the rockers she is learning what to avoid.

Angie returns from the kitchen she shares with several roommates, carrying two glasses filled with vodka. Three ice cubes, precisely. And a rind of lemon expertly twisted on the rim.

"Cheers," the woman says, smiling, clinking Angie's glass with her own.

Angie sips. Sips deep until she can feel the beautiful burning drip in her chest and her head starts to clear.

The woman rolls a joint. They share it. Angie sucks until the burning evaporates into clouds that roll across the horizon of her skull.

This time, when the woman kisses her neck, Angie responds. The woman's hands spread across Angie's back, Angie's breasts, Angie's ass.

"You're so soft," the woman says. You're so damn young, the woman thinks. Too young, the woman almost thinks. You're so soft. The woman stops thinking, because Angie is moving against her. Hard. Hard. Hard against each other in the blurry morning.

NOVEMBER

NOVEMBER

**NOVEMBER**

NOVEMBER

NOVEMBER

The shadows from the suspension cables of the bridge make a grid; the little car is a dot plotting its progress through the graph of traffic. Angie feels safe somehow, in the clot of crawling cars, nearly becalmed over the wide river. She feels rewarded by excellent reception from her favorite modern-rock radio station, comforted. On mornings like these, as she expertly flips a token into the toll basket, she is impressed with her own competence and can even congratulate herself on her own survival and successful self-invention. She is solidly Angie (only Claire calls her Evangelina anymore, and no one screams the Stones song in her face); still radical and lesbian (two words now); still a Stonewall supporter (her name on computerized mailing lists for Pride this and Pride that). Her hair is insistently short, but fashionable—fashion having changed more than her haircut. Her tattoo is indelibly on her thigh, although Claire long ago joined the ranks of the women who have seen it. Angie still knows how to dance and drink and dish, although she is more circumspect now, or perhaps only less anxious. And she still knows how to think and fuck and dress, although she is less circumspect now, or perhaps more anxious. And she still knows what to avoid, although she does not always do so.

Angie also knows that for all her urgent inventing, some things have just happened to her, without intention or cause. Sometimes having a job that could be called a career feels like that, arbitrary and impulsive and lucky. Other times, work feels like her most innovative invention, something that the faggots and dykes and even Mike Jagger, that rock-and-roll economist, had not suggested. Something beyond cultivation or rebellion. If she understood more, she would name it ambition, but she has denied herself that word. Instead it is a whisper, a glance, a scent that she has followed, or that has followed her. It is how she understands herself; how she understands her lover and maybe even their child; how she understands her clients—the ones who are lesbian mothers fighting for custody of their children, and the ones who are lesbian mothers indicted for the murder of their children.

Almost an hour out of the valley, she parks her car on a street of brick buildings in one of the city's less impressive boroughs, attaching to her steering wheel an antitheft device that looks like a red crowbar. Some of her colleagues have had their cars stolen, which only adds to the beleaguered feeling of working at Triple-F. Triple-F is Futures for Families, Inc., so named in the spirit of subversion at the beginning of the Reagan regime, when it had seemed like a reclamation, a resistance to the narrowing definition of *family*. Over the years, it has lived both up and down to its innocuous name. Angie still cringes every time she says she works for an organization called Futures for Families, even though everyone in progressive legal circles knows that Triple-F is cutting edge on poverty issues, reproductive issues, and sometimes even lesbian and gay issues. As the resident dyke, Angie is responsible for the lesbian agenda, an agenda she must fit within the context of families with a future. Lesbian-mother custody litigation is the best fit: What progressive person could doubt that the family should be expanded to welcome even lesbians? Sometimes it seems positively trendy, even as being a lesbian seems trendy. The patina of trendiness, however, does not extend to her work representing lesbians who want less time in prison instead of more time with their children.

Today's first meeting, for which she is only fifteen minutes late, does not involve the lesbian agenda of Triple-F, except to the extent that the people who live in SROs, those single-room-occupancy "hotels" that dot the city, are lesbians. She arrives during a discussion that is not about SROs or the people who inhabit them but about corporate regulations and possible manipulations. Angie likes legal talk, even wishes for more, especially if it would replace the defensive soliloquies that Roger and Steven quickly steer toward. At Triple-F, rampant self-blaming is second only to blaming the organization as the sub-agenda

of every meeting. Angie had long since decided that these big-boy attorneys thought that if only they were bigger, or the organization more
boyish, all problems could be solved by filing a lawsuit. Before the
meeting is over, she excuses herself and walks out, gently gliding on her
privilege as a senior attorney.

"Problems, Ange?" Roger asks her later, his head in her office
doorway. He sounds sincere but also wants to let her know he knows
she came late and left early.

"Not really." Angie looks up from her desk. Then she winks at
him, almost tauntingly. Actually, she likes Roger, although there are a
lot of reasons not to like him. He is a white guy with a brown beard and
a penchant for psychoanalysis of the Jungian variety. With almost no
provocation, he will expound upon the woman who lives in his soul,
usually interrupting real women to give voice to his inner woman.
Angie told him he should name his inner woman, but Roger replied
that names were not necessary. So Angie named the inner woman Octavia. Angie asks Roger about Octavia, familiarly, in casual conversation, so that people new to the office think for months that Octavia is
Roger's lover, or someone both Angie and Roger know and like. Angie
writes Roger memos, telling Roger "Check with Octavia." Octavia
never memos back, but Angie can hear echoes of Octavia in certain of
Roger's memos.

"Come by for coffee," Roger invites. "I have a scoop on tomorrow's litigation priority meeting that might interest you."

"Now?"

"Yeah," Roger answers, stroking his beard. Angie suspects that
Roger only has a beard so he can stroke it at moments like these. Better
than cigarettes. Not as good as coffee.

Angie picks up her mail at the front desk before going down the
corridor to Roger's office. The door is open, Roger is not there, and the
Braun coffeemaker is potless. Maybe Roger is getting the water. Angie
looks around for her cup, sure that she has left it here. She stares at the
German coffeemaker as if it will birth a cup, preferably her aqua one
with the purple patterned cloud, but even a foam one would do.

Above the coffeemaker is Roger's favorite saying, a long quote in
French from the philosopher Foucault about how one could work
within the system and still stubbornly resist it. In needlepoint, no less.

The colors shading from one hue to the next in an imitation of subtlety. She and Roger had talked about it one day after Roger had lost a major appeal on a minor issue. She had sat in his office for hours that afternoon, listening to him talk. He was venting, angry at losing. Octavia apparently did not want to listen to him when he was like that. So Angie did. Even making him a cup of coffee from a fresh pot.

Waiting for Roger to return with the water, Angie sits in one of the vinyl chairs in Roger's office and leafs through the papers in her hands. All the slit-open envelopes are paper-clipped to letters, pleadings, and papers, date-stamped by Walter. Walter would know where her coffee cup had hidden. Dependable faggot secretary Walter, organization personified; a good memory for gossip and not a bad dancer.

Angie is cursing Walter in the next breath. Why hadn't he called her at home to tell her the *Delsarado* opinion had been faxed in? Why hadn't he buzzed her at work? Left a message on her Voicemail? He knew she'd been waiting for this. He had absolutely no sense of how this organization really worked. How important her cases were, just as important as everyone else's. Even if this one was "only" a custody case.

"Fuck. Just fuck." Angie is cursing more than Walter as she reads the opinion. Impossible. Reactionary. Barbaric. Written by the judge who had been so nice to her. The one who had smiled at her as she presented her argument. She had been eerily faultless; even she could not find a flaw. It was one of the best arguments she had given in her long years of practice. Her reasoning was solid; her voice was modulated. She did not even point her pen (like a gun, she'd been criticized), for she often did when she was riding her argument toward the shore of the judges' bench. She had responded to the questions of these five individual men, who looked rather cranky in their robes but had not lost the threads of her ingenious argument constructed around arcane state statutes. She had been the quintessential professional. But she had lost more than threads, she had lost, whole cloth.

And, shit, the Deuteronomy quote. Those solid black lines lifted from the King James version. In a footnote, but still there, supporting the judgment that denied her client custody of her child. Denied her client visitation with her child. For being a lesbian—not even an abusive or murderous one, just *one*. Maybe a little silly, a little too trusting, and maybe even a little confused about her sexuality, about whether or not she really is *one*. But she loses her kids for thinking she might be a lesbian, and maybe for thinking she should confide in her stupid fundamentalist husband about it. Sure it was North—or South—Dakota, but so what? These things just did not happen anymore. Not anywhere.

The words are so ugly Angie wants to scream. Not ugly in ways Angie admires, not ugly like *dyke*, like *fuck*, like *cunt*. No, these words are officially ugly in their multiple syllables: words like *deviant* and *sodomy* and *homosexuality*. Words that are clinical and legal and ugly. Words that win any argument, even against the words she had so carefully chosen for their comfort. But no words were comforting enough, not soft enough or absorbent enough. The judges refused to buy what she was trying to sell. She had lost. Lost.

Resistance is possible and necessary within the system, according to the French needlepoint above Roger's desk. Angie climbs onto the desk, taking the needlepoint down. She hoists up the window, looking at the alley three stories below. Let Octavia make another one.

"What the fuck are you doing?" Roger has the coffeepot, filled with water, in his hand.

Angie just looks at him. She will tell him. They will talk. But before she swallows again, so that she can speak, Roger is stammering at her.

"It isn't my fault," he protests. "Sit down. Let me make you a cup of coffee. And anyway, I think if we strategize a bit we can work this out. It's only *some* of the attorneys who are objecting to your newest cases. I'm on your side, Ange. We just have to come up with a principled reason why defending dykes who have killed their kids is within the mission of Futures for Families."

"Dykes?" Angie asks, finally putting down the needlepoint on Roger's desk.

"Well, I mean that only in the same spirit that you say it. 'Dykes.' Like it's some great accomplishment. I'm using it a friendly sort of way. Although maybe when we are talking about the murderers we should say 'lesbians.' It isn't such a great accomplishment to shoot off your own kid's head, is it? Yes, 'lesbians' definitely sounds a lot more friendly, don't you think?"

"What are you talking about?"

"I thought you heard."

"Heard what?"

"About tomorrow's meeting."

"What about it?"

"Steven and Terry want to reevaluate your current caseload for conformance to Triple-F priorities and consistency with the mission," Roger recites, then adds: "Something about kid-killers not really fostering a palatable future, even for lesbian families."

"Oh, Jesus."

Angie leaves Roger's office. Roger, most likely listening to Octavia, decides to leave Angie alone.

Angie closes the door to her own office. Takes out the catalog. *HOME,* the sun-*O* smeared with ink from her briefcase. She flips pages. Looks at the sheets. Towels. There's a madras shower curtain. Pure fun with a coordinating rug. The photograph has a baby in a footed bathtub. She takes out her Book. Grids a list of things to do. "Telephone Sharon Delsarado." Angie wishes she could write her client a letter, her only agony whether or not to enclose a copy of the opinion. But she will write only after she calls. Speaks to her; listens to her. Hears some whisper that follows her, or that she follows.

Angie flips through the pages of her Book, as if it is a catalog. Calendar pages by month and by week. Dotted with her own handwriting, sometimes obsessively neat and sometimes a scrawl. Lists of things to do. More lists. Addresses and phone numbers. She picks up the phone, does not check her messages, speed-dials Rachel's office. Leaves a just-tell-her-I-called message for her not-back-from-court-yet lover. Re-checks her calendar. Her day to pick up Skye. Checks her watch. Five hours. Dials Kim's home phone number. Gets the answering machine. Hangs up without leaving a message.

Looks in her Book for the page entitled "Sharon Delsarado," in her special section for pending cases, the hot-pink index tab announcing "Current Projects." After the client's name and address and phone number is the name and address and phone number of local counsel: that member in good standing of the state bar who vouched for Angie's integrity; that necessary signature on Angie's pro hac vice motion allowing her to practice law in a state in which she is not a member of the bar; that closeted-dyke attorney who should have telephoned her about the Delsarado opinion instead of merely sending it by fax. She looks at the attorney's number. Decides to call. Picks up the receiver. Does not dial. Looks at Sharon Delsarado's number. Decides she cannot call. Not now. Closes her Book.

Leafs through the rest of her mail. On the front page of the *Law Journal*, there is Chelsea's case. And inside, Chelsea's photograph. Smiling. Angie thinks she should telephone Chelsea, congratulatory. Or walk down to her office. But she does not think she could negotiate the conversation without betraying her own resentments.

Some people were born to privilege, Angie knows. The right schools, the right contacts, the right parents who made it all not only possible, but probable. Had there ever been any doubt that Chelsea would have her photograph in some newspaper smiling? Years ago, her options for publicity would have been limited to her debut, her engagement, her marriage, and her election as chairwoman of the Garden Circle. But thanks to women whom Chelsea would disparage as unprofessional, she can flash her newsprint smile as the postfeminist version of a debutante, a successful career woman—although married, of course, as she reminded people with incessant references to "Chad, my husband, who is also an attorney."

Angie does not feel better because Chelsea's case is something about which Angie cares, the enforcement of a protective order for a battered woman. Angie feels worse. Angie knows too many women, many of them dykes, who worked in the shelter movement and were now without work. Gradually expelled from the battered women's shelters, from the domestic-violence projects, from the movement fast becoming an agency. For being dykes. For not having credentials. Not welcome at the conferences, in the courtrooms, as the social science and psychological experts. Instead, people like Chelsea win the cases and have their smiling photographs admired. It seems as if this simply happens.

Angie is still looking at Chelsea's photograph when Kim walks into Angie's office, knocking but not waiting for a reply. Kim is one of the things that happens to Angie, has happened. Maybe every person in her life has merely happened to her, Angie thinks. Even Skye, almost an accessory of Rachel. Maybe even Rachel, the coincidence of mutual attraction and the opportunity to explore it. Definitely Claire, for what could be more accidental than one's mother?

Kim's ambition is to be inevitable in Angie's life. It is an ambition that she cannot articulate, perhaps because it encompasses all her other ambitions. To be popular and pretty, but also to be daring and independent. To be an adult who does not need a father to pay her tuition or a mother to introduce her to yet another "nice young man." Kim has lost count of the times she has come out to her parents. Told them over and over and over that she is a lesbian. Told them that there is nothing wrong with being a lesbian; that there are lesbians in every profession. And she is going to be a professional lesbian. With a lover who is also a professional, and is very well respected and almost famous.

Kim keeps only her hair ambiguous, either brown or blond, depending more on the disposition of the describer than on the season or the shampoo. It is cut bluntly, with an almost sinister slant to the jawbone, a reiteration of her jutting bicuspids. Angie thinks the hair rather silly but the mouth inexplicably sexy.


"Such a pretty mouth and such silly words," Angie says.

"I'm serious. I want you to masturbate while I watch." Kim is looking at Angie.

"You might very well be serious," Angie sounds—even to herself—like the senior attorney Kim expects her to be. Kim is an intern at Triple-F, a law student at a local school, and still negotiating the boundaries between fantasy and reality, especially with respect to Angie.

"Well, why not?" Kim is challenging, coaxing, struggling for the right tone.

"I don't."

"Masturbate? Or do it in front of people?"

"I don't."

"Never? I don't believe that." Kim has abandoned her efforts to look sexy.

"Believe what you want. I don't."

"Well, would you like to watch me?"

"Not really."

"Okay. Sorry." Kim pouts.

"Look, don't get insulted. I'm just conventional."

"I'm not insulted. I just want to make you happy."

Angie does not take Kim's cue.

Kim becomes more obvious:

"You know, if I had only six months to live, or even a year, I'd want to spend every second with you." Kim's fingers are circling the tattoo of the woman she calls her lover in conversations with people who do not know Angie.

Angie closes her eyes against Kim. But she moves her head closer to Kim's mouth. Kim takes this as a positive sign, as she has learned to take any of Angie's ambiguous signals. She strokes Angie's short hair.

Angie misses Rachel in the stupidity of afternoons like these. Rachel's love is soft, enduring, comfortable. Angie tries to remember a time when Rachel's love was jagged and insecure, but she cannot. Just as she cannot recall being an adult without being with Rachel. Rachel does not think love is tested in melodramatic devotion.

And neither does Angie. Besides, Angie has had enough of devotion; she has Claire. Claire who says she would die for Evangelina; Claire who says she has sacrificed her life for Evangelina.

Claire believes in sacrifice, in melodramatic devotion, in having only six months to live. Claire watches them on TV. Talk shows having replaced soap operas, but all of it is daytime drama. *Lesbians Losing Children* instead of *The Days of Our Lives*. Sharon Delsarado instead of a character actress playing Nurse Hughes. Claire rushes home from the seven-to-three shift at the textile factory to keep appointments with her favorites.

"What are you thinking about?" Kim asks, almost hopefully.

"Sharon Delsarado," Angie answers.

Kim sighs. This is the kind of drama she craves. When Angie tells her about the decision, Kim sits up in bed and makes bold proclamations about resistance, as if she is at a pep rally for the lesbian revolution.

This time, Angie is the one who sighs, exhausted. And then she is out of Kim's bed, looking at the list of things to do in her appointment Book. And then she is dressed and in her car. Alone, in her phoneless car, but somehow never less lonely than when she is cradled in her well-worn seat. Driving carefully on crumbling highways above frozen water, home toward Skye, toward Rachel. Home toward the telephone.

＊　＊　＊

Almost dark in the almost winter, but from this part of the bridge
Angie thinks the landscape looks like somewhere in northern California. A hump of backlit lavender, jutting into the water. The hills had
looked like a postcard to Angie, beautiful because they did not look like
the hills of her childhood, the ones turned inside out. And now this
piece of East Coast valley looks like the mist on the Pacific Rim. Nothing ever looks like itself, thinks Angie. It looks like something else. Or
not something else.

Even her house looks not-like-Claire's-house. The floors, the furniture, the ceilings, all struggle to be different from Claire's floors,
Claire's furniture, Claire's ceilings. Planked hardwood, not cheap shag
wall-to-wall; Swedish pine, not painted pressed wood; beamed and
peaked, not flat and low.

The differences are most exaggerated in the smallest of details:
Claire's house has no calendars, or maybe one, hidden in a kitchen cabinet, numbers floating, not even protected from each other by straight
black lines, on cheap tear-off paper stapled under a reproduction of a
covered bridge. Angie's house has thirteen calendars, counting as one
the three calendars in her Book (yearly, monthly, weekly), and as another one the three calendars in Rachel's Book, and not counting the
calendars in the checkbook registers, or in Rachel's watch, or in the
computer, or in the answering machine, or in the alarm clock, or in
the cars in the driveway. Counting the *365 Things Every Child Should
Know* daily calendar in Skye's room and counting the black-and-white
lunar calendar spiraling with its thirteen cycles in the hallway. And
counting the nine other dependable arrangements of grids, excuses for
twelve illustrations of this year's trendy theme: *Frida Kahlo* or *Georgia
O'Keeffe* or *Photographs by Annie Leibovitz* or *Intriguing Women* or
*Dykes to Watch Out For* or *Garden Herbs* or *Heal the Earth* or *Sacred
Places* or *A Celebration of Civil Rights.* Mostly the calendars are gifts,
perfect and inexpensive, from former clients, former lovers, and present
co-workers. If Angie and Rachel receive more than thirteen, they often
recycle them as presents to other former clients, other former lovers,
and anyone else they may have overlooked in the grim winter rush of
bestowing gifts.

The month showing on each calendar is always correct in Angie and Rachel's house, unlike that on any calendar that inhabits Claire's house. It is Angie who is scrupulous about meeting the deadline imposed each month, even the irregular lunar cycle. She turns the page of each calendar, flooded with reward. Her satisfaction is not due to the novelty of the image, or even derived from the implicit promise of new possibilities, or even attributable to the illusion of progress that marking time bestows. Instead, it is her ritual of polishing one flank in the suit of armor she wears in her constant battle to defend the present against the nasty surprise attacks of the past.

She checks the answering machine, knowing it does not register hang-ups.

Angie looks out the window, through the bare branches, for Skye. Happy, always happy, Skye. Running down the driveway from the yellow bus after a day at school. Knowing one of her mothers is always home, waiting for her. Waiting to say yes when she asks if she can have a fruit-by-the-foot, some sticky glucose marketed as healthy, as one hundred percent fruit. Waiting to remind her to put away her purple knapsack, which does not belong on the bench in the hall. Waiting to ask her if her coat is hung up in the hall closet, even if it always falls off the hanger when the door is slid shut.

Angie is amazed at Skye's happiness. She wants to pull the child toward her, as if by surrounding the small body she can absorb some of Skye's mystery. Absorb it before it disappears, for Angie is sure that Skye is soon to be a sullen adolescent, sure that there is no other way to be an adolescent than to be sullen. Just as Angie had been sure that Skye would turn gloomy the moment she became a third-grader, or started school, or went off to pre-school. The child who sang and skipped would soon be a memory. Happiness could be nothing if not temporary.

There are people, even people who call themselves friends of Angie and Rachel, who think it is only natural that Skye would be happy. "What a lucky child!" they exclaim, assuming that Skye is grateful for living in America with two white dykes, cushioned by their professional jobs if not their sexual status; assuming she is thankful for the chance to have a dog as a pet instead of as a meal. They overlook Skye's dull hair, her inability to draw, her lateral-S speech defect, and all the other imperfections that would cause them to fuss endlessly over their own children's happiness. They measure Skye against the tragic life they believe she would have led, in some country they can never remember, if she had not been rescued into civilization by adoption.

At dinner, Skye half listens to Rachel talk about her day, which is half more than Angie is listening. Angie is looking at the kitchen clock. Not tasting the takeout that Rachel brought home. Asking Rachel for the third time what time zone North—or it is South?—Dakota is in. "One hour behind us? Or two?"

"Isn't there one of those area code–time zone maps in your Book? Before the phone numbers?" Rachel asks.

Angie ignores Rachel's preferred solution of looking at the map in her Book. She does not want helpful suggestions from Rachel. She does not even want to talk to Rachel about this case, does not want to quell Rachel's anxiety or share her own, because underneath everything it is always there: the thick dread of every lesbian mother on the planet that her child will be removed from her. Removed by some ex-husband, some sperm donor, some relative. Removed by her own mother, her ex-lover, the state child protective services. Removed.

She wants some solution that will mean she can postpone calling Sharon Delsarado, forever.

The phone rings. Once. Twice. None of them moves to answer it. On the third ring, the machine blasts Angie's voice requesting a message at the tone. The dial tone blares.

"Another hang-up," Skye announces matter-of-factly.

Rachel's eyes and Angie's eyes exchange Claires.

Rachel waits a moment, then tries to make conversation: "This tea is so sweet it makes my teeth sing."

"Teeth don't sing," Skye announces.

"Mine do," Rachel says, "with tea this sweet. You should try it."

Skye takes a sip from Angie's offered glass. And then shakes her head against the taste.

"Too sweet?" Rachel teases.

"No. It tastes bitter or like mustard or something."

"Give me some," Angie says, taking the glass. Then: "Shit. How much sugar did I put in here?"

"Are your teeth singing?"

"I'll say. I don't see how you can drink this shit. It's not even summer."

"Do teeth really sing?" Skye asks, suddenly younger. She is at that incredible age where she teeters between adult and childhood realities—or perhaps every age is like that. But these days she is too old to hold Angie's hand on the street, and not too old to hug her white bear to sleep.

"No. It's just an expression."

"I don't think it is."

"Like a saying."

"But we haven't done that one at school." Skye's grade is collecting expressions, which appear on large sheets of paper at the back of their classroom at Meadowlark School. One evening, Skye and Angie and Rachel sat at the kitchen table thinking of all the expressions they had ever heard and letting Skye write them down. Letting Skye write down "A stitch in time saves nine," A penny saved is a penny earned," "Curiosity killed the cat." But not "Blood is thicker than water," which neither Rachel nor Angie said out loud although both of them thought of it.

" 'Teeth singing' is a different kind of expression."

"Oh. Like 'Spare the child and spoil their rods.' "

"That's 'Spare the rod and spoil the child.' " Rachel laughs. The saying that none of the children brought to the school. That none of the children knew. That Skye refused to believe was really a saying, really something anyone ever said, really some reality. Skye's proof was that the three of them had not thought of that saying on the night they laughed at the kitchen table remembering all the sayings they had ever heard. All the sayings. "Sticks and stones." Even after Rachel's patient explanation about rods being sticks, about beliefs that children who misbehaved should be hit, about slashes on flesh that could turn to scars, Skye did not believe.

It is still dinner, that private garden of innocuous and continuous conversation that the three of them have spent years cultivating, when Angie stands up, announces she is going to "make a business call," and goes into the room painted Apparition Blue, into the room that serves as a semi-office, into the room with the white phone dangling its extra-long powder-blue cord. From her Book, from her list of "Things to do," she finds Sharon's number, dials it. Waits for the answer. Three rings.

Sharon's voice is slurred. Loud. Oh shit, a drunk client when Angie needs to tell her something important. Something she will not be sure Sharon will remember and she will have to telephone her again tomorrow.

But Sharon already knows. She's describing the phone call from the fundamentalist former husband. She's saying how he said she'll never see her kids again. She's calling herself a dyke, a whore, a cunt-sucker, a butch, all the words the court did not use, did not have to use. She's announcing she does not want to stay in any godforsaken town, that she won't see her kids at all if she can only see them in the presence of some fucked-up relative, that she's moving to New York or San Francisco or somewhere civilized.

"Are you there alone?" Angie asks.

"What the hell do you care? I'm just another case, just another mother, only this one is one of your damn losers. Don't ask me if I'm alone. I'm not. I've got a hundred women here waiting to fuck the shit out of me, as soon as I get off this phone with my prissy-assed pussy-licking lawyer. Damn important New York lawyer. With some fancy organization. *'Can help me,'* she says, *'can win my appeal.'* Thinks she knows so much. Thinks because some shit-kicking rancher judge smiles at her she going to win my case. Don't know nothing about men, about people, about the kinds of people that live in places that ain't New York City. I wouldn't move there if you begged me. California is much more human. But I'm not staying here. I can tell you that."

"Sharon," Angie says, "Sharon, I'll file a motion for reargument."

"Do you think that will do anything?" Sharon Delsarado's hostility dulls slightly.

"It's possible."

"I'm not asking what's possible." Sharon's voice is sharp again, sharper. "I'm asking you, do you think it will do anything? Do you think the highest court in this state is going to change its mind about some fucking dyke and her two lousy kids? You already told me that there's no place else to go. No other court is—you said—'a realistic possibility.' Saying it to me as if you were using really big words that I might not understand. Like I don't know what *realistic* means. I'm being realistic. There isn't any other court that would help me."

"You're right. There's really no viable appeal." Angie remembers explaining to Sharon the enormous odds against the United States Supreme Court agreeing to review the case, and the even more enormous odds against that Reagan-stacked Court disagreeing with a state court in favor of a lesbian mother. But when she had explained that to Sharon it had been abstraction; now it is hopelessness. Angie wants to offer hope: "But we can try the South . . . the North . . . the state courts again."

"I'm sick of trying. Just sick of it." Sharon Delsarado is sobbing now. Huge gnawing sobs that would be screams except for their absence of even a hope that someone might pay attention to them.

Maybe, if she were younger, Angie thinks, she would throw herself into her little white car and drive all the way there, even exceeding the speed limit by more than five miles, and sit in Sharon Delsarado's kitchen and comfort her. Maybe if she were younger, Angie thinks, instead of sipping tea in Sharon's kitchen, she would dynamite the Supreme Court building. Or organize an activist group to kidnap the kids, so they could live with Sharon, underground, or in Australia. If only she were younger. Or not a lawyer. Not a prissy-assed pussy-licking lawyer.


Angie does not cry until she is tucking Skye into bed. Skye is feeling too old to be tucked in, so Angie pretends she is merely checking for something, anything. She ruffles through Skye's hair, the hair that should be shiny blue-black but instead is dun-colored and limp. A glop on the pillow, unresponsive as Angie strokes it. Wondering how it is that she has happened to have this precious child in her life, this child whom she loves more than she ever thought possible.

Angie loves Skye's bed, one of the high wooden ones like a bunk bed without the bottom bunk. She had promised it to Skye before she knew these high beds were expensive. But then she had found one, some assembly required. Rachel and she had put it together, the directions from the Swedish company without words, only pictures. Skye loves the bed, but Angie suspects that she loves it more than Skye does. Angie loves it because she does not have to lean over when she pretends she is not tucking Skye into the covers, when she kisses Skye's forehead. Angie doesn't need any mirrors in the room to watch herself mothering Skye. The image would be better, Angie thinks, if she had on a long pink nightgown—maybe with a satin tie at the neck and a bit of ruffle, covered by a matching robe—instead of the ripped Lavender Law T-shirt she wears to bed. She kisses Skye again.

What she wants to do, in this moment, and what she knows she wants to do, in this same moment, is more than a maternal kiss on the forehead. She wants to crawl into the high bed, next to Skye, under her girls-in-bonnets quilt. What stops Angie is knowing the bed would break. What stops Angie is knowing that even if the bed did not break, she could not have what she wants. What she wants is Skye.

Skye's body. To take Skye's body as her very own. To snuggle in the bed all night and in the morning have Rachel call her for toast. To sleep without waiting for angry voices or police sirens and in the morning have Angie brush her hair. To be Skye. Someone else could go to Triple-F tomorrow, write Sharon Delsarado a letter, draft a motion for reargument, and catch up on the work she should have done today. Someone else could decide whether she should represent a lesbian mother in a custody battle who shot her baby daughter in the head with a rifle. Someone else could talk with Claire. She could be Skye. Sleeping. Instead of Angie, crying.

Crying, almost savoring the wetness on her cheeks because she feels as if she is liquid, wants to evaporate. Maybe she is losing her edge, she thinks, some sharpness she struggles to keep honed and shiny. Perhaps some bit of complacency has crept into her style, undermining her. Probably Sharon Delsarado is right, she had been lulled by the judges. Her oral argument had been too polite, too controlled, too confident: that was its latent flaw.

All of Angie's guilt congealed in the lawyers' expression that cases are not won, only lost, at oral argument. And she had lost because she thought she would win. Would win because that spring month was a winning one, she had already scored twice. "Important victories for all women," as *The Times* had quoted some pundit; "a step ahead for all lesbian and gay families," as *The Voice* had quoted a different pundit. One was a custody case for a model mother, perfect except for her lesbianism, which was itself of the most perfect variety: discreet, monogamous, and apolitical. It helped, of course, that the former husband was a drug dealer. The other case was an adoption for the so-called "other mother," so that the child now had two legal mothers. It helped, of course, that both mothers were wealthy and professional. The dates of both decisions were marked by little red stars on the monthly calendar in Angie's Book, on the same page where *Delsarado arg. 9 A.M.* appeared in Angie's most careful script. The nights of both decisions were marked by celebratory dinners with Rachel and Skye, at their favorite restaurant near the river, the one that turned into a lesbian and gay bar after midnight.

Rachel is not a patient woman. She is a tenacious attorney, a considerate lover, and a trustworthy mother. But she is not a patient woman. When Angie finally comes to their bed, Rachel is not waiting for her. Rachel has learned not to wait for Angie.

Still, it is difficult. Difficult for Rachel to make Angie wait for her, instead of her waiting for Angie. Difficult not to seek solace for her own anxieties about another mother losing another child—another mother who could be her, and another child who could be Skye. Difficult not to pose the unanswerable question, to ask Angie why she persists in doing lesbian custody cases. Difficult not to feel a momentary satisfaction that her own cases are "only" economic: clients losing their homes in eviction actions; clients losing their skimpy welfare payments in administrative hearings; clients losing their jobs and fighting back by filing discrimination complaints. All of Rachel's losses cause her pain, but she feels a distance from them that she cannot maintain when a lesbian mother is losing her child. And distance, Rachel knows, is necessary to being an effective attorney; it is inherent in the very word *represent.* Rachel suppresses any thought that Angie can preserve her distance when she represents lesbian mothers because she does not really feel like Skye's mother. Rachel takes a certain comfort in Angie's entanglement.

Still, it is difficult to casually read her book, to let Angie start sliding next to her, wrapping an ankle around her own so that her legs spread slightly, a small patch of suction that she had not known was there being released with a sigh. To let Angie want her. To let Angie start to talk about her case, her telephone call, her conversation with Roger, about her day. Difficult not to press her about Claire, about some other nagging doubts. To let Angie finally ask Rachel about *her* hearing this morning, about *her* day, about *her, her, her.*

It is midnight and they are still talking. One woman in a ripped T-shirt from a long-ago conference. One woman in an oversized button-down shirt. Almost-empty water glasses on mismatched wicker nightstands. Hand on thigh, higher. Giggle. The Federal Rules of Civil Procedure standards on a motion for summary judgment. A button undone; shadowless breast. Sitting up and shifting to think, retrieving some strategy from the recesses of intellect. Minds like file cabinets. Good memories. But not perfect. "A case from the Fifth Circuit, I think." Look it up tomorrow. Stretching a mouth toward a skull's lowest shelf, toward an ear, toward a long scar. Lick. Tip of a tongue across a face, across evaporated tears, across. The thick pink candle, which has been flickering for hours, is too hot now, the wax sliding down through a rupture in its thinned shell, down to a safe ceramic hollow of glazed and fired pottery. Smoothing a stomach. Flinch. Relax. Rolling over and pressing against the bed. Arched ass, cupped. Mouth on mons, nuzzling. Exploring for a clit, as if in unfamiliar territory instead of surrounded by paths well blazed by tongue and well marked with old chapping and new wetness. Taste like nothing else, no one else.

Rachel and Angie are not themselves now, or each other, but some creature they become together. A creature with its own personality, its own shifting moods, its own desires. Awkward moments with jutting elbows and tangled ankles, but a creature confident of some elegance, some entitlement to existence, some satisfaction. Pleasure so certain it can be repeatedly deferred. Until it cannot.

Angie is stretched across an empty bed in her head. Solid ash and spindle headboard. The sheets are cool, cotton, some muted natural color; there's a matching comforter with graph-paper stripes. Blue; yes, blue. Because the bed is on a beach. Summer sand, blue-white against the blond of the bed and the corner of the comforter. A blue ocean, aqua almost, and a blue sky with a stream of clouds like a ruffle. Tropical. Or summer. Angie is drifting into sleep, cradled by a page from a catalog. Rachel's breathing is a breeze, expertly tailored, an excellent value, suitable for even the most particular pussy-licking lawyer. The telephone. Clear lacquer. Supervised visitation. Button closure on quilt cover. Traffic. Imported. Resistance is possible. Needs no ironing. Ambition. Fruit by the foot. Grids. Crisp blue. Sky blue. Skye. Dyke. Steel suspension bridge.

DECEMBERS

DECEMBERS

**DECEMBERS**

DECEMBERS

DECEMBERS

Angie's Decembers mean fund-raisers, receptions, dinners that are neither work nor social. A formal benefit for Rachel's job, held in a motel restaurant, hobnobbing with liberal corporate lawyers who believe Rachel should say "welfare" and not "entitlements," lawyers who believe Rachel should solve individual problems but never challenge policies. A less formal benefit for a lesbian and gay legal organization, held in someone's Village penthouse, talking with lawyers who believe Angie should say "gay and lesbian" instead of "lesbian," lawyers who believe Angie should stick to custody cases and avoid involving the movement with murderers.

Tonight's dinner is informal, the most dangerous kind. Without a stated purpose, such gatherings always make Angie nervous. And after the last meeting, devoted to discussing her newest client—the one Roger refers to as "the riflewoman," complete with a few hummed bars of TV theme music—Angie is particularly nervous about socializing with anyone from Triple-F. Knowing he was not invited, she wishes Roger would be at the dinner. Instead, the guests are Chelsea and Chad. At the home of Kaitlin and Coleman. Also Dorothy and Joseph, who at least do not have matching names, who at least do have a child who will be good company for Skye.

Andrew, an ash-blond boy with good manners, is playing checkers with Skye in the living room. The adults, differently complected but all coupled and cautious, are drinking wine in the dining room. There are fireplaces in both rooms. With greeting-card fires.

The house is old, Victorian, being refurbished by Kaitlin and Coleman without apparent financial difficulty. With both pride and nostalgia, they remind their guests of their recent move from the Upper West Side to this nineteenth-century suburb. Kaitlin shows them around, remarking on the work that has been done, the work that needs to be done. The tourists remark on the house's resemblances to their family homes.

"Oh, we had a little landing just like this. My sisters and I gave plays on it." Chelsea says this, smiling.

Oh, we had stairs just like this, only they were outside and the wood was rotten and they were streamed with piss. Angie does not say this, not smiling.

"Oh, look at this bathroom wallpaper. My parents had wallpaper just like this in their bedroom." Dorothy says this, smiling.

Oh, look at this bathroom. My parents never even had a bedroom as big as this. Angie does not say this either.

"Oh, what a wonderful oven. It's industrial, isn't it?" Chad asks.

Oh, what a wonderful oven. It's a bit more versatile than a hot plate, isn't it? It's a bit more efficient than a coal stove, isn't it? A bit safer, too? Angie does not ask.

Angie murmurs, in what she thinks are polite tones, at the wooden staircase boasting its landing, at the authentic flocked wallpaper, at the huge square oven adorned with knobs. She never looks at Rachel, who is looking at Angie, worried. She never looks at anyone, not eye to eye, anyway.

Dinner, produced on the gorgeously industrial cooking machine, is chicken. Sauteed in some sauce, white and creamy. Chelsea must have forgotten she is a vegetarian, Angie thinks, taking some rice. There is always salad. Angie looks at Rachel, spooning salad. Skye, spooning salad.

"Some chicken?" Andrew offers Skye.

"I don't eat animals," Skye explains.

Andrew does not put any chicken on his own plate, as if in deference to Skye's sensibilities.

Angie is waiting for the talk to veer toward Triple-F, fearing that the talk will include the riflewoman. But the dinner conversation is orchestrated by *The Times.* Not that anything momentous had happened at *The Times;* there has not even been an especially pertinent article. The repeating rhythm is "Did you see the piece in *The Times* about this?" or "did you read the piece in *The Times* about that?" Then there is the irrelevant yes or no, followed by an exposition of the article. Angie waits for the analysis, the opinion, a connection. Angie asks first Chelsea, then Coleman, then Chad, "So, what do you think about the piece?" But the answers are always nonresponsive. The only connection is to another piece, also in *The Times.*

Angie feels guilty that she does not join the conversation. But the only recent *Times* piece she can remember is about a woman who jumped from a bridge. Stopped in the slow lane at the apex of the span, left her car engine running, walked toward the guardrail, and jumped over the steel barrier into the cold dirty river. Survived.

And she is too uncomfortable with her colleagues and their partners to refer to attempted suicide, to talk about the vagaries of survival, even to mention a bridge she travels with thousands of other commuters. Angie judges the subject too revealing, displaying an almost embarrassing eroticism. Instead, Angie withdraws from the adult conversation. She talks with Skye and Andrew about the cucumbers in the salad. She sees Rachel taking a piece of chicken. And then another.

By dessert, recollections of pieces in *The Times* are exhausted. Now, Angie thinks, it is Triple-F business. Being with some of her colleagues reminds her that the riflewoman is among the least of the problems at Triple-F. She thinks the entire organization is falling apart. Chelsea's battered-woman case is drawing heat from some major funders for being too radical and being criticized by a feminist organization for being too reactionary. Coleman, the present director of litigation, is being accused of sexually harassing his secretary and of fiscal mismanagement. Dorothy has written a letter of resignation effective next year unless there is compliance with her list of demands, including a new director of litigation. Terry and Roger, both of whom are absent and thus safe subjects, are not speaking to each other. No one has written any grants for the next cycle of funding.

Instead of confronting the problems at Futures for Families, Inc.—the project Angie had assumed as the rationale for an otherwise unlikely dinner gathering—the conversation rambles until it settles on their own families' pasts. Stories of courtships compete with stories of births, always punctuated by their own parents' reactions. Racial and ethnic differences slide into parodies of food and accents. Of course,

Angie thinks, any discussion of the disaster that is their organization would be impolite, excluding the halves of the couples who do not work at Triple-F. Unlike these anecdotes, so polite and inclusive.

Their insensitivity alarms Angie. Or perhaps it is only their heterosexuality. Although she has worked with some of them for many years, she knows none of them know her well; they know Rachel even less well. But she thinks they should know some statistical probability that at least she or Rachel had been rejected by their parents. Hadn't there been a piece in *The Times* about that? They should know that Angie or Rachel's parents might not have reacted so fondly to bringing home a mate that was not a man. That Angie and Rachel did not hold hands at high school dances. Did not have an engagement party. Or a wedding.

And she knows that they know Skye is adopted. They know that Angie or Rachel's parents could not make jokes about genetic resemblances. That Angie and Rachel did not go to birthing classes. Did not decide on a midwife. Or a doctor.

Or perhaps it is only their class backgrounds. *Background,* like something so tastefully blended that it did not warrant comment. Background for things that can be admired: landings and bathrooms and patterns of wallpaper and industrial ovens. Background was something that could not be ordered from the toll-free telephone number on the back cover of a catalog; was something antecedent and irrevocable; was something that could not be an ambition.


Driving home, the three of them squeezed into the small car, Angie tries to decide what bothers her most about her colleagues. Their class. Her queerness. Or the boredom.

"I wish Ellen had been there," Angie says, thinking of the boredom, thinking that maybe the boredom is what bothers her the most.

But Rachel is thinking about class. Because when Rachel guesses that Angie is thinking about class, Rachel can think of nothing else. And not class in any textbook sense or any concrete sense, but class as a distance between them. Their differing backgrounds some unbridgeable gap.

"I always think of Ellen as a middle-class Black," Rachel ventures, but asks for agreement: "Don't you?"

"In a way. But marginal. Her mother and father were social workers, but her aunts did day work and hair and her uncles were day laborers." Angie knows this is sensitive stuff. Geography is the only assurance that Ellen's aunts did not move heavy furniture from room to room for Rachel's mother and that Ellen's uncles did not trim trees for Rachel's father. Class, but something else.

"Oh," Rachel manages, uneasy but somehow reassured that Angie and Ellen do not share identical class backgrounds. Knowing that if she did not like Ellen so much—or if Ellen were not so straight and so happily coupled with a very nice guy—she would be jealous. Jealous not of Ellen Robinson, the high-profile African-American feminist who represents women subjected to involuntary sterilization, but of Ellen on the phone with Angie after some particularly contentious meeting at Triple-F. Complaining and strategizing. For hours. But mostly Rachel is glad that Angie has an ally at Triple-F.

"Ellen will tell me I should have known it was going to be like this."

"Did you?" Rachel asks.

"I don't know. I guess I knew and I didn't. Or maybe I just did not think it would be this awful."

"It was awful, wasn't it?" Rachel asks nervously.

"Pitiful," Angie answers. "I just feel so defeated."

"Defeated? But you didn't even fight."

"I guess not." Angie tries to laugh, but somehow it sounds more like a gasp for air.

Before the span across the river, Angie pulls the car over, safely on the shoulder. Rachel gets out to vomit. Those passing might think they see two teenagers, driving back to the valley from the city after drinking liquors unfamiliar to their bodies. Instead of two middle-aged dykes, one a lapsed vegetarian with a stomach clutched from watching her lover's anxiety, from her own anxiety. Angie refrains from mentioning the chicken, only asks Rachel if she feels better as she starts the engine again to drive the three of them carefully across the river.

" 'Bridge freezes before road.' " Skye's voice startles like a sudden beam of light in the silent darkness.

Neither mother responds.

"Is that an expression?" Skye's voice is less piercing, more plaintive, but also confident in her knowledge that a direct question is never ignored.

"No," Rachel says.

"Then what is it?" Skye persists.

"More like a warning."

"All expressions are kind of like warnings," Skye remarks.

Rachel decides this is not a question, despite Skye's hesitant inflection. So she does not answer, giving her attention to Angie's hunching over the steering wheel.

"I hate this bridge." Angie says when she notices Rachel's observation.

Rachel thinks of Angie as a confident driver; a small startled noise escapes from her still-sour tasting mouth.

"Because bridges connect things!" Skye exclaims, trying to explain something about one of her mothers to the other.

Out of the mouths of babes, one mother thinks.

"We're almost home," the other mother says too loudly, the sounds ricocheting around the little car.

▪ ▪ ▪ ▪ ▪ ▪ ▪

Angie is throwing up in a toilet in a ladies' room in a bar. No one holds her head. A woman waits for her outside, sitting at a table, staring at Angie's drink. Vodka and Kahlua. Wondering how old Angie is. Young. Older than she looks? Younger? Angie is back at the table, running her hand through her cropped hair, looking this woman full in the face. Glad this woman waited. They leave, without speaking.

In this woman's car, Angie looks in her purse for her own address. "I just moved," she tells the woman as if this is an excuse. Angie's purse is stitched cloth from Indian prints, like a patchwork bedspread. It is the last purse she will ever have, but she does not know this. It is not the last time she will let a woman drive her home and come into her bed, and she does know this. She asks the woman her name, again. And again in the morning. The woman is kind, is glad she is not as young as Angie, is listening as Angie stands in the room naked with a phone in her hand. Angie says nothing. Is expressionless, almost. For half an hour. This woman waits. Smokes a cigarette. Practices blowing patterns in the air. Looks at the books by Angie's bed. Nothing erotic. Masturbates. Angie watches, rooted by the phone.

■  ■  ■  ■  ■  ■  ■

Skye is a tree. Or a wood nymph, but looks like a tree. Angie wonders if the blond girls in the class get to be fairies, with gossamer wings made of netting and clothes hangers. Dorothy had told her that Andrew, with his ash-blond hair, had been one of Santa's elves in his school play. At the public schools, there are Santa plays, once a year. At Meadowlark School, there are Solstice plays, winter and summer. Angie never lets herself contemplate whether such differences are worth thousands of dollars in tuition money. She is more distressed about the inconsistencies of her political support of public education and her personal choice to send her own child to a trendy alternative and private school.

In the space rented from a local repertory theater, Skye's crepe-paper leaves crash against the other children's. At least both boys and girls are wood nymphs, Angie thinks. She points this out to Rachel, approvingly.

"Wait and see who the woodsman is," Rachel suggests, withholding judgment.

"I hope there won't be a woodsman," Angie whispers.

"Why not?"

"The woodsman kills the trees."

"Oh, Jesus," Rachel groans, only half-mockingly.

"Am I overprotective?" Angie asks, laughing.

"Because you don't want a tree in a school play to be chopped down?"

"That tree is our daughter!"

"Well, maybe she won't be the tree that's chopped down."

"Even worse," Angie says. "She'll have survivor's guilt."

"Oh, Jesus," Rachel groans again.

"We'll just have to wait and see what happens."

"Didn't Skye tell you? I can't believe she didn't narrate the entire plot over breakfast." Rachel takes breakfast seriously. She always makes something hotly substantial for Skye, becoming impatient with Skye's cheerful soliloquies performed over her cooling eggs, or French toast, or pancakes.

"No, she said it was a secret."

"I didn't think that child could keep a secret." Rachel laughs.

"Get a program," Angie commands.

The play seems appropriately pagan to Angie. Thankfully, there is no woodsman, or woodswoman. The trees survive, swaying with the winter winds, and even sing some Latinate dirge, accompanied by the fifth-grade recorder ensemble. Angie decides to ignore the heterosexuality, the sixth-grade king and queen, in favor of the gendered mix of kindergarten animals. The large paper sun is hoisted at the end to much applause from the audience and the players. Angie can see Skye's branches, clapping.

"Not bad," Rachel pronounces. She is smiling. Then standing.

The children bow.

The music director bows.

The drama teacher bows.

There is more applause, then coffee and juice. Cake and cookies, all homemade, and probably organic. Even the banana bread purchased by Angie at the Good Earth Bakery. Skye and Rachel and Angie mix with the jumbled crowd. And yet they do not.

Skye especially seems set a bit apart. Her differences from the majority of the children are discernible, but are not unique or even among the most dramatic. There are African-American children wearing traditional kente cloth; Korean sisters clinging to Anglo parents; a boy with two mothers and two fathers; and a second-grader balded by chemotherapy. But something divides her from all of the children, some idiosyncrasy that makes her hold back when others push, and sometimes push when others hold back.

Perhaps it is the same something that sets Rachel and Angie apart, separated from the other parents as if by a medieval moat. Certainly, there is their dykiness, but the Meadowlark parents pride themselves on their tolerance and try to include them in conversations, which inevitably and prematurely founder. Certainly, there is their professionalism, but the Meadowlark parents are also professionals—physicians and therapists and architects—and there should be the potential for interactions that are not advice.

Yet Rachel and Angie are less alone than Skye, less obvious, because they have each other. Soon Skye joins them in a triangular fold. They do not touch until they are outside and walking to their car. Then they are hugging and laughing in the winter air, making smoke rings of their breath. Skye joins in the praise of her performance, looking forward to her Solstice presents.

In the car, Angie feels Skye's anticipation and cannot resist teasing.

"I hope the presents are good. I bet they will be. I have a connection with the Winter Solstice fairy, you know."

"Really?" Skye laughs, as if she has not heard this every Winter Solstice of her life.

"Yes, I used to date her."

"You shouldn't tell her that," Rachel says, smiling. "She'll think you loved someone before me."

"I didn't love her," Angie says, turning to Skye in the backseat. "We just dated. You have to know lots of people before you can be sure you have the right one. But we parted on good terms, so don't worry."

"I'm not," Skye declares.

"Just drive," Rachel says. "And look where you're going. She doesn't believe you, you know," Rachel says loudly. "She knows there isn't a Solstice fairy. She just wants her presents." Rachel likes to think she is being the practical parent.

Angie will be not dissuaded. "Is that true?" she asks Skye.

Skye does not answer.

"How old are you now? Thirteen?" Angie rescues.

"Nine. I'm just nine."

"Oh, well. Then I guess you don't need to believe or not believe in the Solstice fairy. Not when you're nine. Thirteen, maybe. Yes, thirteen is a good time to decide about the Solstice fairy. I think that's when I decided."

"That's probably when you dated her," Rachel says, not unkindly.

"No, I was fourteen," Angie squeezes Rachel's knee protruding against the dashboard from the passenger's seat. They have both learned to be generous about certain aspects of Angie's adolescence.

Evangelina's Decembers mean Claire's depressions. Evangelina does not know how to spell *depression*, not yet, but she wants to be able to spell every word in the universe. Evangelina does not know why it is wrong to want that book of maps for Christmas, to want any book instead of a doll. Evangelina does not know how to smile the right smile at Claire, so that Claire will smile back. So she thanks Claire for the underwear on Christmas morning. Lace. She hates lace but she thanks Claire because Claire loves lace and she loves Claire. Claire loves lace and dolls. Claire tells Evangelina that when she was a little girl she always wanted a doll for Christmas, a doll with lace underwear. But she never got one. Evangelina always gets one.

Even this year, when Claire and Evangelina are living far away from Luke, the man Evangelina calls her father. "On our own," Claire says, pretending that this is freedom instead of one of her desertions of Luke.

Maybe, just maybe, there is a book in the torn paper wrapping. Maybe a book in a box. A book Claire could have bought for her at a big store that had rows of books and clothes and dishes and underwear and everything. That big book of maps she saw, with aqua oceans and mosaic continents and the names of cities over thick black dots, all orderly in squares of thin lines that marked east from west and south from north. That book had page after page of places, and if she learned to use that book, Evangelina knew she could follow the lines and get to some of those places. Maybe Claire had gotten that book called Atlas at that big store they went to when they first got here, Evangelina and Claire and Claire's boyfriend, all of them shining under the fluorescent lights. All of them standing in line to get Evangelina's picture taken by the professional photographer, paid for by Claire's boyfriend.

The curly-headed doll with a plaid dress over a lace slip is alone in her box. Claire had stitched the dress, the slip. Even a little ruffle across the back of the underpants. And a matching plaid hat.

"It's just like Shirley Temple." Claire smiles.

Evangelina smiles back.

Claire's boyfriend smiles, too, as he takes off his coat announcing that he cannot stay very long. Evangelina does not smile back.

"That doll looks just like you, kid," Claire's boyfriend ruffles

Evangelina's curls and smiles again. Evangelina tries to smile back, looking at Claire. But Claire is not smiling, only looking at her boyfriend, expectantly.

"I've always wanted a beautiful doll like that on Christmas morning, although almost any present . . ."

"I'm sorry, sweetie." Claire's boyfriend is still smiling.

Evangelina makes herself small, listening to them argue. Listens to the boyfriend slam the slender door, hard. Listens to Claire sob: "All I ever wanted was a present on Christmas. Is that too much to ask? I do everything for everybody else. Does anyone love me? Couldn't even get a goddamn doll when I was a kid and it's no better now."

Evangelina wants to show Claire that somebody loves her, that she loves her. But when Evangelina tries to give the doll to Claire, Claire slaps her hard against her face. "Ungrateful bitch!" Claire yells.

The slap hurts Evangelina. Hurts so much she wants to cry all day with the doll in her arms. But it is Claire who cries, who cries all day. Evangelina reads, her one book, stolen from a school library, over and over, spelling the words to herself. None of the words in the book is *depression.* None of the words in the book gives Evangelina a hint that might help her get a present for Claire. When it gets dark, Evangelina slides into bed as gently as she can. Next to Claire, the doll between them.

▩ ▩ ▩ ▩ ▩ ▩ ▩

Angie surveys the books on her wicker nightstand, trying to decide which one to bring on the plane. Once she would memorize the titles near her head as she rolled toward the edge of her newest lover's bed, as if she could tell something about a person's true character by looking at such books. Soon she decided that no books were best, for their absence meant she would not be tempted by conversations beyond the bodily. She could leave in the morning, without regrets. Now she thinks that the books on a nightstand indicate nothing other than one's current reading interests, although in some part of her she still must regard the nightstand as a reluctant oracle. Which is why she keeps the catalogs under the bed instead of on the nightstand, even the lower shelf of the nightstand.

Not that Rachel does not know Angie broods over the *HOME* catalog, or the one about garden supplies, or the clothes from dozens and dozens of merchants. Or the catalog from Victoria's Secret. It is the last one that she pulls out now, sliding it from the pile and opening to the jarring colors of lace underwear on white women. The molded and prominent breasts invite her gaze and make Angie think she should try to masturbate. But the women's bodies look uncomfortable, their expressions drugged, and Angie finds them decidedly unsexy. She looks for a sexy one, one that might approximate Rachel's complicated androgyny and dramatic profile. But she notices she is also looking for a model with Kim's jutting incisors, but the women are too perfect for that, all infirmities remedied.

Angie knows she should think about Kim, to try to figure out why Kim keeps happening to her, why she is enticed by such mediocre sex. But in this moment she is distracted by her transference of Kim's mouth on the model in the black satin merry widow, with lace underwire cups and ruffled lace edging. Lightly boned. Back hooks. And the straps and garters are removable.

She should telephone Kim before she leaves. Wish her happy winter holidays or something. Maybe she should have gotten her a present. Maybe she should have sent her a calendar. Or a book would have been nice. And not very intimate. She had gotten Roger a book, after all. Maybe she would have time to get Kim something before she left.

Angie goes back to inspecting the books. About six or seven volumes, and half are hardcover, and none of them are library books. The weight of them impresses itself on her. Only once in a while does she experience that weight as oppressive, like a reminder that she does not have enough time to read everything she wants, even half of what she once did. Mostly she appreciates the stacked books as security, the way Claire would perceive a cabinet full of canned goods.

Plane reading should be engaging, but easily interrupted and somewhat unemotional. She picks up *The Roots of Postmodern Poverty.* Could the postmodern have roots? she wonders for a moment, concluding that even fragmentation has a history. Displacement, dispossession, dispersal, deprivation, histories without descriptions in the modern texts. She skims the chapter devoted to Appalachian whites. The chapter that induced her purchase. It does not refer to them as hillbillies or even ridgerunners, like she does, if only silently. Like Claire does. It does depict them, poor and without shoes in the snow. Children sliding down strip-mined mountains on pieces of wood: children at play. Children slithering through small tunnels to extract every bit of coal from the cavities: children at work. Shafts collapsing: children dead. And then the coming of the unions and the machines. Making most of the workers obsolete. And then the depletion of the minerals. Making almost all of the workers obsolete. And then the realization that even rocky subsistence patch farming was no longer a possibility. Making even the most determined of them desperate.

They scattered. They left the hollow hills and dynamited ridges for the factories. In Chicago. Detroit. They followed ambitions for food and work. Sure, they drank moonshine on the way, beat each other, and spent the little money they had on an orange instead of bread. Sure, they were considered stupid, and lazy, and as dishonest and superstitious as gypsies.

The book carefully deconstructs the stereotypes. In its dispassionate prose gleaned from social workers and scholars, the book provides its own realities. Cajoling and convincing its readers with theories of the economies of exploitation. More important, however, the book posits that these scattering people possess no group identity. They practiced losing their accents, changed their musical tastes, and joined unions. Some of them even learned to read, wear mascara, or pay the rent on time. They could not be hillbillies and ridgerunners without hills and ridges. They assimilated. They survived.

But they were not themselves anymore. Another chapter depicts them as working-class and wearing shoes in the snow. Children knocking balls against the factory walls: children at play. Children sitting in small seats in overcrowded schoolrooms: children at work. Fires in tenements: children dead. And then the collapse of the unions and the coming of the machines. Making most of the workers obsolete. And then the moving of the factories south, and then farther south, and then across oceans. Making almost all of the workers obsolete. And then the realization that even waitressing in the diners and restaurants was no longer a possibility. Making even the most determined of them desperate.

They scattered. They left the crumbling streets and the heatless apartments for the sun. In Florida. Texas. They followed ambitions for warmth and work. Sure, they drank Budweiser on the way, beat each other, and spent the little money they had buying lottery tickets instead of food. Sure, they were considered fictional, and brutal, and as rude and foreign as Yankees.

The book ends with these stereotypes. Assimilation is an open question. So is survival. It depends on government policies. Angie snaps the book shut. The government. Apparently, mascara and new music are no longer sufficient remedies for poverty, at least not postmodern poverty.

Probably the worst book she could read on the plane, Angie concludes. The last book to read on the way to see Claire is a social-scientific history of Claire's life.

"What are you doing?" Rachel walks into their bedroom.

"Looking for a book to read on the plane tomorrow."

"There's always that transcript you've been putting off."

"The riflewoman?"

"I thought you didn't like it when Roger called her that."

"I'm getting used to it."

"Sounds like you're thinking of not representing her."

"Why do you say that?"

"You're going to write a brief for a client even you call the riflewoman?"

"Sure, why not?"

"Because it sounds stupid."

"Most things do."

"Oh, you're in a great mood." Rachel teeters between sarcasm and tenderness.

"I don't feel like getting on a plane tomorrow."

"You don't have to, you know."

"I do have to."

"No, you don't."

"Do you think I like leaving you and Skye on Christmas day and flying to see Claire?" Angie sounds like a whining child.

"You must. Otherwise you wouldn't have done it every year for the past ten years. You ruin the kid's Christmas, you know. *The Feminist Atlas* notwithstanding."

"She got lots of presents. I know you think that atlas is funny, but I think she'll like it. It's really a great Solstice present. We always have a nice and wonderful Solstice."

"No one else in the universe celebrates Solstice."

"They do at Meadowlark School. And we celebrate it. It's the women's holiday. Didn't you like your present?"

"I love it," Rachel says seriously.

"You really look gorgeous in it."

"Are you sure I'm not too old for it?"

"No dyke is too old for a new black leather jacket. Only most dykes don't look as sexy as you do."

"Most?" Rachel teases.

"None." Angie steps toward Rachel. "No other dyke in the entire world, anyplace in *The Feminist Atlas,* could look as sexy as you do in that jacket. Or without a jacket for that matter." Angie is now pressing her breasts into the flat of Rachel's back, smelling Rachel's neck, and kissing that Rachel-sweat smell. "I just love you. And I love being with you on the Solstice. It's so special."

"If it were really special"—Rachel pulls away and turns to face Angie—"you'd spend it with Claire."

"That's not fair. Let's not argue, Rachel. I love you. I love Skye. I'll be home on New Year's Eve."

"I love you too, baby. But I worry about Skye. And I even worry about you. You look exhausted. You have rings under your eyes like a raccoon, like you were wearing mascara in the shower or something. You know, someday maybe Claire will really kill herself, like she's always promising, and you'll just fall apart."

"I won't fall apart."

"I'm not so sure."

"I'm doing the best I can, Rachel. The best I can."

"Take the transcript, Angie. It will remind you you're a well-respected lawyer and not a twelve-year-old child trying to keep her mother alive."

"I'll be back as soon as I can. You know that."

"And you know I love you, don't you? Otherwise I'd never put up with this. It's Skye I worry about."

"I could take her," Angie suggests.

"Forget it." Rachel is harsh. "You know how your mother feels about Skye."

"She loves her."

"Angie!"

"Okay, she has a hard time with Skye's origins."

" 'Origins'?"

"Okay, okay." Angie looks at the books again on her nightstand. "I think I'll take the one about the myths of mother-child bonding. That's related to the riflewoman. The transcript is too bulky. It's in two boxes. I'd never get it on the plane."


When Angie gets off the plane, she spots Claire immediately in the near-empty lounge. Claire looks better than ever, wearing creased white shorts and yellow Reeboks. Angie feels her blood rush toward her mother with a childhood longing to be loved, but also to protect. Spiked with their mutual desire for something beautiful, something apricot and expensive that would reflect their slightly tanned complexions and their meticulous teeth. The two of them, a mother-daughter advertisement.

"Hello," she says to Claire, "You look good."

"You look like shit," Claire smiles. "You know, I've been thinking about this. You might get yourself somewhere if you wore a little mascara. And put some Magic Cover under your eyes. And dressed better, like the women who work in stores. And for Christ's sake, let your hair grow out. Short hair is not in this year."

"Maybe. Happy Christmas."

"It's 'Merry.' It's supposed to be 'Merry.' "

"I like 'Happy.' "

"Who says 'Happy Christmas'?"

"I think the English."

"Well, you ain't in England," Claire proclaims.

"I guess not," Angie admits.

There is a Christmas tree in Claire's living room. It has lights that blink off and on. There is roast beef on the table. It is congealed and overcooked. There is a sheet on Claire's couch, because the cushions are ripped. There is a man on the couch. The man Angie calls her father, except when she calls him Luke, is sitting on the couch in his boxer shorts. Drinking a Budweiser and watching television. He greets her as if she has just returned from the store with a pack of cigarettes, instead of traveling by two planes on Christmas Day. She often forgets him, too, as if he is a tiny moon blotted out by Claire's energy. But she is glad to see him.

"Happy Christmas." Angie kisses him on the cheek.

"It's 'Merry,' Evangelina. It's 'Merry Christmas.' I don't know why you say things just to aggravate me," Claire scolds.

Claire hates the bathrobe. It has violets all over it and Claire hates violets. And Angie has to admit that the bathrobe does not look as good on Claire as it did on the lady in the catalog, the lady with the lavender hair. "I'll send it back," Angie says.

Angie hates the underwear. Lace. At least there is not a doll, Angie thinks. Carefully folding last year's wrapping paper, the green foil with the red Christmas trees, so that it can be used next year. "Thanks, I always need underwear," Angie says.

Luke likes the shirt from Angie. The underwear from Claire. Silk boxer shorts. "They are really in this year," Claire says.

■ ■ ■ ■ ■ ■

Evangelina is telling a lie.

They have already had pizza for dinner. Already played cards. Already pretended they were not waiting. Already looked at the clock nailed into the kitchen wall, above the sink. And only now does he ask. And she answers, as if rehearsing.

"I don't know where she is."

"It's Christmas Eve; she's got to be somewhere."

"Shopping?" Evangelina offers.

"Do you think the stores are open this late?" Luke asks hopefully.

"For last-minute shoppers."

Evangelina dusts Claire's dresser again. Picking up each object, wiping it with an oily rag, putting it on the bed, making up stories about each of Claire's knickknacks. When the pressboard surface is clear, Evangelina glides the cloth from one side to the other, back and forth, like skating. She even ventures vertical, brushing the dresser's only slightly cracked mirror with oil, so that she has to remove the printed sayings Claire has tucked into the slit between the glass and frame: "God, Grant Me / The Serenity to Accept What I Cannot Change / The Strength to Change What I Can / And the Wisdom to Know the Difference" and "A Woman Must Always / Act Like a Lady / Think Like a Man / Work Like a Dog." Evangelina does not know that they are bookmarks, cloth rectangles with tassels at the top, but if she did she would love them even more than she loves them now. She hopes Claire really loves them too—that it is not just coincidence that Claire has them on her mirror—because they are like a gift she made for Claire. Cross-stitch. Completed by Evangelina. *Home Is Where the Heart Is.* Evangelina had wanted to find one of the sayings Claire already had; had hoped for the lady one, not just because it was shorter, but because it was about women. And she liked the part about the dog. But *Home Is Where the Heart Is* was the only one the five-and-dime stocked, in a kit with faded red thread.

After she is done replacing the items on Claire's dresser and re-checking her present to Claire, she watches the man by the grey light of the television. Thinking of the other man that Claire is kissing. Probably right now. Right this minute. Evangelina just wishes the kissing is good-bye kissing. Just wishes Claire will come home safe. That man had a gun, Evangelina saw it in the trunk of his car. Wrapped up in Christmas wrapping paper. Just wishes Claire would come home soon. Soon.

Angie does not talk to Luke until Claire is out of the room, surrendered to her tranquilizers and snoring in the bed she does not share with Luke. In the bed under a framed but unglassed cross-stitch Angie made as a little girl, the letters made even more blurry by dust. And under a discount chain-store photograph of Angie as a child, her eyes light and open, framed by a halo of curls. Angie will have to sleep in Claire's bed tonight, and she is postponing it as long as possible, although she is exhausted. She talks to Luke about her job. He likes to hear about the bad things people have done. Bad things that get them in trouble with the law. It is better than TV, although he keeps the color set turned on.

Angie tells him about the riflewoman. Asks him about the rifle. Luke likes to tell Angie about the things he knows.

"Now, no ordinary man would have a thirty-o-six around the house. That's for safaris or stalking. I mean, you could stand on one mountain and kill a dog on the other. It's like long distance. It had a scope? Well, that's definitely long distance. Kill something on another mountain, I'm telling you. Do you know what I'm talking about? Understand me? It's power. Like a power rifle. It's about eight boards. You know what that means? It means if you shoot it, the bullet can go through eight boards. Them is one-inch boards, now. Made of oak, solid. You say somebody shot her kid through the head with that? Must have blasted the kid's head from here to Shinola. Shit. Could kill a kid on another mountain with that power."

"Did you ever have a rifle like that?"

"Me? I'm just a shitkicker. Had a little Winchester, thirty-thirty. That's all you need in the mountains. Unless you was in the union. Then, a pistol was best. Though you really needed a bomb." Luke laughs at his own joke. "I like that Magnum I got now, though. Protection. I kind of miss a rifle, though. The heft of it on your shoulder. I don't like to kill nothing, though—never did. You know that."

They talk more about rifles, about Angie's cases, about some scandal on the late-night news. And finally, they talk about Claire.

"How is she, really?"

"You know how she is."

"I do and I don't. Sometimes she's just so mean to me, I don't know if she's saying things to be mean or is really sick."

"Don't talk bad about your mother." And then his voice gets softer. "It's just the changes, Evangelina."

Angie looks at Luke by the flashing colors of television light. The changes. What Luke has said about Claire for the last thirty years. The world's longest menopause. How Luke excused Claire's infidelities, Claire's hysterics, Claire's unexplained departures. How Luke continues to live with Claire, his wife. How Luke continues to love Claire, his wife—if he does.

Finally, she asks him what she has never asked him before: "Do you really think it's the changes for all these years?"

"Want a roast beef sandwich?" he asks. Angie wishes she were in court so she could object to his answer as nonresponsive. There would be some judge to instruct him to answer. Instead, she waits. Only when he is in the kitchen, standing there with a butcher knife in his hand, does he speak again.

"She was never the same after you were born, Evangelina. It's women's hormones. You haven't had a baby, you don't know. It drives women crazy."

She wonders what the hell she is doing here. Wonders how Claire manages to keep Angie's loyalty and even love. Wonders if Claire was sufficiently stunted by a childhood without dolls to stunt her amazingly lifelike doll of a daughter. Wonders if Claire allowed little Evangelina to develop emotional responses more sophisticated than those Skye had at six.

Rachel is right. She has a choice. And next year she will not come. Will stay home with Rachel and Skye. Will eat dinner with them on Christmas night. Cranberries and squash sculpted into the shape of a turkey, with bread stuffing and mushroom gravy. Maybe invite some friends over. Everyone will drink wine and toast each other. The conversation will be about important issues. Everyone will be witty and no one will comment on her dress or her makeup. No one will comment on the rings under her eyes, because there will not be any. There will be presents that are not lace underwear or any kind of underwear. Books, current and controversial, wrapped in the kind of paper sold in museum gift shops.

She will renounce her absurd loyalty. The loyalty that has been bred into her. Biologized as some dominant gene through the forces of unnatural selection. The ridge rapes with blunt instruments, the castrations with coal picks, the factory "accidents," all insured the disloyal would not reproduce. Psychologized as some dominant trait through the pressures of family pathologies. The pitiful mother who never had a doll, and the guileless father who justified mental illness with maternal hormones, both insured that the disloyal child would not be loved. And before Evangelina had become Angie, she had wanted more than anything to be loved. More than almost anything.

JANUARY

JANUARY

**JANUARY**

JANUARY

JANUARY

Question. Ans—Objection. Overruled. Instruct the Witness to Answer the Question. Repeat the Question. Question. Answer.

Question. Answer.

Question. Answer. Objection. Sustained. Strike the Answer of the Witness.

Question. Answer.

Mark this as State's Exhibit Three for Identification.

Question. Answer.

Question. Answer.

Question. Answer.

Motion to Admit State's Exhibit Three Marked for Identification as State's Exhibit Three.

Counsel?

No objection.

State's Exhibit Three Marked for Identification Admitted as State's Exhibit Three.

Can you describe the exhibit just admitted into evidence?

The exhibit is a rifle.

Can you describe what kind of rifle it is?

Thirty-o-six.

And what is such a rifle used for, commonly used for?

It's a hunting rifle. Big game. Or deer.


The transcript has its rhythms. Questions. Answers.

Objections.

Sustained. Overruled.

Evidence.

Admitted. Excluded.

Rhythms that swirl under Angie, joining a tidal pool of the hundreds of other transcripts she has read, the countless questions she has asked, the thousands of objections and motions she has made, the innumerable trials she has observed. But now her task is to discover any dissonance in the rhythm. Not simply in performance—a question or an objection or a motion she would have phrased differently. Not simply in strategy—a question she would have asked or not asked. But a dissonance that reverberates with the current state of the law as expressed by an appellate court. She is scavenging for some error, preserved in its proper and precious form, some appealable error.

Angie takes notes on a lavender note pad, cousin to the yellow legal pads so favored by traditional lawyers. Even before unconventional colors infiltrated office supply stores, Angie had preferred white pads to yellow ones. But now Angie has blue and green and even pink in addition to lavender. Sheets of receptive paper for her careful black ink that glides when the fountain pen is clean and glops when the pen is dirty. Although Angie likes to hold her pen under a running kitchen faucet, watching the stream of water go from black to gray to clear, she does not do so often, or soon enough. She will throw this pen away, as she has thrown away so many others, in frustration at its deterioration. She consoles herself that she only purchases the ten-dollar art pens rather than those expensive executive pens with gold nibs and gift boxes advertised in the holiday editions of office supply catalogs. Or those several-hundred-dollar—thousand-dollar, even—Mont Blanc pens that Chelsea and Coleman and Steven and everyone else at Triple-F seem to possess. Always casually slanted across a blank piece of paper on their desks. Or protruding from a jacket or briefcase pocket.

Four hours. Five. In the quiet of her after-hours office. Angie reads. Angie writes. The transcript is an experimental novel, full of repetition yet oddly linear, character development incomplete and the voice of the central characters absent. Question. Answer. Question. Answer. The child's body is explained, but the dead child cannot be interrogated. Did the child speak yet? Was her first word *Mama*? Angie refuses to think of such questions. The only questions that merit attention are the ones in the transcript. Question. Answer. Question. Answer. The defendant's action is explained, but the defendant does not testify. Only the confession. In a letter to her mother. Read by the mother on the stand.

> Did you receive this letter admitted into evidence as State's Exhibit Six?
> I did.
> And do you recognize the handwriting of your daughter, the defendant in this case, Cheryl Martin?
> I—
> Objection. Leading.
> Sust—
> I'll rephrase the question. Can you identify the person who wrote the letter?
> Yes, I can. It's my daughter.
> Please state her name.
> Cheryl Martin.
> And is she the defendant in this case?
> She is.
> And how do you know it's a letter from your daughter?
> Her handwriting. I recognize her handwriting. And it's signed. Cheryl. In her handwriting.

Angie wonders if the mother is crying. How the mother sounds as she testifies. Does the court reporter have to strain to hear the mother as she mumbles? Or does the mother speak clearly, defiantly almost, as she looks at her daughter on trial for the murder of a child, her daughter's child, her own grandchild? What is she wearing? No doubt the prosecutor had told her to wear something appropriate. What could be appropriate? "Perfect for a day of long testimony in a murder trial," the catalog description would read.

Angie is trying to imagine an appropriate accent and doodling on her lavender pad. Because she does not want to read the letter. Maybe she should start smoking cigarettes, she thinks. She could light one now, dangle it from her hand, flick the ember into a ceramic ashtray, postpone the inevitable. Maybe she should just read it and get it over with, she thinks, and does.

*Dear Mom,*

*You want me to explain what happened, but I can't. I don't like explanations. You raised me to hate explanations. You had one for everything. And now, they want to explain me by you. I wouldn't talk about you to the psychiatrist, even though he kept asking about you. As if you were the cause of what happened. Like it's all your fault. He asks me what about our relationship made me hate men. Why doesn't he ask why everybody hates women? Even you. You sighed when I called you and told you my baby was a girl. You told Glen you felt sorry for him with a daughter. Right there in the hospital, do you remember that? I remember. You smiled. Glen smiled. I hated you both. I loved only Emily, in her little glass cage, arm banded to her fate: Girl. Martin.*

*I was already a dyke, long before that long labor doused with Pitocin. I'd been diddling girls through high school. Through college. Even after I got married. Although I've never been sure how that happened. And to Glen, no less. Glen, who told me I'd never get through college. Told me I should be satisfied with him. And his family's gas station. I could do the books. His mother would teach me, he said. Which wouldn't have been half-bad, since she's a cool lady. But I'd have to see more of Glen.*

*I got a job in the bank. Went out with women when I said I had to work the drive-through window. Joined a poetry group. Sometimes Glen climbed on top of me like I was a horse or a whore, and those were the only moments I could think clearly, could face the reality of how horrible it really was. But it never lasted more than five minutes, and almost anything is bearable for five minutes. I'd think about Sylvia Plath and Emily Dickinson and Adrienne Rich.*

*You told me I was lucky to have Glen. I told you I was lucky to get a promotion. And then I told you I was pregnant. And that I thought I was gay. You slapped me in the face, like I was some snot-nosed child, instead of a professional pregnant lesbian.*

Angie looks up from the transcript. Not only a professional lesbian, the words she had heard Kim use so longingly, but a professional pregnant lesbian. Angie could write that on her lavender legal pad, but her mind veers toward seeing the words in a catalog rather than in her own handwriting. An enticing description for a maternity dress, navy blue without ducks or lambs or any sentimentalized animal. Or maybe some sort of accessory, even an appointment Book, black leather certainly. "For the busy professional pregnant lesbian." Angie summons the self-discipline honed in law school, which still serves her so well, and returns to the transcript.

*I named her Emily. So white I could see her veins all over her body. She was so real. I couldn't pretend anymore, somehow. When Glen touched her, I flinched. I gagged. I just couldn't stand to see him touch her. He was so ugly when he touched her. I knew he would try to fuck her. I could just tell. And I hated how you held her. Saying she was spoiled. How can a three-day-old baby be spoiled?*

*So I left. Simple. Easy. Gina got me the rifle, from her brother the deer hunter. For protection from Glen. He said he was going to have someone kill me. Not even do it himself. He said he loved me too much. What a joke. Months passed. I was safe. Glen was going to go away quietly. His mother called me, we talked a long long time. I didn't tell her about women, but just said I didn't think I was compatible with Glen. You called me to say you felt sorry for him, didn't ask how I was. I thought I'd move, out of state. San Francisco, maybe. Then he came over screaming that you told him I was gay. Started to choke me. Grabbed Emily and she screamed and he put her down. I got the rifle from the closet. Saw him blurry through the scope. Warned him. Told him I knew how to shoot and I would if I had to. Emily screaming and screaming. And him calling me names over Emily's screams. Said he was going to kill her, 'cause I'd turn her into a little bulldagger. I pulled the trigger like I practiced, but I didn't realize he had picked up Emily again. That bastard. That fucking bastard. He must have used her as a shield. I never saw her. Only him. That fucking bastard.*

*That's the only explanation there is. I'm not talking to the psychiatrist or the cops or any lawyers. Glen's mother got a lawyer to come and see me. Doesn't that sound strange? But I think she's about the only one I trust anymore.*

*Please do not come to visit me. You can write me letters if you want.*
*Your daughter,*
*Cheryl*

The letter's anger dislocates Angie. Somehow she thought it would be softer. Full of *I'm sorrys* and *I love yous.* Or at least something that the mother reading the letter out loud to the jury could emphasize with a trembling voice, letting the jury know that *my daughter is a good daughter; my daughter should not get the death penalty.* But Angie's new client is a not a good daughter. If a good daughter finds herself in jail, she consoles her mother, telling her everything will be fine, asking her for something small like a hairbrush or a Bible. That letter sure did not do anything to make Cheryl Martin sympathetic, even if it did say she did not mean to shoot the baby. Only her husband. Angie makes a note on her lavender pad to check any transferred-intent instructions to the jury.

Angie picks up the telephone. Calls home. Waits for Rachel to pick up the answering machine, but there is only her own voice, then silence. Leaves a message: "It's ten o'clock. I'm on my way." Leaves the transcript on her desk, yellow Post-it notes protruding and the lavender pad marking her place. Does not call Kim. Does not stop for something to eat. Although she thinks about doing both, walking through the large darkness toward her little car.

In the middle of a bridge, fumbling for a toll token, Angie realizes she is incredibly tired; so tired she is nauseated. Her bones feel brittle, too big and too sharp for her cringing-with-cold body, and yet too soft and small to support her sixty-mile-an-hour suspension over the water. A headache nags, claiming its due in the absence of distracting words. The radio is static; she switches from one station to another, pushing buttons. The heater is sullen. She slides the knob to maximum, hearing air.

When she slams on the brakes to avoid an accident, her head jerks and she supresses the urge to vomit. Soon, the motionless car in front of her begins to inch forward. Angie shifts into first and follows, hearing Claire's voice folded into the voice of every other mother: *If every kid in the neighborhood jumped off a bridge, does that mean you'd do it too?* But also hearing the disembodied voices of her legal training, in which the answer to every question is *It depends.*

The pothole is bottomless. Angie can look through the over-tarred surface, through the crumbling sub-base, down the perpendicular tunnel of air, into the water reflecting the bridge's necklace of lights. She eases the car around the hole, feeling as if she could easily disappear down it, some metropolitan Alice without a waiting wonderland.



Rachel is sitting at the kitchen table, demanding to know where she has been, why she has not called, why she is so late.

"I did call. I told you I'd be home later than usual. I thought there wouldn't be a problem. This is your night to get Skye and everything."

"The problem is that it's after eleven."

"I left a message when I left at ten."

"Big deal."

"I was working."

"That's all you ever do."

For Angie, work explains everything. Everything that needs to be explained. For Rachel, work explains nothing. Nothing can explain why Angie is not home, not with Rachel and Skye.

It is an old conflict, embedded in their relationship. Angie had thought that the explanation was class. The working class explains itself with work. The upper class does not need to explain itself. But Angie knows it is something more complicated. Rachel's accusations have the lilt and stress of Claire's rantings. Claire screaming at the adolescent Angie, demanding to know where Angie had been, why she had not called, why she was late. Why she would rather be at the library than with her own flesh-and-blood mother.

"All I ever do?" Angie asks. It feels like a brave question. Angie does not like to invite argument. Does not like the facts and figures that hover just inside her headache. How much money she makes from her work which allows them to afford this house; how far she has to commute because they live here where Rachel wanted; how many nights she waits for Rachel to get home from work or a meeting or some drinks with her colleagues.

Rachel does not answer, except to say, "Come to bed."

"In a minute," Angie says, watching Rachel walk down the hall to the bedroom.


Angie thinks she should call her best friend. Only she does not know who it is. The problem with being a dyke, she thinks, is that you sleep with your best friend, but you call her your lover. And most of the time this works, except when you fight with your lover, because then you do not have a best friend when you need one. Like now. She could call Ellen: too late. She could call Kim: too complicated. She could call Laura: too incestuous. She could call Roger: too strange. Besides, Ellen would want to talk about Triple-F; Kim would want to cajole her into passion; Laura would want to pretend that they had never been lovers or gotten drunk together; Roger would want to reveal his woman within. She could wake up Skye, sit her at the kitchen table, and give her milk and cookies like Claire used to do to Angie when Claire had a bad dream.

If she had a sister, Angie thinks, she would telephone her. Or maybe she could call her brother, if she had one.

Angie telephones Claire. Why else have a mother, she thinks, if not to call her late at night and long distance, feeling lonely and seething with self-pity?

Claire is awake, dying, crying. She had been to the doctor. Although she did not have the money to pay, did not have anyone to go with her, did not have the strength to get back home. There were more blood tests. And a prescription for Prozac.

"I'll send you some money."

"I don't need your money."

Claire does not know whether she should get the prescription filled. People had been on television saying Prozac had made them commit murder. But people had been on television saying it made them be able to live their own lives.

Angie assumes these are two different sets of people. Although that is the problem with the truths of these TV talk shows: There are two sides to every story. Two carefully crafted opposing sides. Never the side about the pharmaceutical companies' profits; never the side about a society that fosters depression in women.

"I don't know much about it," Angie says, "but I'm working on this case—"

"I am not one of your cases. I am your mother."

"I know that. I was just saying—"

"You think you can say whatever you want?"

"No."

Silence. Angie wonders what she would say to Claire if she could say whatever she wanted. Would she tell her about Cheryl Martin? Cheryl Martin's mother? How she has to struggle to identify with her client instead of her client's mother? How she hardly thinks of the child with a gunshot hole through her head?

Or would she tell her how she wanted—more than almost anything—Claire to be another mother, one who would soothe and appreciate Angie. One who did not demand that Angie act like the mother. One who did not have a difficult life, but a life of comfort and brilliant colors. One who Angie almost always expected to find at the other end of the telephone when she called. *Hope springs eternal.* Angie clenches her teeth.


Claire slams down the receiver.

Angie opens her Book. Makes a new list on a gridded sheet of paper:

> *Prozac*
> *—Claire*
> *—Cheryl Martin*

Angie answers the phone when it rings, knowing it is Claire, calling back. Claire crying. Claire apologizing.

Everything Angie could think of to say has already been said, used up, depleted. Even "I love you" seems like a salve gone all crusty at the edges. Maybe just being at the other end of the phone is enough.

It is not. And Claire tells her it is not. "You should be here with me," Claire says.

They say good night. Exchange *I love yous.*

Angie thinks Claire should try the drug. Why not?

Although Cheryl Martin might be able to give some reasons. Angie tries to recall what the trial attorney had told her, in one of those long and threatening-to-become-uncomfortable telephone conversations about the trial. Part of the defense? No, she would remember. Maybe only in the penalty phase? Offered by whom? It is somewhere in the transcript, somewhere in the thousand or so pages she has not yet read.

It is quiet after midnight. Skye sleeps. Rachel sleeps. Angie goes from room to room, looking at each of them. Anxious. Maybe a shower will help relax her. The bathroom is a mess. The rug bunched and the water dripping in the shower. The bath mat still on the floor, instead of draped neatly over the side of the tub. And the shower curtain all pushed to one side, courting mold. Her hairbrush with the bristles flattened on the sink counter.

Angie straightens everything, which she calls cleaning. And then the kitchen. Shaking out the Indian-print tablecloth in the freezing night air. Why is it so cold? she wonders. The trees look silver past the deck. Bare and silver. The winter is so long. So ugly. Maybe a new rug for under the table. Something bright, Mexican or South American. Where is that catalog that markets directly from the peasants? "The people get the profits." Perhaps one of the people getting the profits is Skye's mother, her other mother, her third mother, her biological mother. Angie closes her eyes, ties to close her mind. It is such a struggle sometimes, there is so much to deny.

A hot bath with freesia-fragranced bubbles. A clean bathroom with folded towels. A catalog featuring foot-loomed cloth made by genuine peasant collectives. Only now Angie is thinking about a nightshirt. Something in a cotton flannel. Soft, without a collar but oversized, like a man's giant shirt. Definitely with buttons up and down the front of the entire shirt so that she could button the bottom ones and let the top ones open just below her breast. Maybe Rachel would think her sexy then, so sexy Rachel could not be mad at her when she worked late.

The local radio station pries open Angie's puffy eyes. Coffee from Rachel, like a sugared and creamed apology. Snow. Only a dusting in the city. But the valley has powder. Maybe two inches, more predicted.

School closings: Meadowlark School. Skye is excited. Rachel is waiting for courthouse closings. Delayed openings, one hour: county offices, including county court and all village courts.

"What time is your trial?"

"Two."

"I guess that doesn't help."

"Not really."

"I'll take Skye down to Triple-F with me."

"You're going to work?"

"I have to. If I would have known it was going to snow, I would have brought the transcript home."

"They were announcing it yesterday."

"I guess I didn't hear."

"If you would have called me I could have told you."

"And if you would have answered the phone when I called as I was leaving you could have told me," Angie taunts, almost laughing.

Rachel does not rise to the bait. She needs to save her arguments for this afternoon's court.

At Triple-F, everyone always acts glad to see Skye. She is one of the more well-behaved kids who inhabit the office on the many school holidays that are not work holidays. Well-behaved because she will sit and read *The Boxcar Twins* or *The Baby-sitters Club* or one of the *Nancy Drew and the Hardy Boys SuperMysteries*. Well-behaved because she will not sit on the copying machine with her pants pulled down making copies of her ass. People at Triple-F variously appreciate Skye for getting bigger every time they see her, for answering their questions about school politely, for keeping them company in the lunchroom playing cards or for running downstairs to the vending machines to get Cokes.

"Your office is messy." Skye pronounces, putting down her backpack in her usual corner.

"That's rude." Angie scolds.

"Sorry."

"But you're right, Skye. It is messy. It just is not a very nice thing to say to me after we had to drive so long in bad weather."

"Sorry." Skye pauses, "but I thought you said the drive was pretty."

"I wouldn't say 'pretty.' " Angie is still not inured to the ugliness of this fraction of geography, punctuated with rusted steel: bridges, cars, and refrigerators parked along expressway exits.

"But you said that the river looked like a pretty beach."

"I guess I did." Angie reaches over to smooth Skye's hair, remembering the shimmering fingers of ice stretching like sandbars across the halting river. She had pointed out the scene to Skye, thinking it was enchanting enough to be a calendar photo—"January"—and is now oddly touched that Skye recalls its stark beauty. But Angie's sentimental joy twists toward the cynical as she strokes Skye's static-filled hair, wondering whether Skye will revisit the glittering ice floes or whether the scene will mature into the flat and ugly landscape that is childhood. And as Angie pulls Skye closer despite the child's squirms, Angie realizes she hopes that Skye will kiss Angie's own spikes of soft hair.

*I'm fucking losing it.* The words form in Angie's mind, like a note to herself on the graph paper in her appointment Book. But as soon as she comprehends, she decompensates, more a rearrangement than disassociation. She is responsible for Skye, she chides herself, assuming the expression of accountability she once reserved for Claire.

"Why don't you get us some Cokes." Angie lets go of Skye, almost pushing her away. "The change is in that box on my desk."

"Can I have one?"

"Yes, I said so."

"Before lunch?" Sky asks. Reminding Angie of one of Angie's own rules.

"Yes." Angie is firm. She wonders if she should tell Skye that sometimes it is fine for rules to be broken; that sometimes one should not call attention to an obstacle; that sometimes one should just lie low. That sometimes one should not be such a good girl. Or maybe these are things that a mother should not tell her daughter; cannot.

Skye counts out the quarters, singing a little.

"Remember, I want the diet kind."

"I know," Skye says, "you always do."

"Not always."

"Almost always," Skye insists.

"You don't know what I get when you're not here."

Skye tilts her head, still amazed that people—including Angie—live their lives outside of her own presence. "What do you get?"

"The diet kind."

Skye asks, "Who gets it for you?

"I go to the vending machine myself."

Skye is incredulous. "You do?"

"Of course I do. Who do you think gets it for me, a little elf?"

"You could ask one of the interns." Skye suggests, demonstrating her knowledge of office hierarchy.

"That wouldn't be right."

"Why not?"

" 'Cause some things you don't ask other people that you work with to do for you."

"You ask them to get books and stuff."

"That's the kind of stuff I should ask them. That's their job."

"Oh. You ask me."

"That's different. You don't work here. Now, are you going to go get the Cokes or what?"

"Can I get Sprite?"

"That would be fine."

"Orange?"

"Sure."

"Skittles?"

"No candy. I said a drink."

"Later? Can I have candy later?"

"Skye. What did I say?"

Skye does not answer, but leaves for the vending machines. Angie thinks that perhaps she does not have to worry about Skye being too good a girl after all. Evangelina would never have persisted.


A woman, looking either sexy or mean or maybe both, stares up from Angie's chair. She is black and white and on a postcard, at the very top of the neat stack of morning mail Walter has so scrupulously and demandingly positioned on her chair, one of his many recently developed strategies to improve efficiency in an organization of lawyers with messy desks. She has to remove the entire pile before she can sit down, but she picks up only the postcard. The curve of one breast, almost revealed. A hand under it, fingers spread across the ribs. Hair waved over half the face. The other eye, shadowed and catlike. The dress, striped and catlike. The fingernails, catlike: must be fake or not a dyke. Angie looks at the postcard more closely, recognizing it as a particular type of celebrity photo card, but not recognizing the celebrity. She flips it over: "Jodie Foster. Los Angeles. 1987." She reads the signature: "Kim." With some sort of stylized dot over the *i*. At least it is not a heart or smiley face, Angie thinks; at least it is not a long letter scented with rose toilet water. She turns the postcard back over. Looking at the woman she now knows is Jodie Foster. Wondering what Jodie Foster thought about this photo session; if she even thought about such things anymore after all those years in front of all those cameras. Angie has never really liked Jodie Foster, although she has never really disliked her either. Once, Angie would have looked at the postcard and wondered why the sender chose this one to send. Now, she only thinks fleetingly that other postcards from that series would have been better: Vita Sackville-West or Emily Dickinson or even Janis Joplin. Or maybe even a postcard not in that series: a real dyke, someone with enough guts to call herself a lesbian and take the consequences. Someone who lost her kids for it. Or killed them. Someone real.

Angie puts Kim's Jodie Foster postcard down on her desk without reading it; starts to read and sort the rest of her mail. Pleadings. Letters. Including a letter from Cheryl Martin #156-84G562P. Angie rips it open, wondering why Walter has not slit it with the electric letter opener he had recently purchased. Never enough copy paper, but now there is an electric letter opener. Which Walter is not using on all the mail. Although perhaps Walter judged the letter too personal. Handwritten. A letter from a client in prison more personal than a postcard of Jodie Foster from a legal intern. But the postcard did not need to be slit; it laid itself open. For a moment, Angie wonders if Walter read the postcard and what words he read. She shakes her head. Of course Walter read the postcard, and of course its words were as stylized and vague as the dot in Kim's insipid signature. So Angie does not read whatever it is that Kim has written.

The envelope holds two sheets of yellow paper, filled with words. Angie looks at the handwriting, knowing Cheryl Martin's mother testified that she recognized this as the handwriting of her daughter, the defendant. It is small and exact. Just loose enough not to be cramped, but barely. There are some loops, but not many. Although it is not printing. Definitely cursive, as Skye would say. But Skye does not comment, even though she looks at the letter in Angie's hands as Skye puts the Diet Coke on Angie's desk, in a corner, away from the pages of transcript and the lavender legal pad. Skye opens her own Sprite, carefully holding the can away from her body, and settles in a chair to read her book: *A Nancy Drew and the Hardy Boys SuperMystery: Trial by Fire.* Sometimes Angie will ask Skye about a book, interrupting as Skye laboriously relates the plot with detailed twists and turns and self-interruptions. But today Angie only mumbles thanks for the Coke as she harmonizes Cheryl Martin's letter with the letter she read in the transcript last night. The letter starts off businesslike, but then slides into the rituals common to all prisoners. First the blaming: her attorneys, her ex-husband, her mother, and all the "scummy fat cats who only pretend to care." Then the stroking: her faith that Angie is different because they are both "gay women" and have known the "hate that men have in their hearts for women like us." Then the prize: "My case shows how gay women cannot get a fair trial and if I would have been a straight mother who accidentally shot her baby daughter when her husband was using the child as a shield and was going to kill her, would I have got the death penalty? No way!"

Angie does not need the letter for assigning blame, being cajoled, or providing political incentives. She has already accepted the case, already agreed to write the brief on appeal, already filed her *pro hac vice* motion supported by local counsel, already made plans to get some lesbian organizations to join as amici. Angie only wants information from Cheryl Martin's letter, something that might lead to some appealable error. But Angie will read every letter from Cheryl Martin—and she is sure there will be many more—twice. She gets a file folder and writes out a label: "C. Martin: PERSONAL CORRESPONDENCE." She will two-hole-punch each letter at the top and clasp it to the left side of the folder. She will write once a week, but no more, keeping a copy of her letter clasped to the right side of the file folder. She will continue to work, harder and harder.

Still, the first letter from a client always has a certain impact. Cheryl Martin's handwriting stays with Angie when she returns to the transcript, rereading the letter Cheryl Martin's mother read into testimony. Now Angie knows where the exclamation points and underlinings would be. Now Angie knows where the little smiley face would go, above Cheryl's name and without an outline. Only two eyes, a dot nose, and an ambiguously curved mouth. Just like the one at the end of Cheryl's letter to Angie, the letter in the new file folder on her desk, among the sliding sheets of transcript.

After the guilty verdict, after lunch with Ellen and Roger at the kosher pizza parlor chosen by Skye, after Skittles, after a long phone call from Gertie Geldenshel, Cheryl Martin's (former?) mother-in-law, after a meeting called to review current litigation but devoted to a discussion only of Chelsea's newest case, and after an extended argument with Walter about whether it is possible to get some support staff assistance with organizing the pages and pages and pages of the Cheryl Martin transcript, Angie packs up the still unorganized and unread portions of the transcript, her lavender legal pads (now three) of Cheryl Martin notes, her unanswered mail, and her child.

"See you tomorrow, Walter." Angie wants to make sure there are no repercussions from her disagreements with him. They both know he could make her life hell.

"No, you won't, sweetheart," Walter answers cheerfully.

"Going somewhere?"

"Lots of wonderful places. To see lots of wonderful boys and do lots of wonderful things. Like you should do on Saturday. Not the boys part, but the wonderful things. Tomorrow is Saturday, which means not even you should be working."

"I wish."

"You're not wishing on the right stars," Walter says softly. "Angie.

Take the advice of your best butch secretary. Take a break. Let's ask for an extension to file the brief. Let's say you're sick or something, before you really are."

"Other things will just pile up."

"Let them. Take tomorrow off, at least. Get religion or something. You know, if you don't relax—and I mean *relax,* if you know what I mean but can't say at the moment"—Walter pauses for effect, nodding toward Skye—"you are going to just keep getting bitchier and bitchier."

"Oh? Is it that bad?" Angie tries to sound light.

"Actually, it's getting that way. And if you can't get it at home, just try that Jodie Foster look-alike intern with the fangs who is always following you around with her tongue hanging out."

"*Walter.*" Angie refrains from asking Walter if he thinks Kim really looks like Jodie Foster.

"That is, if you haven't already."

"Walter. *Really.*"

"Hey, my lips are sealed." Walter slides his index finger across his smile. "But if you want my opinion—or even if you don't—what you've got at home beats the Foster clone by a mile."

"Do you have all your books?" Angie turns away from Walter and toward Skye.

"Yes."

"Then let's get the heck out of Dodge," Angie says.

"Yes, let's," Walter agrees.

"Want a ride to the subway stop?"

"No, I'm riding into the city with Steven. You two just go along."

And they do. Angie and Skye in the little car, snuggled in their seat belts, going across bridges and into the valley, home. An "outlying area north and west of the city" where it is starting to snow again, at least according to the radio.


It is winter-dark in the valley. Angie navigates off the highway, sliding past the village courthouse to see if Rachel's truck is still in the parking lot, gathering snow. Angie pulls next to it, refrains from telling Skye that maybe Rachel could not get the truck started again, tries to sound as if she has just had a sudden inspiration to check if Rachel's trial is still going on.

It is. Judge Burnstein is not one to adjourn court early, even if it is snowing, especially when the trial would have to be put over until Monday morning. Angie and Skye push open the heavy squeaky door and sit in the back of the small courtroom. The judge nods at Skye almost imperceptibly, recognizing Rachel's daughter as a child who will cause no trouble. Skye is as comfortably quiet in court as someone who has regularly appeared in courtrooms since she was a baby, being hoisted by one mother or another, being held in the back by a client or a paralegal or a student intern or her other mother.

Skye smiles as she listens to Rachel cross-examine a witness. Or maybe it is the direct examination of a hostile witness; or maybe Rachel is taking advantage of a non-objecting opposing counsel. However allowed, Rachel is dancing the dance of leading questions. She plunges and pirouettes while the witness is immobilized, sweating through his suit. Angie figures out that he is the manager of a ramshackle apartment building near the river: a slumlord.

"No further questions." Rachel announces.

"That guy is a creep," Skye whispers as the manager exits the courtroom.

"The defense rests," Rachel's opposing attorney declares, standing up. Then sitting down.

"No rebuttal." Rachel announces, rising.

"Arguments?"

"I have some motions." The opposing attorney stands up again.

"Why don't I just consider that all motions are renewed? And any other motions can be submitted in writing within ten days. I think we should get on with the closing arguments so that we can get home while the roads are still passable."

The judge's clerk sighs. The attorneys nod.

"Counsel?" Judge Bernstein turns to Rachel.

If an opening argument is a map, then closing argument is the final sales pitch. Angie and Rachel and probably every law student who took trial practice or clinic in law school heard metaphors and maxims about trial arguments, but none of the wisdom ever made sense until each of them stood up in a courtroom in front of a client and performed. Rachel's performance sparkles; it is rehearsed without being stilted, a catalog of the evidence presented, arranged under each item she has to prove to win her case. And Rachel wants to win; Angie can sense that and assumes everyone else can. It gives her an attractive edge as she sits down, yielding to her opposing attorney as he puts on his glasses.

The opposing attorney's closing argument is not bad, although Angie resists thinking that it is as good as Rachel's. He is pointing out the defects in Rachel's claim of damages, just as Rachel had pointed out the defects in the apartment building. He has a confidence about him—an aura of success—and when he takes his glasses off and holds them in his hand, Angie just hopes that Rachel can win back her advantage. But instead of sitting down, he continues talking, casually and almost conversationally, to the judge.

"Your honor, while I'm sure there are some heartfelt feelings about this case on the side of plaintiffs and their attorney, that really isn't the issue here. Nor is the issue their loss of some insignificant pieces of property due to any supposed problems with the apartment building in question. No, the real issue here is the sanctity of private property. This really isn't about these tenants against a landlord; it's socialism against democracy. Yes, that's right: That's what's really at stake in this case. They are just complaining because we don't have a socialist system, and my client, Redwing Housing Incorporated, must insist on democratic freedom. To find in favor of the plaintiffs would be to find in favor of socialism. And therefore, because we live in a democracy, judgment must be entered in favor of my client. Thank you."

Rachel stands up. In front of an elected judge in a small county. So Rachel cannot laugh, cannot say that if she had known socialism was part of the stakes in this trial she would have prepared better, cannot say that in every case she litigates the contours of capitalism are the underlying issue, cannot say this is fucking ridiculous, cannot do anything other than begin her rebuttal argument in a serious and studied tone. She reiterates the defects in the apartment building, reiterates the evidence that proved the defects: her clients' testimony, the public health inspection, the county building inspector's report, the apartment building manager's admission made on cross-examination. Then Rachel invokes democracy, the role of the rule of law, the law's equal application to rich or poor, the law's purpose of preserving individual liberties even against the free enterprise of corporations, as the law protected citizens against the robber barons of the nineteenth century.

"Objection. I think we can be spared the history lesson." The opposing counsel stands, putting a hand on his hip.

"Overruled." The judge pronounces. "You opened the door on this one, counsel, so you will have to endure it." The judge smiles at Rachel. "Although I trust counsel will only provide us with the broad outlines of the New Deal and the War on Poverty and the Rise of the Welfare State."

"Only the broad outlines," Rachel agrees. But she spends at least five minutes, saying things that Angie knew that Rachel knew, but had never really heard Rachel utter with such conviction, or at all. Speaking long after Angie would have sat down, thinking her point had been made, thinking she had won her case with the judge's reference to the war on poverty. Rachel yokes history to her clients, their "insignificant possessions," their tenancy at an apartment in horrible disrepair, their requests and pleas and demands for hot water and a door with a lock and things "most of us are lucky enough to take for granted." Rachel is making a closing argument meant for a jury, while the judge sits impassive. When Rachel concludes with a "Therefore plaintiffs respectfully request" and a "Thank you," Angie can see the sweat through her lover's black jacket.


"You were really great," Angie tells her. They are sitting in the health-food bar, the only place open on this snowy Friday night. When their fruited sparkling waters arrive, Skye says "Let's toast!" She lifts up the Boysenberry Delight bottle, waits for Angie's Peach and Rachel's Kiwi-Strawberry, and shouts "To court!"

"Shhh!" Rachel scolds, but she is laughing.


Angie refuses to romanticize work. Still, it is hard not to feel guilty after seeing Rachel's performance. Angie is suffering by comparison, resolving to work harder, to hone her desire to win, to be more focused. To stop fucking off.

To stop fucking that intern.

Steam rises from the bathwater, scalding Angie's testing foot. The water is always too hot at first, she thinks, turning on the cold. Always too hot, always the same pattern. Even when she knows it will be a mistake—or maybe especially then—she feels incapable of change.

So much in control, she is out of control.

When the water is cool enough to her toes—too cold, really—she lowers her body into the porcelain tub. Then she turns on the hot, full blast. The water reddens her skin with resolve.

Tomorrow will be the day—no, Monday—to speak with Kim. To tell her it has all been a mistake. Some momentary lapse of morals, of judgment. Angie imagines herself gracious, if not honest. She will refrain from the impolite words—*monogamy, mistake, power*—and the impolitic sentiments—*the sex was never very satisfying.* She will not compare herself to Kim, or Rachel to Kim, or herself to Claire. She will not confess: *I've got no fucking idea . . .* She will only extract, escape, efface.

She will only work, harder and harder.

She feels clean, as if everything is solved.

Yet the details of work still seem overwhelming. She is both disappointed and shocked when she returns from the bathroom to the extra room that is her study. The computer glows with WordPerfect blue, a false azure Mediterranean touted as restful for the eyes, ricocheting off the Apparition Blue walls. The floor is carpeted with photocopied cases, pages bent across the staples, and Post-it notes sticking only to each other.

Certainly she had known it would be like this. When she was in law school; when she took the job at Triple-F. Certainly she had known. Confident in her capacity for work. Reveling in her work because it was not a factory, not a rocky field or someone else's kitchen; because it was not the work Claire did; because it was not the work anyone ever thought Evangelina would do. Her work: day after day. Every night until midnight. Year after year, learning to be a mother, first bathing Skye, then reading to Skye, then checking Skye's brushed teeth, then enforcing lights-out. Always, always tucking Skye into bed, even if Skye was already asleep and well loved by her other mother, even now that the custom has become superfluous, tolerated rather than craved by Skye.

Certainly she had known. But she had not. Or had not known she had known. Not known how work would drive her, her inner taskmaster more demanding than any boss she had ever had. And had not known, and still could not admit, how work could be anesthesia, the insulated container for every rage, every pain, every unnamable absence.

How work could organize life, almost completely. But tonight, there is a bag of potato chips, empty. Three Coke cans, half empty. No cigarettes. Still the longing for one, after all these years. Still the longing for something slender in her fingers, something slender and hot that she could suck on and that would seem almost to suck back.

On the white melamac desk are pencils sharpened by Skye. A lead pencil, a gift she had given to Rachel and then appropriated. Her good pen: the ten-dollar art pen. Cap open, ink dried on the tip. A stack of lavender legal pads, half used.

The computer table is piled with borrowed lawbooks: rules of procedure, rules of evidence, rules of rules. And for Cheryl Martin's case, there are medical dictionaries, psychology treatises, and firearms manuals. Some books she will catalog as secondary sources in the table of contents to her brief. But some sources are not for citation, only for her own understanding. Another page marked by another postcard from some legal intern, to check someone else's understanding. Possible guideposts in the search for the Holy Grail of appellate attorneys: appealable error, perfectly preserved.


She is making grids in WordPerfect. Tables with columns and rows. Listing possible issues in the trial. Relevant testimony. Relevant pages of the transcript. Relevant precedent: Favorable / Unfavorable.

Rachel is luminous in the reflection from the blue screen. Standing there in a nightshirt, brushed cotton but with satin piping, ordered by Angie from a catalog. Angie remembers that the color is called Evergreen Dreams.

"That color looks good on you." Angie turns away from the computer screen to face Rachel.

"I'd never know you thought so."

"Why not? I've told you before."

"For all the attention you pay me."

"Hey. What's the matter? I told you I need to outline this Cheryl Martin brief."

"It's eleven-thirty on a Saturday night. We should be out dancing."

"We haven't gone out dancing in years, if we ever did."

"That's my point," Rachel says.

"Are you saying I'm boring?"

"No. I'm saying that I think we could at least have a conversation on a Saturday night. Maybe even a glass of wine. Sit and talk to each other."

"What do you want to talk about?"

"At this point, anything except the Riflewoman."

"Don't call her that."

"Oh, shit, Angie. You know if I had to compete with someone real I might be able to do it. Maybe even with some of those little interns that run around your office thinking you are just the most amazing thing since sliced bread."

Angie decides not to reply.

"But I can't compete," Rachel continues, "with all these tragic dykes who will die unless the great Angie Evans comes to their rescue."

"That's not fair, Rachel. I don't accuse you of wanting to rescue your clients. You know this is lots of work. It's not like you're some little housewife. You work hard, too. You just worked really hard in that trial. You work hard a lot."

"That's right, I do. That's why I know you're going overboard. That's why I know that the world will not collapse if you take a few hours to spend with your lover on a Saturday night. Maybe if I was some little housewife you could fool me. I'd believe it was all so important and I was lucky just to be in the presence of someone so great."

"I don't think I'm so great, Rachel."

"I know you don't. I'm not saying that. I'm just saying that you aren't the world's mother, Angie. You need to forget about all this shit once in a while. And you need to pay some attention to me."

"I don't think I'm everybody's mother, Rachel."

"Don't get mad. Just come to bed. Leave this stuff for the morning."

"Okay. I'll be right there."

"Why don't you come now?" Rachel invites. "Let's sit in bed and have a glass of wine."

"We don't have any."

"I bought some red," Rachel says. "Warms you up on a cold snowy night."

"Okay. I'll be right there. Just let me finish filling in this section so I don't lose track of the work I've done tonight."

"Promise?"

"Yes. I like that color on you," Angie winks. "It will look good against the sheets. Or on the floor."

"I'll get the wine." Rachel's voice drifts from the hall, toward the kitchen.

Angie taps ALT-F7 to make another WordPerfect table. "Get back to basics," she says to the computer. She labels a column "Elements." The structure of every criminal offense is the same: actus reus, mens rea. The weak link has to be mens rea: intent. Angie moves her cursor to the mens rea row, making the boxes bigger and bigger with the return key. But still blank.


"I don't fuck after midnight," Rachel says as Angie slides next to her, as Angie slides her hand around Rachel's abdomen, spreading her fingers across Rachel's rib just under the breast.

"Have you turned into a little pumpkin?" Angie teases.

"I would have rotted by now."

"Don't be angry at me, babe."

"I'm not angry," Rachel says. Angrily.

"Come on, Cinderella, let me take you dancing."

"You're too late. Case closed." Rachel takes Angie's hand and places it on Angie's own stomach.

"I'm appealing." Angie puts her hand back, this time closer to the breast.

"You've got no grounds." Rachel removes Angie's hand again. And then Rachel turns over.

Angie looks at the glass of wine on her wicker nightstand. It is empty, with only a tiny concave memory of cabernet. Angie looks at the clock radio on the wicker dresser. It is 1:33, with the digital precision of liquid crystal display. Angie thinks she will have troubling finding sleep, but it finds her.


"We'll see you later."

"Where are you going?" Angie sits up. There is sunlight in the bedroom.

"Skiing." Rachel announces.

"Skiing?" Angie asks, as if it is a foreign term.

"Yes, skiing. You know, snow and mountains and those long flat blades at the end of your legs."

Skye is at the bedroom door, giggling.

"Oh. You want me to get ready?"

"No. We're already late. Remember our date with Laura and Vickie and Jesse? You know, our friends. You remember them, don't you?"

Skye giggles again.

Angie does not answer.

"See you later."

"What time will you be home?" Angie asks.

"You'll probably still be working," Rachel says. "Come on, Skye. Jesse wants to have someone her own size on the slopes."

Angie listens to the car start. Wondering since when Rachel wanted to ski. Wondering when she last saw Laura and Vickie and their kid Jesse. Wondering if Rachel left her any hot coffee.


Angie is making a list of articles to locate: "Serotonergic Mechanisms Promote Dominance Acquisitions in Adult Male Vervet Monkeys"; "Biological Predictors of Depression-Related Anger Attacks"; "Fluoxetine and Violence: A Meta-analysis of Controlled Trials of Treatment for Depression."

The expert testimony in the penalty phase is convoluted, but luckily Angie has the trial attorney's excellent memo outlining the relevant studies. Cheryl Martin's doctor testified that he had prescribed Prozac, generically known as fluoxetine, to the defendant for her depression. Cheryl Martin's expert testified that, on the basis of studies of patients without a "notable" history of violence, he believed Prozac could obscure judgment and make an otherwise nonviolent person subject to uncontrollable acts of aggression. The state's expert testified, on the basis of studies of monkeys, that Prozac did not—and could not—increase a person's capacity for violence. The jury, now charged not with determining guilt or innocence but with recommending whether Cheryl Martin should receive the death sentence, is the arbiter in this battle of the experts. Angie has to find out why they gave the wrong answer. Within this morass of scientific jargon, Angie thinks, there must be appealable error. But first, Angie has to understand the morass.

Question. Answer.

Question. Answer.

Encoded physiologically as altered neurotransmitter systems.

The relatives of dysthymic women may be biologically predisposed to act aggressively.

Clinical psychopharmacology is not an exact science, your honor.

There are hardly any objections.

Angie has three pages on her lavender legal pad of sources to obtain when she reaches the end of the medical testimony. She skips over the testimony of Cheryl Martin's mother-in-law, Cheryl Martin's mother, and even Cheryl Martin. She will read these when she is not so tired, when her head is not spinning with chemistry's syllables.

She marks her place with the Jodie Foster postcard. Goes to the window, looking for Rachel and Skye. Makes a pot of coffee. Thinks about a cigarette. Goes back to the transcript. Flips through the unread pages, idly.

Strangely, she is reading the jury's recommendation. And even more strangely, what she is reading is that the jury is recommending life. Eight to four. A majority of the jury members do not recommend the death penalty. Why didn't she know this? Why didn't that stupid trial attorney tell her? She flips to the trial judge's sentencing opinion. The judge imposes death. Overriding the jury's recommendation.

Angie remembers the case, but not its name. The case holding this unconstitutional. The case from the United States Supreme Court. The case that states that a trial judge cannot impose death when the jury recommends life. Angie remembers.

"Fuck science!" Angie says out loud. "Fuck Prozac and those fucking witch doctors with their big words and monkey torture. Who needs them? I've got the law. The law."

"And fuck Indiana!" Angie yells, scattering the copies of cases from the Northeastern Reporter, Second Series, across her small study. "I've never understood what Indiana was doing in the Northeastern Reporter, anyway. But now it doesn't matter. I've got the Supreme Court. The Supremes!"

She telephones Kim before she realizes what she is doing, excitement surging through her synapses. "I found it. I found it," she tells Kim. "Now I want you to find me that case. Get to the law school library as soon as you can. Find me that case. We are going to win Cheryl Martin."

"You sound so happy," Kim says.

"I am."

"I'm glad you called *me.*" Kim hugs the last word close.

Angie flinches. Does not explain that her intentions were only pragmatic: Kim as legal intern, the only person Angie could command to do research. Not Kim as lover.

Angie vows to explain everything to Kim the next time she sees her. To do it over the telephone is simply too cruel. And by then, Kim will have the research completed. Angie imagines taking Kim to lunch. They will drink cappuccino from mugs, like the ones in the *HOME* catalog, eight ounces of tempered glass in the classic Irish-coffee shape. A bit of whipped cream will settle on Kim's lip, above her bicuspid, as Angie congratulates her on a job well done. And then Angie will explain, gently, the way she rehearsed it in the bathtub.

As she cleans up the study, waiting for Rachel and Skye, Angie is amazed at how simple everything suddenly seems.

Then Angie cleans up the kitchen, waiting for Rachel and Skye.

Angie telephones Laura and Vickie, looking for Rachel and Skye. No answer. No message.

Angie drinks red wine, in bed alone, wondering where Rachel and Skye could be. It's a school night, after all. And it has been so long since she and Rachel have made love.

FEBRUARYS

FEBRUARYS

**FEBRUARYS**

FEBRUARYS

FEBRUARYS

The boys are brutal and the girls are bitchy. Even Skye seems strange to Angie, less individual and more gendered. But across any sexual divides, the children are unanimous in their complaints about the party favors.

"I'm really disappointed about this," a girl named Deirdre tells Angie.

"Don't you think balls are boring?" a boy named Justin asks Angie.

The cake is no success either. Angie finds herself appreciating Tod, the one child who eats only the icing and asks for more, discarding the uneaten portion in the middle of the floor so that the other children can grind it into the wood with their heels. Cleaning the floor is something Angie can do, later, alone. But she has no remedy for children who sneer at cake.

"I don't like cake," one child declares, while another challenges, "What's that in the middle of it?"

"Strawberries," Angie answers.

"Strawberries?" the child repeats in disbelief. "That's disgusting!"

"Well, how about some pretzels?"

"I hate pretzels."

"Oranges?" Angie asks.

"Who would eat oranges at a birthday party?" the child replies.

"Perhaps you would like to starve," Angie hisses, stalking into the kitchen, a child-free zone of wine and cheese, baguettes and herb butter, blue-corn chips and freshly cilantro'd salsa.

"Back to the land of the tall and the reasonable." Angie laughs, appreciating Rachel, appreciating Laura and Vickie, appreciating Ellen, appreciating Dorothy, even appreciating Marty, one of Rachel's new colleagues, whom she does not know very well. Adults. Some are the parents of children in the next room busting balloons, and some are not parents. But all are wonderfully adult, sipping wine, except for Laura and Vickie, who drink sweet iced tea.

Seventy-nine-cents-apiece balloons. Skye had stood at the counter of the discount party store this morning, choosing colors from an impressively varied palette.

"Pick out three colors," Angie had instructed. "We'll get five of each."

Skye had grown solemn.

"Hurry up," Angie half scolded, half coaxed, glancing at the line forming behind them, glancing out the window for Rachel hovering in the car.

Skye remained reflective. Only when she was ready and two other people had given their balloon orders did Skye reach consensus within her turning-ten-year-old self: "Wine. Teal. Peach."

"Five of each," Angie repeated to the teenager next to the helium tank. As the balloons collected, inflated and bobbing next to each other, Angie kept shaking her head at their muted severity. Maybe a silver anniversary, but a kid's birthday party? Even the three silver Mylar ones boasting declarations of "Happy Birthday" did not interfere with the muted effect.

"Three purple," Angie added. "And three of the green. And three of those neon blue. And the hot pink—three of those also."

The teal and wine balloons are being coveted by the children in the living room.

"What a great color," announces Deirdre, apparently recovered from her disappointment over the party favors now that she has a teal balloon floating above the string tied to her wrist.

Angie is standing by the front door, a glass of wine in her hand, waiting: waiting to be rescued. Thinking that the magic of money and knowledge of the yellow pages could produce a black car in the steep driveway. The white man wheels his paraphernalia into the living room. The hired entertainment has arrived: the magician.

With his incessant patter, including an emphasis on gender roles as the underpinning of verbal gags, he performs with rings and cards and a finger guillotine. Angie and the other adults watch as even the most sullen children smile, and then laugh. Watch as each of them volunteers to be his trusted assistant. Of course he picks Skye, identifying her as the "birthday girl, what a wonderful young man—oh, I'm sorry, a young woman!" The children laugh. "Ha. Ha. Ha. A young wo-*MAN*," the magician echoes his own joke. The children laugh, impossibly, even more. Laura and Rachel and Vickie and Dorothy and Marty pass baleful looks at each other, arching sympathetic eyebrows. Embarrassed in front of a non-mother, Angie avoids making eye contact with Ellen.

Angie brings a bottle of wine into the living room, refilling some of the adults' glasses. She opens another bottle, enduring Laura's scowl and Vickie's exaggerated toast: "To iced tea!"

Rachel catches Angie's eye, with intentions more like a mother's than a lover's. A mother who can chastise with an articulate glare: "Can't you be more considerate?" Angie ruffles her short hair, flashing a defiant smile perfected in adolescence and accentuated by alcohol. Rachel sighs, taking another sip of her own glass of wine and avoiding Laura's eyes.

For Angie, the wine dulls the rest of the magician's patter. It soothes the part of her that would say to him: "I find your comments offensive. Did you ever think that the birthday girl might be transsexual? Or that one of her mothers might be transgendered?" It flattens any residual guilt over the cost of such frivolity as she writes out the hefty check.

And it is the wine, but only partly the wine, that allows Angie to observe Skye approvingly as she opens her presents in the midst of crowding children. Rachel supervises, but does not need to remind Skye to be polite. "Thank you, this is great." "I love this." "I've always wanted one of these." "This will be fun to play with." Skye's lies and truths are so seamless Angie cannot tell the difference.

Angie is grateful for the absence of dolls.

She slips her glass in the kitchen as the Meadowlark School parents arrive to pick up Skye's classmates from yet another birthday party. If

Angie answers the door, they recognize her as one of Skye's mothers. If Rachel answers the door, they recognize Rachel as one of Skye's mothers. Always they look in confusion for the other mother, knowing they have met her at Meadowlark functions. In a moment, their gaze settles satisfactorily, but they often bestow the nod of recognition on Laura or Vickie or even Marty. Then they gravitate toward the cake, which still reigns on the birthday table. Some cut themselves a piece; some snarl at its sugar. One father takes a handful of orange quarters and puts them in the pocket of his ski jacket. As the parents claim their children, Angie tries to find some correlation between adult and child attitudes toward the food, but if there is any, it is not obvious to her.

When the only adults remaining are friends, and the only children battering balloons in the living room belong to these remaining adults, Rachel brings more wine into the living room. Ellen moves the cake into the kitchen, Marty starts picking up paper plates, and Laura gets more salsa and chips, more iced tea. Skye takes Jesse and Andrew and Marty's children, Shanara and Seth, into her room. Soon, racing cars and racing necklaces screech across the bare wooden floor, crashing against the metal baseboard heaters. The children scream with enthusiasm.

"Should I go check on them?"

"No, they sound like they're having fun."

"That's what I'm afraid of!"

"And what was Deirdre's mother afraid of?"

"Was that the one who looked around and couldn't tell which one of us was Rachel?"

"Yeah, all dykes look alike."

"But she thought it was me"—Marty laughs—"and I'm not a—a lesbian."

"You're not?" Rachel teases her co-worker.

"Me either," Ellen adds, laughing.

"Thank goodness," Rachel says.

"What's that supposed to mean?" Ellen looks at Rachel, half serious.

"It means Rachel's had too much wine," Angie says.

"Look who's talking!" Vickie interrupts.

"I only mean," Rachel explains, "that if you were a dyke, I'd be a little more worried about all those hours on the phone with my lover. I'd think surely they couldn't be talking about Triple-F for hours."

"We actually don't talk much these days." Ellen's gentle chiding is overrun by Angie's defensiveness: "Sometimes we talk about other things."

"Like what?" Rachel asks.

"Probably," Laura interrupts, "she talks about how boring her other friends are, since she never has time for us, her long-lost friends. Rachel doesn't have to worry about Angie spending hours on the phone with this dyke; she never even calls me. I don't know what you do with your time, Angie."

"I buy balloons," Angie says, smiling. Knowing very well that if she did spend hours on the phone with Laura, neither Rachel nor Vickie would be very happy. Knowing she could have said, "At least I don't spend it at twenty hours a week of recovery meetings," but also knowing she could not have said that.

"And you do a good job of it, too." Vickie rescues. "Although that faded blue and maroon were a little artsy."

"Tell me about it," Angie answers. "And if you knew your balloon colors, you wouldn't be saying 'faded blue' or 'maroon.' Those colors are teal and wine. And Skye picked them out. I had to insist on purple and pink or something lively. You'd think she was sixteen and ready to be depressed."

"Jesse's favorite balloon color is beige," Vickie announces.

"Yeah, especially at the Pride Parade." Laura then launches into a story about the little prizes being thrown from the floats at last year's Pride Parade, Jesse wanting them and Vickie trying to explain what condoms are.

"So, what are they?" Rachel asks. Some of the women laugh, and some do not.

Despite the ebbs in conversation and eddies of tension, Angie feels lucky. And maybe it is not just the wine. Maybe it is people in her living room, laughing. Friends she has known a long time, and a woman she has just met and likes. To gossip. And Angie feels lucky because no one mentions Skye's birth mother; no one asks how Angie and Rachel know that this is Sky's birth day, if it is; no one wonders aloud whether

Such possibilities become anxieties for Angie in a gradual slide, an assemblage, a tumble of tired days. There is no decisive moment, no photograph, no flash of recognition, no day on the calendar, no month. Even now, rocking the heavy Skye, playing with Skye's coarsely brittle hair, Angie barely recognizes the inexorable fierceness of love.

■ ■ ■ ■ ■ ■ ■

"Good night, birthday girl!" Angie yells into Skye's room, hoping the child is already asleep. Angie pulls Rachel close, so that the light from the full moon slants across her face. Normally Angie would light a candle next to the bed, but tonight there is no need. They kiss, softly and carefully. Angie knows that the aftermath of the wine makes her aggressive, so she checks herself. Also she knows that the moon makes her hungry, so she hesitates. Balancing on one elbow, above Rachel, she waits. Waits for Rachel to catch up, as sometimes Rachel waits for her. So many years together teaches one to wait, Angie thinks, but not always how.

How to wait, without the mind wandering. Work is her usual destination, easily accomplished without even a single bridge to drive across; she is suddenly in her office composing a list of things to do and writing in her appointment Book. Call Kim again. Why hadn't Kim called her with that case for Cheryl Martin? Maybe Kim suspected Angie's strategy, so that she was stringing Angie along until Angie lost her resolve. Maybe Angie should ask Coleman for another intern to do some research, or try to convince him again to hire another paralegal. Or maybe Kim is just not very good. Angie strays into a tangle of Kim's kiss, quickly looking down at Rachel's mouth half open and expectant. "Rachel," Angie says, and means it.

"Angie. Angie." Skye calls out desperately.

"What's wrong?"

"I need you."

Angie looks at Rachel, who closes her eyes. If Skye is calling Angie, instead of Rachel, it means that Skye is feeling seven instead of thirteen.

"Ten is going to be a difficult age," Angie says, kissing Rachel's or how or why Angie and Rachel have explained adoption to Skye, their daughter.

■ ■ ■ ■ ■ ■ ■

Perhaps if she had met Rachel sooner, about a year sooner, she would not be sitting in this chair rocking this baby—a baby who should "no longer crave rocking," according to *Baby's First Three Years* on the bookshelf behind her; a baby who should already be walking; a baby who should no longer be a baby. She would not be hushing this baby, would not be talking to this baby about a case she had to argue this afternoon, would not be worrying that Rachel would not get home in time, would not be making her contingency plans of diaper bag and briefcase and asking the client "Could you just hold my baby for a minute while I talk to the judge?"

Would not be assuring people that the large discolorations on the baby's thighs and arms and sometimes even on her face were not bruises, but only erratic pigmentations.

Or perhaps if she had not met Rachel, ever. But Angie cannot imagine that. Rachel feels inevitable, intentional, absolute. That precise moment in the woods when Rachel turns her back to take off her sweater, the T-shirt underneath riding up to her shoulder blades. That moment, like a photograph Angie preserves in the slotted vinyl compartments of her mental appointment Book. An image of Rachel's back shadowed by the blades of winter trees.

But if Rachel does not seem accidental, Skye does. Despite Rachel's incessant planning for Skye, plans that floated around Angie like casual clouds, Skye still seems like something that has just happened. Like something that could un-happen.

Skye could be dead in her crib one morning, quiet as a doll without eyelids. Skye could be gone one day, taken by the workers from the social service agency. Skye could be lost, crawling along a highway, tracing her mother's scent like a loyal dog. Skye could evaporate, dehydrate, disappear.

forehead almost maternally. "I'll be right back. Wait for me, baby."

Angie looks at the digital clock, especially luminescent from the moon's reflection. Nine. Five. Seven.

"What's the matter, baby?" Angie strokes Skye's forehead.

"I feel guilty."

Angie acts neutral as a defense against the newness of guilt.

"What do you mean?"

"Like I've done something wrong."

"Is there anything you want to tell me about?"

"No."

"Anything you can think of?"

"No."

Angie falls back on her legal training, posing hypotheticals to her child: "If you could change one thing about today, what would it be?" "If you could say you're sorry to one person, who would that be?" "If today were yesterday, what would we do different?" "If we could invite one more person to your birthday party, who would you have come?" If. If. If.

Skye has no answers. Only half sobs. Only vague notions.

After forty-two minutes, Angie stops exploring emotions. There are times to be dogmatic, she thinks. "Skye, let me tell you something. You have absolutely no reason whatsoever in the world to feel guilty. You had a nice party and invited your friends. The ones who came all had a very good time. You were polite and nice to everyone. No one got hurt. There is no reason to feel guilty. You are a wonderful wonderful ten-year-old. Who needs her sleep."

Angie kisses Skye on the cheek and gives her a hug.

"Good night, baby."

"Good night, Mommy," Skye says to the woman she knows as one of her two mothers, the woman she almost always calls Angie.

Back in bed with Rachel, the bedroom door pulled shut and the moon shifted, Angie whispers, "What kind of ten-year-old kid feels guilty after her birthday party?"

"One who picks out wine and teal balloons," Rachel advises. "She's not just any kid. What does she feel guilty about?"

"I don't know. She couldn't say."

"She probably snitched one of the rainbow balls from the party-favor bags so that someone she doesn't like wouldn't get one."

"I don't think it's that simple." Angie shakes her head.

"Do you think we've made her this way?" Rachel asks.

"Talk about guilt." Angie's laugh is low.

"It's contagious," Rachel declares.

"I suppose," Angie agrees.

Making love after such a conversation seems impossible. But it is not; it is only different than it would have been an hour before. It is more direct, and the moon less comforting. Instead of passion, what rises in Angie is a huge blank space—no work, no love, only a boundary of sensation. A boundary she cannot cross no matter how Rachel touches her, no matter where. Until she conjures that sharp sound she uses to command herself to orgasm when all else fails. *Sotto voce.* Anonymous voice. Not Rachel. Not Kim, not some nameless lover, not Claire, not the woman who gave birth to Skye. *Sotto voce:* Dyke. Whore. Dyke. Whoredykewhore / dykewhoredyke / whoredykewhoredykewhoredykewhore.

■  ■  ■  ■  ■  ■  ■

"Little Evangelina. Little Evangelina. Thumbelina. Just like a faggot, can't even run."

All the other kids laugh at Carol's taunts. Carol, the tomboy, older than her cousin Evangelina by several years, stronger by all her years on the dirt farm. Evangelina cannot keep up with Carolina, whom no one ever calls anything but Carol; cannot find the trail in the snow-blurred woods; cannot understand why her cousin holds her close when she shares her bed at night and whispers, "Sweet girl, you kiss so fine," but acts as if she hates her in the light. Evangelina is stuck on a some bare bush branches, unlacing the stickers from the ruffles that poke out below her jacket, on the dress that Claire made, plaid with white ruffles. Evangelina is trying not to slide into the slushy mud, slanting her heels that should be in boots, on shoes that Claire told her not to wear outside, patent vinyl with a ribbon bow. Evangelina is crying for Carol. Who comes back for her.

"Your mother is going to slit your sorry throat," Carol sings. "Your dress is torn and your new shoes all mud. And I'm going to watch while she gives you a switching."

"My mother doesn't switch me."

"Oh? I forgot, nobody switches precious little Evangelina. Ha! Nobody makes *her* get a branch from the yard and pull down her underpants. Ha! Your mother is going to switch you good for getting such a mess. And I'm going to watch."

"She's not my mother."

"What?"

"I said, she's not my mother."

"You're crazy."

"Not my real mother, anyway."

"Auntie Claire is real enough."

"Yeah. But she's not my real mother. I'm adopted."

"Don't make me laugh."

"I am."

"Are not."

"Am."

"Why would she adopt you? She didn't need no kid. You think a sixteen-year-old girl is going to go out and adopt her a baby?"

"She was lonely."

"Even if she was, little Evangelina, she couldn't adopt any baby. You got to be twenty-one. And married, even. She wasn't married to Luke then. Even I know that."

"Do not."

"I remember when you was born, little Evangelina. Thumbelina. Little doll baby. I thought you'd be a little doll for me to play with. Auntie Claire was big as a house, then you popped out."

"I did not."

"You did. I was there. I saw it all."

"You didn't see it."

"Just about."

"You were just like a doll, Thumbelina. Only you shit on everything."

"I did not. I *am* adopted. I am."

"I'm going to ask Auntie Claire."

"Don't."

"Why not?"

"You'll hurt her feelings."

"So what?"

"Don't you hurt my mother."

"She *is* your mother, then."

"My adopted mother."

"Then she don't have real feelings. Not for you."

"She does."

"I'll tell her what you said, about being adopted and all, and we'll see what she says."

"And I'll tell on you."

"On what?"

Angie stalls, watching her own breath, warm and important in the cold air. "On how you kiss me at night in bed."

"Go ahead. Nobody will believe you, little Thumbelina-Evangelina."

"They will."

"Then I'll tell them how much you like it. How it was your idea. Something you learned from some dirty boy."

"That's not true."

"With your mouth wide open, like you really like it."

"You told me that's the way to do it."

"You don't like it?"

"I'll tell. I will. Carolina."

"You call me that again, I'll slap your face."

"Carolina. Carolina. Carolina."

"Shut up, you little whore."

"Carolina. Carolina. Carolina."

"I said, shut up, you fucking whore."

■ ■ ■ ■ ■ ■ ■

Angie is holding the phone, tight. Listening to Claire navigate memory lane with an inaccurate map of the present.

"Remember when you used to tell everyone you were adopted?"

"I guess."

"I thought you hated me."

Angie notices the past tense. Thinks she can hear the Prozac vibrating in Claire's arteries, humming through Claire's synapses.

"I just thought being adopted would be interesting," Angie allows.

"As if I'm not interesting enough! Your cousin Carol used to think it was so funny, you telling her you were adopted all the time. She was always jealous of you, you know. With your beautiful hair. And that you had me for a mother. I think she had a crush on me or something."

"Carolina used to tease me."

"Really, Evangelina, if you can't say something nice about someone, don't say anything. And why do you insist on calling her Carolina? She likes Carol. And you have to admit, she doesn't seem like a Carolina."

"Some people don't think I seem like an Evangelina." Angie feels bold.

"What's wrong with your name?" Claire's voice borders the shrill. Angie thinks she can see the Prozac stretching.

"Nothing. Just that some people prefer Angie to Evangelina, just like some people prefer Carol to Carolina."

"What's to prefer? Carolina is a silly name. And it doesn't suit her. You just don't call a woman like her Carolina."

"I guess."

"With her as a model, I wonder why you didn't turn out better."

"I'm very different."

"I'll say. And they say all you lesbians are the same. Look at Carol! A happy girl with a nice girlfriend—a girlfriend who treats your aunt Sally like gold—and a good job. And she doesn't go around telling newspapers she's a dyke, just minds her own business. Her softball team last year came in first in the division on her home run."

Carolina. Rents an old farm with her "roommate." Operates heavy equipment for the county. Captain of her softball team. And thinks she's closeted. Little Evangelina should have done as well.

"I thought she was coaching softball."

"High school girls. She still plays on her own team."

Angie suppresses any thoughts of Carol putting her arms around some tenth-grader at second base, putting her tongue inside some tenth-grader after practice.

"Oh."

"You should really call her. You kids should be closer. All of you kids, but you and Carol special. Since you have so much in common."

"I'll call her when I get a chance."

"You're too busy for your own family?"

"No. Tell her to call me."

"She's always out working or practicing ball. Or visiting your Aunt Sally. Besides, she don't have lots of money to be calling long distance."

"I'll try."

"That's a good girl, Evangelina."

■  ■  ■  ■  ■  ■  ■

"Evangelina? Are you still there?"

"Yes."

"I guess you're finding out about the hand that rocks the cradle. Ha! You're finding out what it's like to take care of a brat, day after day after day. Aren't you?"

"I guess."

"Now you know how I worked like a dog for you. A dog. Now who's going to take care of me? You're too selfish. And you're too selfish to take care of any kid. All you've ever been interested in is your little jobs. Those and going to school. You can't take care of a baby. You couldn't even learn it when they tried to teach it to you in school. You failed Home Ec, for chrissakes. Couldn't even give a doll a bath. I don't see why you even want a baby, except I guess the brat comes with your newest girlfriend. What is she, so rich she can just scrape babies out of the gutters of Mexico or wherever? You'd think she'd be rich enough to take care of me. And you. You always hated dolls, so how are you going to take care of a baby? Just tell me that, will you? Just tell me that."

But Angie has nothing to tell. Nothing except the way she becomes numb. And she does not know how to talk about that. Not even to Rachel. Not even to herself.

Angie is sitting in her messy office reading the Hague Convention on Intercountry Adoption. When the telephone rings, she hopes it is Kim with news about the Cheryl Martin research. But it is Rachel, without news and just wondering if there are any plans for dinner.

"Get some Chinese," Angie advises.

"Skye said last time that she hates Chinese."

"Then get pizza."

"I'm getting to hate pizza."

"We could always cook."

"On a weeknight? And eat at nine o'clock? It's too late and I'm too tired."

"Okay. I'll pick something up when I pick up Skye."

"Great," Rachel says. "Mission accomplished. Then I can work here and finish up that housing-project brief."

"Are you still working on that?"

"What do you mean, still?" Rachel sounds anxious.

"Nothing. I just thought you were done." Angie is noncommittal.

"Almost. Almost. And what are you doing?"

"Reading the Hague Convention on Intercountry Adoption."

"How exciting. Why?"

"They want me to give a talk at the Lesbian/Gay Adoption Group."

"You're not going to do it, are you?" Rachel asks.

"Maybe."

"You're going to talk about Skye?" Rachel's tone approaches incredulity.

"Of course not. I'm going to talk about the legal aspects. They want me because I'm a lawyer. I can say things like 'Article Thirty-two of the Hague Convention on Intercountry Adoption prohibits "improper financial or other gain" from an adoption.' "

"Yeah, right. What's improper? And you know at those groups people always ask personal questions. Share experiences." Rachel says *share* five octaves higher than her normal speaking voice, and one octave higher than her best falsetto.

"I'm not into sharing." Angie laughs.

"You may not have a choice. They strap you to one of those folding chairs and suck your blood."

"Sounds fun."

"You're going to do it, aren't you?"

"I might."

"In your spare time, I suppose?" Rachel is caustic.

"It's only one night. We could all go."

"Not on your life. So Skye and I can sit there and be inspected? So Skye can hear all the dykes moan for perfect little babies?"

"It isn't that bad."

"It is."

"Got to go, babe," Angie says as her office door opens to Kim's protruding smile, which fades at Angie's "Love you, too" into the telephone.

"What's up?" Angie tries to bring back Kim's smile with one of her own. Still, she thinks, that's what Kim gets for coming in without knocking.

"Not much. Classes are so boring, though."

"Already?" Angie does not know if she means this early in the spring semester, or this early in law school.

"Unfortunately." Kim sighs. Then smiles. "Hey, how did your daughter's birthday party go?"

"Fine." Angie is cold. Wonders how Kim knows.

"I think it's really great that you have a kid. I hope she'll like me. I mean, I know she'll like me. All kids love me. How did you get her, anyway?"

Angie deflects this with a smile. "You're not asking me where babies come from, are you?"

"You mean you were married?" Kim tries to be sophisticated rather than incredulous.

"That's not what I said."

"Oh. I didn't think so. But then, how did you . . . ?" Kim bites off the question she really wants answered: How much of the how requires Rachel? Kim assumes that the Angie who fights for other lesbians to retain custody of their children would never surrender her own child, so she is trying to assess how much of an obstacle Rachel can be.

"Why don't you tell me how the research is going?" Angie deflects Kim again, this time without a smile. She never explains Skye to anyone who asks for an explanation.

"Not so good." Kim's lips rise above her jutting bicuspids.

"You couldn't find anything?" Angie thinks she should not have Kim doing this. Still, Kim has had a legal research course, Angie reasons.

"I found it. But I don't think it says what you want."

"What do you mean?"

"It says the opposite of what you said it would say."

"What?"

"It says it's fine, I mean constitutional, for a judge to override a jury's recommendation of a life sentence. Like, only a few states have a death penalty scheme that lets the jury recommend—and not sentence—and sometimes this works to the benefit of the defendant and sometimes it doesn't. And there's nothing wrong when it doesn't."

"*Nothing?*"

"As long as the judge bases the decision on the state statute. And the state statute is good, I mean constitutional."

"Did you bring me a copy of the case?"

"Here it is."

"That's it?" Angie says, skimming the typewritten sheets that Kim hands her. "Thanks. But could you also get me a copy from the United States Reporter?" Angie is trying to be tactful. "I know everyone these days uses the computers, but I'm such an old-timer I like to read the opinions from the bound volumes."

"I didn't know that," Kim says defensively. She remembers learning about the bound volumes in the first semester, but law students always use the computers. "I thought you needed this right away. The computer is so much faster."

Angie does not mention the time she has been waiting. Angie does not say it only takes a minute to pull the volume down from the shelf and copy the relevant pages. Angie does not say that the typewritten pages seem less real to her than copies from the official United States Reporter; Angie does not say, You could have typed this opinion on your computer just to make me crazy and I might never know.

Angie does say: "I do need it. I just feel better with the copy from the official reporter. But I'm glad you found it, even if it isn't good news."

"Is there something else I should look up?"

"I don't know yet."

"You don't seem very happy." Kim sighs.

"I'm not, Kim. I mean, I was hoping this opinion would help Cheryl Martin. And it doesn't. So I've got to see if I can make it help her, or I've got to find something else." Angie is silent, trying to remember what else she needed from Kim, something about cappuccino. "Oh," she says finally, "I want to schedule a lunch."

"Lunch?" Kim is slightly excited, but also slightly threatened. They have never had lunch together. "You should come to my apartment for dinner. Tonight. We could get some Chinese. Or I could make some soup for you."

"I've got to work, babe."

"You could work at my place."

"That would be difficult." Angie smiles, trying to seem gracious.

"I'll help you. And you know, when I get on law review you can work at my apartment all the time. I'll have access to the computer bases, you know, WestLaw and Lexis, and I'll be able to use them from home. You could come over and do research on my computer. My dad bought me this great computer when I started law school—you know, the laptop I have. Well, when he said I would need it really outfitted, I laughed, I mean, I don't really understand all these things. But it does have a modem and that's what I'll need. I'll be able to hook up anywhere. Get you all the cases you'll need. And you could come over and use it. And it's so easy, on that little laptop. We could do it in bed!"

There is so much that Angie does not say.

M A R C H

M A R C H

**M A R C H**

M A R C H

M A R C H

Angie is trying to write her weekly client letters, rereading the contents of the file labeled "C. Martin: PERSONAL CORRESPONDENCE." It is full of poetry. Bad poetry. Nouns surrounded with dashes and capital-G gods dangling at the ends of the short lines. Emily Dickinson in prison. "Thank you for the poetry," Angie types. On the keyboard of her office computer, the words float on the too-perfect blue.

Angie gets up without saving her file, wanders down the hall. Ellen. Angie thinks she could talk to Ellen about Cheryl Martin and about bad poetry. But then Angie remembers that Ellen is not here. Ellen is in the Caribbean, vacationing. Angie imagines her swimming in blue waters, the mild salt sliding down her quickly darkening body. Angie notes a flash of resentment, but attaches it only to Ellen's neglect to telephone Angie right before leaving. Ellen should have been more considerate of Angie's frustration with the Cheryl Martin case, with the winter, with Triple-F politics; Ellen should have consoled and cheered and commiserated with Angie before getting on Virgin Air with her bathing suits and her novels nestled in her leather suitcase. Everyone is always reminding her of her own neglect, but not realizing how they neglect her. Or so Angie thinks, feeling sorry for herself. But Angie also thinks that self-pity is something to be immediately staunched, not with pills or therapists but through determination and concrete plans of distraction.

Her solution is a colleague. She immediately rejects Coleman (one does not seek solace from one's nominal boss) and Walter (or from one's supposed support person). She does not seriously consider Chelsea (whose patina of privilege would only aggravate) or Dorothy (whose relentless heterosexuality would only embarrass). She has to mentally walk the halls before she remembers Steven and Terry, both of whom seem vaguely adversarial these days, although she is not sure why. That leaves Roger.

Roger. Roger and Foucault, in needlepoint. Roger and Octavia, his woman within. Roger and coffee.

Roger and Angie talking. About Coleman and the ongoing rumors of sexual harassment and fiscal mismanagement. About Chelsea and her criticism of the "radical feminist agenda." About Steven and Terry and their rumblings of reorganizing Triple-F. About Cheryl Martin's poetry.

"It's really awful," Angie is saying.

"She's probably just trying to express herself. She's been through hell. It's good for her, gets her in touch with her own feelings."

"But why do *I* have to be in touch with her feelings? I mean, why send it to me? I'm a lawyer, not a therapist." Angie tries to sound harsh.

"Thank heavens." Roger is shaking his head. "I can't think of a worse person to be a therapist."

Angie tilts her head toward Roger's needlepoint, trying to decide whether or not she should be offended.

"You don't even go to one, do you?"

"Some people might consider that a personal question."

"Ange, really. You take everything personally. It's no more personal than discussing restaurants. Or vacations. I went to Greece last summer because my therapist suggested it. Toured the ruins. Communed with the ancient spirits who still sail around the islands. It was great."

"Sounds like you enjoyed it."

"I did. You should go away. I mean, even Foucault took a vacation every year. He spent every August with his mother."

"How nice for him," Angie sneers. She is beginning to think coffee with Roger was not a good idea.

"Not anymore. He's dead. But anyway, I'll give you my therapist's name so you can figure out a vacation."

"I think I'll use a travel agent."

"Seriously, Ange."

"Have I ever told you I can't stand to be called Ange?"

"A therapist could help you with that, too."

"You are hopeless, Roger."

"That's why you love me. Ange."

"Is that what your therapist told you?"

"Saved by the bell," Roger says at the knock on the door. Walter. "Come on in."

"Thanks. But I'm looking for Angie." Walter leans his body half inside the door. "Can I talk to you a minute? Will you be in your office later?"

"Roger and I were just concluding our discussion, which has degenerated beyond belief."

"She doesn't want to admit she loves me." Roger laughs.

"Sometimes I don't know whether that man is just weird or really crazy," Angie mumbles to Walter in the hall.

Walter closes Angie's door behind him. Not a good sign, Angie thinks. Maybe she could just tell him to come back later, when she has recovered from Roger. Maybe she could just say "Now is actually not a good time," in a Chelsea tone of voice. Instead she tells him to sit down.

"I have some news." Walter shifts nervously in the chair.

While Angie waits for Walter to continue, she looks at him. Looks at his perpetual black turtleneck and black jeans. Looks at the long silver chain and the single long silver earring. Looks at his dark hair shaped in what Luke would call a crewcut. Angie finally prompts him: "What's up?"

"I did what you told me to do. And I'm done. I did it."

Angie is still looking at Walter, still waiting for him to continue.

"I finished early. I got the paralegal certificate."

Angie leaps up and gives Walter a hug. "Congrats!"

"I just want to thank you. I'm not very good at things like this, but I just want you to know that if it weren't for you—"

"Don't be ridiculous," Angie interrupts. "You worked for it, not me."

"Yeah, but you encouraged me. Made me believe I could do it."

"Lots of people around here know how great you are."

"Maybe. But no one else had the time of day for me. No one else looked at my applications. No one else wrote me a recommendation.

And no one else cosigned a student loan for me."

"I just recognize talent." Angie blushes. "And we'll have to arrange an announcement. Make sure we impress this on Coleman so you can get a raise and pay back that loan."

"I've already done that."

"I didn't hear any announcement."

"That's what I'm here to tell you. As soon as I got the certificate in my hot little hands, I made an appointment with Coleman. Told him I wanted a promotion or I'd resign. Just like you and I talked about when I thought about going into the paralegal program."

Angie does not display her lack of recall for that part of the conversation. She's holding her breath until the punch line. Walter is enjoying the suspense.

"I got the promotion."

"Coleman gave it to you?"

"He did. And even better yet, I'm all yours."

"Mine?"

"Yes, all yours, baby." Walter twirls the chain around his neck. "Almost all, anyway. I promised that if Terry or Roger or even Princess Chelsea requires my meager services I'll assist."

"How did you manage this?"

"I just laid it on the proverbial line for Chief Coleman. Said you were the best damn attorney in this rotten place and certainly worked the hardest and did the most interesting stuff. Besides, you and I dress the same and have the same haircut, us being queer. Although I didn't have to remind Coleman of that! He probably would have appointed me to the board of directors if it meant that he could keep his desk securely between my private parts and his. That man is so afraid I'm going to jump his bones."

"Well, whatever he's afraid of, I'm glad. Two weeks ago he was saying how Triple-F couldn't afford the five paralegals we have and we should train support staff to do paralegal work. Without a raise, of course. And you talked him into a promotion."

"It must be my boyish charm."

"It must. When do you start?"

"I'm at your service. But I still have to slit open your envelopes until they make some reassignments. But I'll do anything as long as I don't have to make Roger another pot of coffee ever again. I'll even make your coffee."

"I get coffee from Roger. I always thought he made it."

"Only if he thinks you're looking."

"Well, get to work."

"Well, tell me what to do."

"How about starting on Cheryl Martin? I'm writing the brief. But I'm having trouble with local counsel not returning my calls. I need to check on a local rule regarding page length. Maybe you could call? You're so good on the telephone; I just hate it. Meanwhile, you can go through that stack of death-penalty cases. I need to know what issues have been raised on the state level and which have been successful."

"In Indiana." Walter points out the window. "Isn't that somewhere over there? Tucked between Illinois and Ohio? Or is it Wisconsin? Or maybe even Iowa? All those hunky farm boys!"

"It doesn't matter where it is. It only matters that this is the state that convicted Cheryl Martin for first-degree murder and sentenced her to death."

"I'm going to love working with you in this new capacity! You are such a fun girl!"

"I never said I was fun." Angie is slightly apologetic.

"Oh, but you are. So rad you don't even know you're rad."

"Rad? Never mind. Just get to work."

"I'm working, I'm working. Consider me already immersed in the Northeastern Reporter. I just love the Northeastern Reporter. I love the legal sense of geography. There are millions of lawyers in this country who simply accept that Indiana is in the Northeastern Reporter, when any fool knows Indiana should be in the Midwestern Reporter. But there isn't even a Midwestern Reporter. Does that make sense?"

Angie laughs in spite of herself. "Having a Midwestern Reporter would make it too easy."

Walter picks up the neat pile of cases that Kim photocopied at her law school library. "I'll do it right and do it quick. That's my motto. And I'll even do it in those little boxes you like so much. Like a chart."

"Do what you think is best."

"I'm starting to, my dear." Walter starts singing even before he leaves Angie's office.

"That's great," Rachel says, pouring the spinach ravioli into the colander. For a moment, she is engulfed in steam.

Angie sips a glass of red wine, stirring the tomato-and-cream sauce. She thinks it is good to be in the steamy kitchen with her lover, exchanging stories about their workdays. Good to watch Skye concentrate on cutting the cucumbers for the salad. Good to feel good.

"I really am glad to have Walter as a paralegal. Though I would have liked to be a fly on the wall when he talked to Coleman."

"What do you think he said?"

"I've got no idea. But I've decided to just be glad. Not look a gift horse in the mouth."

"What's a gift horse?" Skye interrupts.

"It's an expression."

"Like 'Spare the child'?"

"That's 'Spare the rod, spoil the child.' "

"Like the witch's tit?"

"I told you not to say that," Rachel scolds.

"You said not to say it outside the house." Skye corrects.

"Good memory." Angie smiles.

"Don't encourage her. What I mean is that there are certain things that children should not say. Even when adults do."

"I know that. Like the F-curse. And the A-curse. And all those S-curses." Skye giggles.

"Add *tit* to the list," Rachel announces.

"The T-curse!"

"It's not a curse," Angie tries to explain. "It's just not a very nice way to refer to women's breasts."

"I know what the T-curse means." Skye pats her chest, giggles again.

"Let's eat." Rachel sighs, putting the platter of ravioli on the table.

"Can I have Coke?"

"The C-curse!" Angie yells. And after a half smile of hesitation, Skye punctuates Angie's voice with her childish laughter.


It is snowing. Still. Or again. It is difficult to decide. Winter is a blur, indecipherable into days or nights, into separate storms, into distinct incidents. And yet, Angie knows only fragments. A wind warning and a school closing. A piece of coat caught in a car door.

The snow is white. It startles Angie, although she knows the snow will be white. Knows it as everyone who lives in this valley for even a single winter knows it. Knows the whiteness has no comparison, it *is* the comparison: as white as snow. Like a line from Cheryl Martin's poetry, with capital *S* snow. Not like the covers of the catalogs. "Spring Is Here!" Short-sleeved mesh shirts on sale. Daffodil yellow. Primrose pink. Lilac.

Angie cannot shake a bone loneliness. Stumbling from room to room, seeking the comfort of some spray of sun caressing the floor slats. She loves the warm wood of the floor, but wants it shinier, reflecting the light like high-gloss linoleum; she wants it softer, diffusing the light like an expensive carpet. She wants the floor to be like a lover, to be everything she wants, to shift as she shifts.

But in her bones with her loneliness is the belief that to buy something—a new shower curtain, a rug, a set of breakfast bowls—will change life for the better. A belief that keeps the working class working and the middle class owing. Even those college texts with Marxist rhetoric on capitalism, even those trendy magazines with postmodernist deconstructions of consumerism, could not reset her bone-deep belief. A belief more bodily than envy, perhaps more bodily than lust. A belief something like hope.

In the white and early morning, Angie settles down on the couch to ravage a stack of catalogs. Leafs through pages and pages, looking for the perfect panacea. But something—her premenstrual stress, her dormant Marxism, her superficial postmodernism, or simply the snow swirling when "Spring Is Here!"—provokes her cynicism. She holds a little competition: most offensive ad copy; most offensive model; most offensive product.

The catalog attracts Angie with its shape, long and slim, although its title repels her: "The Spoils of Civilization." She leafs through the pages, looking for the red rug featured on the catalog's cover. On some middle page, it appears with its non-identical twin. Two patterns: "Spirit" and "Tattoo." "Nadjima is fifteen years old. She made her first rug when she was nine. It vibrates with life. I own it. Offered here are original rugs made by girls like Nadjima from the Bedouin tribes in the Middle Atlas mountains, handwoven and vegetable dyed; no two are alike, but each bursts with primitive sophistication. Price: $3,750 U.S. funds." Angie wonders how she got on this company's mailing list. How she can endure such blatant exploitation. How she survives; how Nadjima survives.

Forget the competition. Nadjima's life is obviously more difficult. Angie tries to feel content, if only by comparison. Picks up an old garden catalog. Bulbs. Bulbs. Bulbs. The ad copy promotes brilliant color as a defense against winter; it does not mention any girls who might have been Angie's daughter digging in fields. Offers a subscription to the bulb of the month. On the end table next to the couch. Angie looks at the forced bulb in its handthrown pot. Not ordered from a catalog, but purchased from the woman who worked in the Garden Shoppe on Hudson Street. The woman with the long hair and deep voice. The woman who invited Angie into the back room for coffee. The woman who was no longer there. The amaryllis is nothing except garish. The red-orange trumpets, a quartet, blast from the thick green stem. Tropical jazz. But like so many things in her life—she appreciates the concept of it more than she appreciates the sensations. The flower irritates. Varicose-veined petals. Protruding pistils. Like an imitation Georgia O'-Keeffe. At least Cheryl Martin does not paint. Like bad sex. At least Rachel is passionate.

She should make her lover coffee. Bring it to her in bed. Seduce Rachel into a morning that is hours old, seems years old. Show her the snow. Give her a kiss. After making love, they could desecrate the virgin yard with their footprints, squealing like children, with Skye. They could make snow angels; they could be snow angels. They could fashion a fort to protect their encampment from unknown invaders, then stomp on their fort, then turn on each other with blizzards of loose snowballs. They could, they could, if only Angie would not sit on the couch with her catalogs. Until Rachel wanders into the living room.

"Why didn't you wake me?"


"These are things of beauty."

"I hope that means you think the work is good," Walter says, placing a huge stack of papers on the floor as insurance should Angie ask him for something not in his memo or outline or cases.

"It seems good. I mean I haven't really looked at the substance yet. I've been so wowed by the presentation."

"Maybe I could do a commercial for WordPerfect. I could be the employee who impresses his boss with a flawless presentation."

"Only if I can be the boss."

"Or maybe you can be played by a celebrity."

"Elizabeth Montgomery? Or Elizabeth Taylor?"

"How about Annie Lennox?" Walter nudges the postcard on Angie's desk.

"She can't act, can she?"

"You don't have to act to be in a commercial. Besides, your biggest fan thinks you look like Lennox. I, myself, don't see the resemblance. Except for the flattop hair, of course."

"I haven't read the postcard." Angie sighs.

"I have." Walter feigns a drawl. "A postcard just begs to be read, and I can never resist when begged. No one thinks a postcard is private. And that's her point."

"Let's go over the cases."

"Yes, boss. But you know what that girl is doing don't you? Just watch your ass."

"What's the most compelling issue that might be applicable to Cheryl Martin?"

"From the vampire to the riflewoman. You sure know how to pick them. But there may be something in that jury override issue. That U.S. Supreme Court case you gave me says it's constitutional, but the state supreme court says that in order for a judge to impose death after a jury has recommended life, the jury's recommendation must be unreasonable."

"Year?" Angie asks.

"Recent. Last year. But it's applied in some other cases, too. Look down at the middle of the page." Walter points at the grid. "It seems the pretty well established standard. The *Martinez-Chavez* standard."

"Great."

"Yeah. The court overturns the judge's death sentence because there is room for 'reasonable disagreement.' I think we can make the same argument for Cheryl Martin. Don't you think?"

"I do. Are all those cases there?"

"On the grid, listed under issue number one. And then there are two sets of copies. The cases you gave me, with some other ones I added from research. And then another complete set with the relevant passages highlighted and the issues indicated in the margins."

"Any other possible issues?"

"Well, some evidentiary ones. But those got pretty convoluted for me. They seem pretty weak, but I'm not sure."

"I'll take a look."

"How about Prozac?"

"What?"

"Prozac. What do you think about Prozac?"

"I only know two people who take it. I guess it helps them, but—"

"No, I mean as a mitigating factor. Didn't I tell you to do the Prozac cases?"

"If you did, I don't remember that at all. Maybe you have me mixed up with your lazy law student Jodie Foster the rich-bitch vampire."

Angie sighs. Although she does have to admire Walter's thoroughness. "Okay. I want you to do a computer search. All cases from all states. I want the citation for every case that mentions Prozac. And a copy of the case. And then an outline of how each case concerns Prozac, organized by subject. In other words, there might be suits against the manufacturer but I'm obviously interested in how Prozac is used as a defense or mitigating circumstance to a crime."

"Got it. I'll do another beautiful grid. But how should I do the computer search?"

"I just wish Triple-F would subscribe to some legal database. Coleman would rather take expensive jaunts on business than get us what we need. I guess you don't still have access to the computers at the paralegal school?"

Walter shakes his head.

"Ask Kim," Angie suggests.

Walter shakes his head, side to side, but only after he bends down to collect the papers on the floor.


The border is bent, jutting from her appointment Book between "Projects" and "Expenses." When she slides it from between the leather covers, the eyes dominate. Angie knows she is supposed to be captivated by that domination, but she resists the manipulation. She judges the eyes too made-up, with eyebrow pencils and shapers, with mascara and maybe even false eyelashes, with eyeliner and smudged shadow. Dark on the pale face; the face pale white against the faultless black background; the face bleached-white as the half-inch hair.

The whiteness of the nakedness, all shoulder as the hands collar the neck and the arms hide even a hint of breast.

Angie stares at the photo postcard for several minutes, as if it is supposed to tell her something. As if it is about her. Or what someone thinks of her. Someone she does not think enough about to decipher the handwriting smudging the other side. The side that should be blank. White.

She slips the postcard back into the black leather jacket of her Book.


Pulls it out later to save her place. Rachel always bends the pages. Angie hates that. Especially in hardcover books. But Rachel is not reading this book, some psychiatrist's treatise on Prozac. It is supposed to pose popular questions, postmodern questions. Questions like whether there is such a thing as personality, and if it can be changed by pharmacology. But Angie is more interested in violence, insights buried in convoluted passages about monkey synapses, about serotonin, about the differences between depression and sensitivity and compulsiveness. The research cited seems to conclude that a mere drug cannot provoke murder or suicide. But then again, Angie thinks, the author—and probably the researchers—regularly prescribe Prozac. Prescribe it to women like Cheryl Martin, a drug probably powerful enough to make her believe she is powerful. Powerful enough to pull the heavy trigger of a rifle. And maybe even powerful enough to insure the bullet enters only her husband's forehead. *Prozac allows patients to conceptualize solutions to their own problems.* Not little Emily's head, certainly. Not Cheryl Martin's daughter, who would grow up to be a great poet.

And prescribe it to women like Claire.


"Evangelina?"

"How are you doing?"

"Better, better. But I didn't sleep all night."

"Why not?"

"Luke was gone and I kept hearing sounds. Like someone was trying to break in."

"Did you call the cops?"

"What would they do? Those bastards. Haven't you heard the stories about how all these cops have been raping women?"

"I guess."

"Cops. The worst of all. The worst."

"Did you ever get to sleep?"

"Yeah. When it got light. Not even an hour, though, and then I had to get to work. At least it's safe there, though."

Angie always struggles to think of Claire as fearful, instead of as someone to be feared. But the two hundred dollars a month is not for sedatives, but for Prozac, capsules prescribed to dissolve dread. "Probably all women are afraid," Angie finally says.

"Not like me," Claire insists. "Not like me. You've never been afraid, have you? You've never had to be afraid. Always had me to protect you. I hope you know how lucky you are."

"I guess."

"Really. You just don't know what it's like to spend every single day of your life depressed. You should be thankful for that."

"I get depressed."

"I'm talking about real depression. Not being in a bad mood because you had a bad day at work. You're lucky you don't have it. You're lucky you don't have to take these pills."

"Are they helping?"

"Yeah, I think so. Though I'm scared. I saw on TV that people kill themselves on these things, have you heard of that?"

"I think." Angie does not remind Claire that they have had this conversation before, several times.

"I know. There have been women on TV and everything. But then some say it helps them. Some say they can't live their lives without these pills. Say these pills have saved their lives."

"Well, just be careful."

"Of course I'm careful. How do you think I've stayed alive this long? With all those rapists out there? You're the one that needs to be careful. I bet you don't even have locks on your windows. And you, living alone."

"I don't live alone."

"You know what I mean. But I can't stay on the phone like this. I've got things to do, you know. You aren't the only one who is busy."

"Talk to you later," Angie says.


It is always there. Like a small indentation. Flesh, like softened ground. Filled with bruise-brown mud, bubbling. Usually covered by the thick undergrowth of her life. Then led down the path by the sentimental strings of a rock ballad, finding it there. Depression, here in the breaths between Mick Jagger's tiresome attempts at seduction. Here, on the radio that battles the static in the morning fog. Here, long past any forks in this road. Angie knows she is being manipulated by the rock star as well as by herself, knows she surrenders like a predictable adolescent, to a grief as unbearable and as inarticulate. She wants to give herself over to it. To have her constant hollow turn itself inside out and erupt, through her own voice melding with the singer who sings with such studied anguish.

It is always there. But when she is not driving in the car she trudges so far away from it, trudges on the trails she has cleared by hand and the ones she has traced with maps. And even when it is close, so close she can smell the scabs, put her teeth underneath the healing and taste its gentle metal, she possesses a critical distance. The rock song has a grammar mistake. Not "she that." It should be "she who."

Such a careless mistake. In Angie's office is a copy of *Good Grammar for Lawyers*. With its glossary to decipher the difference between *that* and *who, that* and *from, that* and *which*. A trick she learned in law school, on law review, as an editor correcting other people's grammar. Like their mothers had corrected them, they told her. Not like teachers, like mothers. Like whose mother? she wanted to say. Or was it, like the mother of whom?

She still has to look at the book. Writing a brief, a pleading, even a letter to Cheryl Martin. Still has to check herself, check the memorized rules. As if to see whether the rule is still the same, still there, still as reliable as that cavity, hidden in the middle of everything, just waiting for her tongue to find it and rest against its sharp edges.

It is always there.

She calls it her clients.

She calls it Claire.

She does not call it anything.

Maybe she should try that Prozac stuff herself, she thinks.

"*Prozac* is a term in fifty-seven cases." Walter is standing, twirling the long chain around his neck.

"You did 'All States' and 'All Feds'?"

"Just like you said, Boss Angie."

"Was Kim helpful getting access to a computer?"

"I have my own sources, you know. I don't need to ask her."

"Whatever. What did you find?"

"The cases tend to address procedural considerations rather than substantive issues concerning Prozac," Walter reads from his own notes, then looks up. "A few divorce cases, where the wife in Connecticut is noted as taking Prozac."

"Always the wife?" Angie asks.

"Yes, always the wife. And always in Connecticut." Walter laughs. "Then there is another case trying to use Prozac as a defense in a murder prosecution, but the attorney did not raise it at trial, so the appellate court did not decide it. But there's a good case, from Florida, I think— or, let me see, Texas, yes, Texas—where the defendant put on evidence that he had taken Prozac, Xanax, and some liquor. An expert testified,"

Walter starts to read from his notes again, "that the levels of Prozac and Xanax were in the toxic range and that the side effects could include paranoid reactions and hallucinations. And the appellate court found that Prozac and Xanax caused a loss of ability to moderate the intentional and more impulsive actions by the judgment part of the brain."

"Pretty good. What happened?"

"The appellate court reversed because the judge did not give the jury the defendant's requested instruction about hallucinations."

"How old is this case?"

"Last year."

"Great. Call up the attorneys and find out what happened, will you? And what experts they used."

"Did Cheryl Martin hallucinate?"

"There's nothing in the transcript about that. We really need to get in touch with the trial lawyer. Would you call again? What other cases did you find?"

"Suits against the drug manufacturer. Saying the drug caused suicides and murders."

"Get me copies of those."

"I did. But there isn't much in the cases. It's all procedural, stuff like statutes of limitations and demands for discovery."

"Nothing from Iowa, I suppose."

"Indiana, you mean? Not one case with the word *Prozac*. I even looked up fluoxetine, the chemical name. Could not find anything in Indiana."

"Anything else?"

"One more I thought you might find interesting. A client claiming his lawyer rendered ineffective assistance of counsel because the lawyer was taking Prozac during the trial."

"The courts never grant ineffective-assistance-of-counsel claims," Angie declares.

Walter puts a copy of the case on Angie's desk.

Later, she pulls it out of her briefcase, opening it on the smooth red vinyl of the passenger seat, reading it as she inches her way across the steel spans suspended above the wide water.

APRILS

APRILS

**A P R I L S**

APRILS

APRILS

Only the calendars acknowledge spring. Angie waits for a bud of pink-ish green, for the morning she will look out the bedroom window, turn to Rachel, and say, "Spring is finally here." Rachel will pull Angie close then. And the world will open.

The ground erupts with clenched fists unfurling in white gloves. Velvety and parasitic. Angie conjures a rendering from a schoolbook—*Our Natural World*—and decides the plants are Indian pipes. Delicate, and maybe even poisonous. Rather perfect for the shadow of the house.

Cultivated by the previous owners, no doubt. Sprouting now for her. For her and Rachel and Skye.

Angie wonders if the pipes appearance is usual for April, wonders if the grand entrance is early or late. Angie has no history: no history with the pipes on the side of this house in this valley; no history with any pipes at any house in any valley. She thinks she should have heard some gossip about the arrival of the Indian pipes this spring. But her conversations about timeliness are grounded in the rules of appellate procedure and statutes of limitations, not in the soil of her yard mixed with memories of slush.

There must be a book. *Our Natural World,* the adult version. The bookcases in the living room faithfully support the needing-to-be-dusted reference books. *The Color Dictionary of Flowers and Plants for Home and Garden.* No Indian pipes next to the impatiens, also known as touch-me-not, blooms in late spring and summer and need a shel-tered sunny bed. *The Pictorial Guide to Wildflowers of America* has no entry for Indian pipes, although innocence blooms in the spring and early fall in the sandy coastal plains of warm climes.

There must be a book. If not on her shelves, then in the library. She will take Skye into the little library on Main Street, across from the post office, near enough to smell the river. They will research it together, the way they researched the wombat for Skye's school report. Copy the important pages on the library's old copy machine, fifteen cents a page. Staple the papers together, then staple them to her copy of her report. Watch Skye, the way she stands with her hand on her hip, her right leg thrust forward; the way she stands just like Angie. Make a little file for her animal projects. And soon they will start one for their plant research.

Perhaps buy one of those garden diaries she saw in the gardening catalog. So they would know next year, early or late, the Indian pipes. Like an appointment Book, only without lines, so that Skye could draw with colored inks. Spring, beautiful April. She will order a garden Book and take Skye to the library. They will walk outside, Skye's arms full of books, the sun caressing Skye's hair, making it look almost shiny. Skye will sing and the two of them will laugh. Maybe go to the ice cream parlor for the first ice cream of the season. Eat the cones sitting on the curb.

But before Angie has time to take Skye to the library, the Indian pipes have ruptured into thick green ferns.


Angie wraps herself around the telephone receiver.

"I thought you'd be here by now."

Angie recognizes this whining voice as her own. Inserts a bit of professional distance, straightens her shoulders. "I mean, I thought you had to come down this way to file that brief with the Second Division."

"I do. But we've had some computer glitches. I won't be down until late this afternoon," Rachel explains.

"I guess I'll have to go to lunch with Roger, then. I didn't bring anything. I thought we could have lunch together. I was going to take you to that new Mexican health-food place."

"Mexican health food? Sounds great. Why don't you go with Ellen?"

"She's doing a trial in Arkansas. She's never here anymore."

"Why don't you give her a call and talk to her? You seem like you miss talking to her."

"It's either the vending machines or Roger."

"Give Ellen a call."

"She's in court."

"Then leave her a message."

"And say what? 'You're in Arkansas working hard on an important case and I want to tell you how my girlfriend said she'd come for lunch but now she can't and so I have to have lunch with Roger, poor me'?"

Rachel laughs. "How about, 'Hope your trial is going well. Call me if you have a chance.'"

"That sounds like a good idea. I guess I'm being snarly. You're right, I do miss her. This is a crazy place and she's one of the few sane ones around. So, you'll come by later?"

"Yeah. I'll drop by before or after."


In the car, Roger buckles his seat belt. Checks it.

"I'm really a safe driver, Roger."

"You are one of the most careful drivers I know." He is proud that he remembers Angie's habits of driving, one more example of his sensitive manliness.

"You know," Roger continues, "I wouldn't have thought that. Wouldn't have thought you were so careful." He pauses. "Driving is a lot like sex, don't you think?"

"No. But then again, I haven't been in therapy." Angie feels combative.

"I didn't learn that in therapy. It's just true. And even if it's not, I just wouldn't think you'd be such a careful driver. You're just not a cautious person."

"Maybe. Or maybe I'm so cautious that I don't want anyone to know that I'm cautious. Anyway, the most reckless driver I ever knew was a very cautious person. This judge I clerked for after law school. He did everything so carefully. Went to a safe law school, married a safe woman and had a safe number of kids, worked at a safe law firm. As a judge he wrote safe opinions and made safe decisions. But driving? He was hell on wheels. Drove ninety miles an hour, and I'm not exaggerating."

"He couldn't have been all that safe. He hired you."

"Yeah. Big risk," Angie says sarcastically, "top of class and editor of law review. But I was—as a matter of fact—the first woman he hired. Although every other judge was also scrambling to hire women. You could say it was not safe to not hire a woman that year."

"But what I hear you saying—"

Angie sighs.

"—is that because you're so reckless in everything else, you've decided to be a safe driver."

Angie slows for the stop light, stopping ten feet before the white line. "I'm not really saying that. I'm just saying, Why take stupid risks?"

"And is that scar going down your neck one of your stupid risks?"

Angie does not shudder, only because she has practiced not shuddering. She should have worn a scarf; she should be in her office eating lunch from a vending machine. Coke and stale potato chips would be better than this. "I had ear surgery," she answers smoothly.

"More like switchblade surgery."

"Actually," Angie says only a little less smoothly, "it was not a switchblade, per se."

"Excuse me for being so stupid that I don't know the finer points."

"Excused." Angie laughs. "Although you know quite a bit, it seems. You aren't nearly as dumb as you look." She laughs a little more.

"Gee, thanks. But maybe you are. Expecting me to believe that scar is from surgery."

"People believe what they want to hear. And no one wants to hear about ugliness, violence, about dykes who murder their kids. Or did you miss the last staff meeting?"

"I was there, Ange. Or maybe you forgot I was there, defending you. Me and Ellen, did you forget?"

"No, I didn't. That was just a rhetorical question. I left you a message on your voice mail, thanking you for your support. I do appreciate it." Angie is apologetic, but Roger does not want to be mollified.

"You forget about me, Ange. Forget I'm not just some guy you can just cross off your list. I was a Communist, goddammit. I went to jail for burning my draft card. I grew up on a fucking pig farm. Fucking pigs! Watching my father fuck my sister, watching my mother trying not to watch. You think I'm just another liberal. You are dead wrong!"

Angie glances away from the traffic to catch Roger's expression. What she sees is Roger's hand approaching her arm.

"We've worked together for years, Ange. And you've forgotten I'm the kind of person who could love you. And who you could love back."

"And you've forgotten I'm the resident queer?"

"Oh, goddammit, Ange. I'm not forgetting that. But don't be so rigid. I mean, being a lesbian doesn't mean not sleeping with someone because he *happens* to be a man."

"You've been reading *The Village Voice* again," Angie mocks. "And besides, I thought we were talking love here, not sex."

"I get them confused," Roger admits. "At least that's what my therapist says."

"Well, if Octavia ever becomes your outer woman instead of just your inner one, we can talk about this again."

"Don't you think it's weird, though?" Roger sounds serious again. "I mean, I know you're a lesbian, but there's just something between us."

"Maybe it's your past."

"Mine?" Roger looks at Angie, who is looking for a parking space.

"You know: I remind you of someone in your past."

"You mean my aloof mother or my cruel father?"

"More like one of the little pigs. You remember, the cute one with ear surgery?" Angie laughs.

And then Roger is giggling, his face flushing pink through his beard and red like a mask in the hairless places. Both of them laughing, without rancor and without responsibility. Their breath mixes in the cool air as they leave the car for the restaurant. Not forgetting the conversation, but not making any effort to remember it.

The Mexican health-food restaurant is not as good as Angie had hoped it would be.

❊   ❊   ❊

Kim and Walter are standing outside Angie's office, outside the shut door, overhearing Rachel. Rachel's voice is angry. Yelling something about postcards.

"Those fucking postcards!"

"They're only postcards. This can be worked out." Angie's voice is low, placating, a tone Walter does not recognize as within her repertoire.

Walter escorts Kim away from the door. "Come back later," he says when what he means is "Do not come back, ever." He should have torn those stupid things up. He thinks Kim is ridiculous for sending black-and-white postcards of famous women to someone she thinks she loves, someone she could just call on the phone or even drop by and see, someone she is supposed to be working for, if she ever did any damn work.

Or maybe, Walter thinks, Kim is dumb like a fox. Maybe Kim's stretch of the lips is an attempt to conceal a smile. Hearing Rachel's jealousy drift into the hall. Sending the postcards because she hopes someone will see them, someone like Rachel. Kim has to know about Rachel, about Rachel and Skye. Everyone knows about Rachel and Skye. There's even some poster-sized photograph of the three of them standing in front of some mountains, the Tetons maybe, or the Rockies or even the Smokies, taking up practically the entire wall in Angie's office.

Walter feels protective of Angie. Feels protective as he deposits Kim into the waiting room. Feels protective as he stands like a casual guard outside Angie's still-closed office door. But there are limits, he thinks when Angie opens the door, looking for him, saying: "Maybe Walter can help with this."

"Hello, Rachel." Walter says.

"Hey, congratulations on your promotion, Walter. I haven't seen you for a while, but I've heard all about it. Don't let this woman work you to death." Rachel smiles, nodding toward Angie.

"Look who's calling the pot."

"You're as bad as Skye. That's the pot calling the kettle black."

"Whatever," Angie says. "What do you know about this Second Division postcard requirement? It's not in the rules, but the clerk over there says he can't perfect the appeal without a set of postcards to notify everybody and their damn brother."

"Postcards? *Those* postcards?" Walter's laugh ranges through the higher octaves.

"I say," Angie continues, "that we just type up everything and take the man what he wants."

"I don't have postcard stamps," Rachel says.

"Use first-class. I've got a bunch in my Book."

"The clerk says they've got to be postcard stamps."

"Oh, bullshit. He was just being a jerk. Just calm down and I'll help you with the postcards."

"I don't know why things like this get to me," Rachel says apologetically.

"It's the little things that always get you," Walter suggests. "Anyway, who's the clerk over there these days? I used to know some guy who worked there. A faggot friend of a friend. Nice butt, too. I'll give the office a call, see if he's still there. I'll take it over there if you want. Maybe get myself a date."

"Walter," Rachel protests, "you don't have to do that. That's way above and beyond. Running errands for your boss's girlfriend?"

"So, you'll owe me one. Maybe take me out to lunch next time you're in the neighborhood. Since my boss never takes me out to lunch." Walter looks at Angie. "Although she goes to lunch with Roger. And, like I said, maybe I'll get a date."

"You've got one with me," Rachel promises.


Kim waits for Rachel to leave. Watches her. A dyke stride and high cheekbones. A little on the fragile side. Sort of sexy and sullen and bony, with unmemorable hair, except for a shadow of it on her upper lip, a mustache. Dark barbiturate eyes, like some passé drug dealer from the seventies, or even the sixties, looking too important to focus on anyone else or even to glance at her own reflection in the window. Dressed in a black suit and a white shirt like some art photo, too stark and ultimately all background. Kim violently wishes that she could appear half as interesting.

But what is important, Kim reminds herself, is that Rachel is leaving. Leaving her lover Angie behind. Behind for Kim.

Kim approaches Angie warily. Kim thinks she needs a supplement in order to seduce. Kim and Chinese food. Kim and something she found in her copy of the Cheryl Martin transcript, in her apartment, on the desk in her bedroom. Kim and conversation, some story about some lesbian who left her lover for a man. Kim, wanting to know what Angie thinks about this, about everything.

"Rachel and I have this ongoing discussion about which is worse, to have your lover leave you for another woman or for a man."

"What do you think?" Kim asks, resolving not to be stung by Angie's reference to Rachel.

"I belong to the worse-if-it's-a-man camp."

"So do I," Kim pronounces, as if she has given the dilemma careful consideration.

"Why?"

"Well . . ." Kim struggles for the right answer. "It seems to me that it implicates basic identity questions."

"Whose?" Angie laughs.

"I guess both. The one who leaves for a man wasn't really in love with the one who thought she was a lesbian and she wasn't really a lesbian anyway, was she?"

"Why not?"

"Because she left for a man." Kim knows she is faltering, so she turns to smile at Angie.

"That means she isn't a lesbian? Wasn't one?"

"Not deep down. Not really," Kim concludes.

"Only a little deep down?" Angie laughs.

"What do you think?" Kim smiles aggressively.

"I think being left is being left."

"But you just said—"

"I told you what camp I belong to. But that doesn't mean that's what I believe. Deep down." Angie laughs again.

"I don't understand."

"I belong to certain camps because that's the way I came out. It's sort of like being raised. I mean, I'm certain ways because my mother was my mother. And I'm other ways because I was brought out by dykes who were dykes. And I belong to the dyke camp: Real lesbians don't leave their lovers for men. And the dyke camp says that every lesbian deserves anything I can do for her. Even if she's a shit."

"Even if she's been convicted of murder?" Now it is Kim's turn to laugh.

"That's my camp."

"But what do you really believe, deep down?"

"I believe what my mother taught me: Life sucks, kid." Angie enjoys referring to Claire in such a superficial manner, enjoys the fact that Kim does not know her relationship with Claire is anything but superficial.

Kim nods.

"Now tell me what you think is so important in Cheryl Martin's transcript that it can't wait until tomorrow."

What Kim shows Angie is nothing Angie has not seen before.


"What did you do, go with Walter on his date?"

"There was a lot of traffic, Rachel."

"Skye wanted to tell you something about school. About some spring thing they're going to do."

"I'll go talk to her."

"She's already asleep."

"I'll talk to her in the morning."

"I'm going to bed."

"I'm right behind you."

Angie slides around Rachel, wanting Rachel's body to soften around her own, wanting Rachel.

"Claire called."

Angie's stiffness now competes with Rachel's. "What did she say?"

"Nothing. She hung up."

"It could have been a wrong number."

"It could have been you calling to say you'd be late. It could have been Roger calling to see if you'd gotten home yet."

"Roger?" Angie thinks she is being deflective.

"Yeah, Roger. You think I'm stupid? You think I don't know what's going on?" Rachel sits up in bed and turns on the lamp. "Walter practically told me you spend all your time with him. And you're always making little jokes about Roger. Roger this and Roger that. It's obvious as hell he's got a crush on you, I've seen him look at you."

"That's ridiculous," Angie protests.

"Oh, is it?"

Angie can feel the heat of a blush on her neck, burning her behind her ears. Knows Rachel can see it. "He's just being silly," Angie attempts an explanation.

"And how do I know you aren't?"

"What?"

"How do I know you aren't having an affair with him?"

"With *Roger?*"

Rachel just stares back at Angie, her eyes shining wet, her eyes looking away.

Angie cups a hand on each of her lover's shoulders, kisses each side of her neck, then kisses her softly on each cheek. "Believe me, I am not having an affair with Roger."

Rachel just nods.

"Look at me," Angie coaxes. "Look at me. Believe me. And I'm sorry for whatever I'm doing that makes you think something so ridiculous."

"You swear you're not having a fling with Roger?"

"Rachel, I swear."

"Or with anyone?" Rachel presses.

"Or with anyone," Angie echoes.


In the bathtub—another sleepless night—the hot water reddens her ass and thighs, spreading in a blotch across her stomach. Sex. Sex. Sex. The only cure for insomnia. The only cure for guilt. The only clarity, because it is the ultimate confusion.

Angie cannot even decide if what she wants with Rachel should be called sex. Maybe something else. Maybe something close, close and far apart at the same time. That feeling of being utterly connected and yet utterly singular. All hard and all soft, simultaneously.

Angie tries not to think about Roger. Sex with a man, even a man with a woman within, seems adolescent to Angie. Something she thought about at fifteen, sixteen. How could Rachel have imagined that? How could Rachel even be serious? Maybe their relationship is falling apart, Angie thinks. After all, Rachel did ask her if she was having an affair.

Angie tries to think of Kim. She knows she must break up with her. But then, what's to break up? She has had sex with Kim seven, maybe eight times. Sex she can barely recall. Does it count if she doesn't come? Is that sex, really? Does it count if she didn't want to? Is that sex, or just stupidity?

All these years with Rachel, and only half an affair. Most married men have at least one affair for every year they are married, at least according to some article Angie had read in the waiting room of Skye's dentist. And heterosexual women? Ellen has had at least two affairs that Angie knows about and that Ellen's boyfriend supposedly does not; one of them serious. And Angie knows that Dorothy had an affair with an immigration attorney, while she was pregnant with Andrew. And she certainly would not put it past Chelsea.

And then there was Claire.

The memories make Angie want to put her head under the water.

As if water could cure the fluidity of time, of place. As if water—or any substance—could fix Angie in the here-and-now and only in the here-and-now. As if all her practice could make her perfect.

And Angie had practiced. Had practiced her lies so well they seemed as accurate as truths. Had lied to Luke: "I don't know where she is." Had lied to the boyfriends: "I don't mind if you come with us." Had lied to Claire: "I like this newest one the best; I think he really likes you." Had lied to the mirror of the world: "I am not scared, lonely, confused."

Had promised: "I will never let this happen again." Had believed she had power even as the promise transformed itself into a lie, again and again, and she told Claire, "I like this newest one the best; I think he really likes you," again and again.

Until Angie made the promise come true by leaving Claire behind. In a different time she called the past. In a different place she rarely named. It stopped happening to Claire, at least as far as Angie knew. And started happening to Angie.

Angie runs more water into the bath, wanting it hotter and hotter, wanting it scalding. Before Rachel, women had happened to Angie.

Each woman had been nice enough, at least out of bed. But naked, or half-naked, Angie could never fit, body to body. Only a few glasses of vodka, or some dope, smoothed the edges, at least temporarily.

Sometimes she had thought it was sex itself that was deficient, but then some other woman would stand close to her, and her posture would become a promise. A promise that everything would be all right.

Maybe, she thinks, it is not that Rachel is so right, only that she is not wrong. Sex with the wrong person is like diving into a camouflaged pond that looks so inviting, so clear. Diving in from a smooth ledge of rock with a perfect dive, feeling that everyone—and no one—is watching her faultless form. But the water she had convinced herself would be refreshing is always too cold, so cold it it numbs the blood that rushes to the surface of the skin. Once underwater, she craves only surface, only the sun on her skin, only evaporation. Complete and quick.

Sex with a person who is not wrong, sex with Rachel, is what she wants. What she has always wanted. Wanted during all those years she had considered other people's sexual escapades from a comfortable distance; during all those years she had pretended to forget Claire's boyfriends. Angie judged fidelity an accomplishment, much like her other achievements. She had felt invulnerable, not only because she was satisfied with Rachel but because there was no room in her appointment Book.

But then Kim had happened. Has happened. But how? How could this be happening to her?

It seems as if it is happening to someone else. Because it is not Kim who Angie wants. Not now. Not ever. It is Rachel. Now. At four o'clock in the morning. Waiting for dawn so that everyone will stop blurring together, present and past, sex and not-sex. Everyone reminds her of someone else: Roger of some long-ago professor; Kim of her third-grade teacher; Skye of herself as a child. But who is Rachel? Angie wonders. And who is she, herself? Angie curses because she does not even know that; cannot surface on the other side of the lies; cannot admit she is scared, lonely, confused. Angie only dips her head into the water, again and again. In her perfected repetitions, she barely notices that the water in the bathtub grows colder and colder and the night grows shorter and shorter.

Angie is a new attorney, a public defender. She represents men accused of misdemeanors. The men are white, or black or Hispanic, or sometimes Asian or Native American. There is a monthly report with columns in these categories: White, Black, Hispanic, Asian, Native American. And Other. The misdemeanors are drugs. Or gambling, or driving while intoxicated, or disturbing the peace. The monthly report has columns for the criminal charges, categorized by penal code number: 133.45. Or 137.12. Or 142.6. Or Other.

Angie misses women. The courtrooms are stuffed with men. Loud voices and extended elbows. She protects her male clients from other men. She likes misdemeanors, not because the stakes are lower, but because there are no victims. In felonies, the victims are women. Rapes. Assaults. Murders. Angie does not want the promotion to the felony division.

There is one woman judge. Angie always wants to sit next to her at the lawyers' monthly luncheon, but Angie feels too shy. She knows she wants too much from the woman judge, wants her as a mentor, wants her as a professional mother. So Angie avoids her.

There is one woman prosecutor. Angie hates her. She wears expensive suits and sheer stockings, with spectator pumps. She has already announced she wants to be a judge. She always asks for the maximum sentence.

There are women secretaries, women court reporters, a few women courtroom clerks. Angie likes them and she thinks they like her. But there is some unspoken rule of hierarchy that they all understand. Even the court reporter whom Angie saw in the bar on women's night and thought about asking to dance understands what Angie understands: There is something between them that prevents anything from ever being between them.

There are women clients. Few and far between. Women clients charged with womanly crimes: Shoplifting. Welfare fraud. Prostitution.

Candy is white. Penal Code section 375.7.

Angie stands close to Candy in the courtroom of men. No woman judge today, no woman prosecutor. Candy's white hair is stiff with dirt. Her white nail polish is chipped and her white lipstick uneven. Candy is strapped into fuck-me shoes and has a fuck-you smile.

The judge interrogates the plea bargain.

"Time served? On a third conviction? I don't know."

Angie has bargained hard on this one. Time served is less than twenty-four hours.

"Your Honor"—Angie looks at the judge—"given the unusual circumstances here, I believe the bargain is a fair one. However, if the court rejects the plea and sentence, my client must insist upon her speedy-trial rights. The demand has been filed. And the last day is tomorrow."

"Counsel?" The judge turns toward the prosecutor.

"The state is satisfied with the plea and sentence."

The judge looks at his calendar. "As is the Court."

"Adjudication withheld requested," Angie says.

"Does the state agree?" The judge looks at the prosecutor.

"We never discussed—"

"I'm asking the state if it has any objection."

The prosecutor looks at Angie. "Not in this case."

"Time served. Adjudication withheld." The judge pronounces. "But don't let me see you back in this courtroom again, young lady."

For a moment, Angie thinks the judge means her instead of her client.


"That was bitching," Candy says out in the hall. Candy knows enough to know when she has gotten a good deal.

"I told you I didn't think prostitution should be prosecuted," Angie tells her client. Which is true, but maybe there is something else.

Something else, which makes Angie want to see Candy again; that makes Candy know she will be welcome when she comes back to Angie's office, just to "check on her case." Something else, which makes Candy wait in the courthouse hall one morning after misdemeanor calendar call.

"How about lunch?" Candy asks. There is a hint of hesitation in her voice. She is wearing jeans and sneakers. And no makeup.

"I can't today." Angie opens up a large notebook as if to illustrate. It is a calendar filled with little grids and lots of writing. "But how about tomorrow? Saturday?"

"Sure."

"Where should we meet?"

"Somewhere other than the courthouse," Candy suggests.

"That sounds nice."


"Don't feel awkward. I can separate business and pleasure," Candy says. She is sitting on the back of Angie's wicker couch, in Angie's living room, during Angie's Saturday afternoon.

"I'm not sure I can."

"I didn't figure you'd be uptight about my work."

"It's not *your* work I'm worried about," Angie explains.

"That's okay. I'm used to it."

"It's *my* work, don't you get it?"

"What's wrong with your work?"

"Nothing. It's just that you're—"

"—a fucking whore." Candy stands up.

"No, a client."

"A client?"

"Yeah. I think it would be the same if I defended you on welfare fraud or shoplifting or drugs. It's the fact that I represented you, not what you were charged with."

"Oh. Does that mean you're not allowed to kiss me?" Candy leans over.

"I don't think it means that." Angie whispers, convincing herself.

"Then what's the problem?"

"I guess there isn't one." Angie says. But she is not sure. Not sure as they kiss. And still not sure as they move into the bedroom to continue kissing. And still not sure when the kisses move across the face to the breasts and thighs and become strokes at the clitoris. And still not sure when Candy gets up from Angie's darkening bed to go to work.

Only sure that the sex had been exceedingly ordinary.

The professor with the beard sits behind his desk. He is Angie's adviser, and what Angie needs is advice. Advice about courses and about degree requirements. She wants to graduate early. She got into college early and she wants to leave early. Wants to go to graduate school. Political science. Or social philosophy, maybe. Wants to become a professor, even. Like him. Like the few women she has seen on campus. Like the person she wants to be.

He is telling her he is an existentialist. Her head spins with his ideas. She does not agree, but she does not know why.

He is telling her that he believes in free love, but there are certain limitations. Like the fact that she is still in his class on American Social Theory. That would not be ethical, he says, nodding. Angie is not sure she knows what he means.

"Next semester," he says, "don't sign up for a class with me. And then we can begin our affair."

"What affair?"

"Our love affair."

Angie stands up. Her face is red. "But I'm a dyke, Professor."

"I know you think you are. I know all about you and Jennifer. And perhaps we can all work on this together. Jennifer is a lovely young woman; it is no wonder you are attracted to her. But such attractions are a phase that many women go through as they mature. It's an understandable reaction to the men you find yourself surrounded by, the immature men in your own age group. You are a mature young woman and you need a mature man."

"Y-you're my teacher," Angie stutters.

"Exactly." The professor leans back in his chair.

Angie mutters something vague that serves as a retreat. In the hall, she looks for Jennifer, who said she would wait after her own appointment. Angie has to see Jennifer, has to tell her this, has to hold her and turn it into a joke. Has to forget that she had thought the professor liked her, had thought he believed she was smart, had thought he would help her get into graduate school. Has to figure out how to get another adviser.

But Jennifer is nowhere to be found. And when Angie finds her, later, she is distant. No telling, no holding, no joking. And then Jennifer is gone from the college hallways. She is spending her time with the professor, in private. And Angie is gone. Reading social theory at home, and back hanging out in the bars with women. Back in the bars.

■ ■ ■ ■ ■ ■ ■

"See that woman who just walked in?"

Angie tries to bury her fingers in her hair, forgetting it is now short. She tries to decide if she should think the woman is cute or not. Or recognize her as someone's girlfriend.

"Yeah."

"Don't get too close."

Angie nods. Must be someone's girlfriend. Someone tough.

"You know why?"

"Someone's lover." Angie says. Proud of the way she says the word lover.

"Worse."

"What?" Angie is curious. She looks at Bucky, bar dyke extraordinarie, Angie's professor of dykedom.

"She's a political lesbian."

Angie nods.

"She's just slumming here with us. Experimenting. When it ain't fashionable no more, she'll be gone. Back to some husband in suburbia."

"Really?"

"All them political ones are the same. Don't ever say no one warned you. *I'm* warning you. Listen to Bucky about this, even if you don't listen about nothing else."

Angie nods.

"I'm not saying don't fuck them. No, I'm not saying that."

Angie looks at Bucky, swirling the ice cubes in her glass.

"Though I don't know why anyone would want to get it on with them. Terrible at it, those girls. Just terrible. But what's important is not to fall in love with them. 'Cause they ain't playing for keeps, honey. They're just playing."

Angie nods again. Orders herself another drink. And gets one for Bucky, too. Looks at the political lesbian, sitting on the bar stool. The woman looks lonely, looks cute. But Angie listens to Bucky. Swears she will never go to bed with a political lesbian, just hopes she can always tell who they are. Just as she swears she will never go to bed with Bucky, the one who is giving her lessons on being a dyke. No, never with Bucky. That would be like fucking a professor, like fucking her own mother.

She swears she will never fuck Bucky, even as she steadies herself against Bucky's arm, after "Last call for alcohol!" echoes through the emptying bar and the lights come on, making the women squint and blink and some even cry. Even after watching that woman, that political lesbian, get up and walk out, alone and still sexy. Even as she regrets not asking a woman with an unbelievably wide belt to dance, watching her lean against the wall like family, like Carol and maybe even Claire. Even as she feels so lonely and empty and more Evangelina than Angie.

Outside, she does not drop Bucky's arm. A kiss seems more and more possible. More and more necessary. She could guide them into a side street, tuck them between two cars, point out the moon like a pickax beyond the streetlight.

But five—or maybe six or seven—steps allow them to hear some screaming, some yelling and hissing, and a man's voice laughing "Bulldagger!" and another male voice whining "Me next." The side street is blocked with blood. A man starts to whistle. The crowd compresses itself, and one or two drift away. Angie can see them under the streetlight, see that they border on being boys, that they are probably the same age as she is.

"Go back to the bar and get help," Bucky commands Angie.

Angie does not move. Bucky moves into the crowd. Toward the woman on the ground. Toward that woman, that political lesbian, that woman who no longer looks cute or sexy or anything but scared.

One of the boy-men jumps on Bucky. She punches him in the face. Gives her hand to the woman on the ground.

"Don't touch her or I'll slice your pretty little girlfriend's face off." The one who holds Angie has strawberry-blond hair. Angie tries to study his face, the whiteheads like a cap of snow across his mountain of a nose. Angie tries not to look at the knife, the edge not as shiny and sharp as it would be in a nightmare or a movie.

The streetlights blink.

Someone says "Oh, shit."

Angie twists toward the woman with the wide belt walking with a woman who did ask her to dance; lurches back to the bar with its bouncer and its gun-equipped owner; yells out to the clot of dykes walking too slowly up the street. The women start to run toward Angie, whom they can see, toward the men, whom they can sense, and toward Bucky and the political lesbian, whom they are afraid to imagine. Bucky grabs the political lesbian, pushes her to her feet, positions her against a car, then drags her through the ones who are looking at each other's eyes for clues.

Then, like a flock of startled grackles, the boy-men dissipate into the night air.

The woman with the wide belt runs after one of them, catches him, and tears off his shirt. The bar bouncer and bar owner flank him. Bucky approaches, with the knife that had fallen to the ground—the knife that had scraped against Angie's face, landing on the bone behind Angie's ear.

"Take off your pants. And underwear, if you wear any."

Bucky laughs. The woman with the wide belt laughs. The bar bouncer giggles, the bar owner snorts. There are other women, other sounds, indistinguishable.

Angie and the political lesbian close their eyes against the blood that seeps through their fingers as they clutch their split flesh, against any vision that will become a haunting memory.

"Now walk home. And if we catch you around here again, you ain't going to leave intact, if you get my meaning."

The caught one does not move.

"Go on." And the women turn from him. And he runs.

They all walk back to the bar. The owner unlocks the door, ushering her customers.

"Don't get any blood on my floor."

Angie wants to feel happy that no one got killed, but she does not. Instead she feels like maybe they should have killed that kid. Murdered him. Sliced him open until his blood saturated the road. Taken his body and thrown it into some ditch.

No one calls the police. No one gets stitches. No one leaves until the sky is saturated with sunlight.

※ ※ ※ ※ ※ ※

Evangelina is sobbing over her third-grade teacher, the tall woman with the protruding incisors.

"Grow up," Claire scolds. "So your teacher's getting married, so what?"

"Evangelina is such a crybaby, Auntie Claire," Carol announces, tugging at her cousin's curls.

"I always cry at weddings," an aunt says. Maybe Carol's mother. Maybe someone else's mother. Not her own mother, not Claire.

Claire laughs again, stubbing her cigarette into a plate on the kitchen table.

"Someday, Evangelina," the aunt says, "you'll have your own wedding."

"I won't," she pouts, trying to invent a future she cannot imagine.

"Yeah, who would want to marry you?" Carol taunts.

"Evangelina is beautiful," Claire says defensively. "She'll have men begging her to let them run their fingers through her beautiful long hair. Men love curly hair." Claire fluffs her daughter's curls. "Carol is just jealous," Claire half whispers to no one in particular.

"You'll get married, little Evangelina." The aunt reassures. "And with any luck at all, I'll be around to cry at that wedding, too."

I won't, she says again, only this time silently. Even little Evangelina, best reader in the class, knows it's stupid to love your third-grade teacher and want to marry her. But she also knows she does, stupid or not. It makes so much sense that it does not make any sense.

Like other things that did not make sense. Like Carol. Carol sweet. Carol mean. Like Carol's games, of safety and danger. Stranded on a desert island in a war waiting to be rescued, but meanwhile living in a wilderness of women's darkness under the covers without any clothes. Or hiding against the hunting season in a cave, a doe and fawn, licking each other to keep from freezing to death, tasting the salt. Or sequestered in some terrible prison for spying on the Earthlings, searching for their lost powers in each other's hidden folds.

"You be the mother and I'll be another mother and our husbands and babies will be trapped in the mineshaft and we'll be worried and have to get very very close," Carol says.

And Angie agrees.

■ ■ ■ ■ ■ ■

Morning. Late. Stumble for coffee to cure the hangover of insomnia, followed by a surrender to dawn. Look at the mail on the kitchen table. Catalogs and more catalogs. Sip some coffee. It is almost noon; it should be warm. Should be able to sit in a garden and watch something bloom. Something new. Something she has never seen before.

She dials her own office. Checks her own voice mail.

Six new messages. Cheryl Martin's mother. Cheryl Martin's trial attorney. Kim. Two from Walter. One from someone who wants her to speak at a conference on lesbian and gay legal issues.

The phone rings as she puts it down.

"I was just about to call you. I got your message. What's up with Cheryl Martin?"

"Are you sitting down?"

"The prosecutor saw an advance copy of our brief and knows we'll win and so he's agreed to a new trial?" Angie almost sings.

"Angie, sit down."

"What's wrong? Walter? Walter?"

"She's dead. She killed herself in prison."

"How?" Angie sits down. "Prisoners don't get anything they can kill themselves with."

"She hung herself."

"With what? That's just not possible."

"I haven't gotten all the details. A sheet, maybe."

"Fuck. Jesus Christ. Fuck."

"I know," Walter says.

"Walter, could you just return the phone calls from the lawyer and the mother. Ask them if there's anything we can do. I don't think I can come in today. Just call me and let me know if they want us to do anything. And then take the rest of the day off yourself."

"I've already talked to the lawyer. He just called to tell us. And the mother called to say she wants to sue. Sue the prison."

"That bitch."

"Just take it easy, Ange."

"I'll see you tomorrow, then. Just take the day off. Tell someone you're going to the library."

"Take care of yourself."

"You, too."

Angie hangs up the phone. Hangs up. Hanged herself. Or is it hung? Another dead dyke in a world that likes its dykes best when they are dead. Another mother who lost her kids and then lost herself, in a world that likes its mothers best when they are lost. Another lost case, another loss that should have been won.

When Skye comes home, she finds Angie rocking back and forth in a wooden chair on a wooden floor with the afternoon sun slanting through the wooden windows.

Rocking. Rocking. Rocking.


"The world," Angie says to Rachel.

"Is nothing but," Angie whispers.

"Dead," Angie says.

"Dead trees." Angie looks at Rachel.

"You did the right thing by calling me, honey," Rachel tells Skye. "Now, she's just upset about something. She'll be fine. Go into your room a little while." Rachel watches Angie rocking back and forth; watches Skye go down the hall to her room, not closing the door. "What is it, babe? What's happened?"

"Nothing."

"What are you saying?"

"It's a poem. A poem."

"Oh."

"You know. Emily. Emily Dickinson. The dead poet. And Emily. That dead little girl. Shot dead. By her mother. With a rifle."

"Your client?" Rachel struggles to remember the client's name.

"Dead. Dead trees. She's dead, too."

"Who?"

"The mother. The one who wrote all that poetry. Sent it to me. Not on postcards, but in little envelopes. All that poetry. And now she's dead."

Rachel and Skye put Angie to bed. And both of them rock her and smooth her forehead, as if she is a child who is not too old to be rocked. And they are perfect mothers.

M A Y

M A Y

**M A Y**

M A Y

M A Y

Angie is sitting. On a chair, behind a table, between two other women, facing an audience. It is Law Day. A day declared in defiance of the Communists' May Day, itself an edifice constructed on the ashes of the pagan May Eve. A day when attorneys appear on podiums in high schools, on public service announcements, and on panels at conferences on topical topics. This conference is entitled Lesbian and Gay Rights. This panel is on "the family." All the panelists are women. Almost everyone in the audience is a woman. Angie assumes all the women are lesbian, or at the very least bisexual.

Angie uses thirteen of her fifteen minutes. She talks as if a button had been pushed, as if she had been wound up, as if she is on automatic pilot. Heads nod when she talks about the work of Triple-F; more heads nod when she talks about her own work on appeals of cases denying child custody to lesbians. Stillness when she talks about criminal defense, about cases in which lesbians are charged with murder. Murders of lovers seem marginally palatable, murders of children do not. Angie concludes with a thank-you.

During the question-and-answer session, someone asks Angie about that terrible case in yesterday's newspaper about a lesbian losing custody of her children to her mother. It happens all the time, Angie explains. The audience murmurs with outrage. A mother, suing her own daughter—even a dyke daughter—for custody appalls them. Angie envies their anger, even as she distrusts it. Angie knows that some of the murmuring lesbians are lawyers, lawyers who have litigated and lost. Angie knows that some of the murmuring lesbians are mothers, mothers who lose sleep to anxiety.

Someone else asks Angie about another terrible case, this one also from yesterday's newspaper. Angie feels as if she is on a TV talk show. Or on the witness stand, being cross-examined. Does she really think that the mother who let her baby suffocate in a closet is worthy of scarce legal resources? Does she really think that the mother who let her baby suffocate—and maybe starve—in a closet is important just because she is a lesbian? Does she really think that the mother who let her baby suffocate—and maybe starve—and had sex with her lover while the baby screamed with pain—is human? Angie says she does. She does. She does.

The people in the audience, people she knows and people she does not, shake their heads. Suspending disbelief and disapproval to listen to Angie's political explanation, compressed into three sentences like a sound bite. Diversity. And each and every lesbian. Deserving. Most of them start to shake their heads again, before she is finished speaking. But one or two lesbians, and then a third, talk to her when the panel is over and she is leaving the room. One or two lesbians, and then a third, tell her they think her work is important. One or two or three lesbians, but none of them is Cheryl Martin.

Cheryl Martin. A page in an appointment book. A file in an office. A name on a list of things to do. Cheryl Martin. Dead. Dead. Dead.

Even work cannot change some things.


Angie is listening. In her bed, between sheets of one-hundred percent Supima cotton. It is the new moon, no moon. Darkness on both sides of the wooden windows. Rachel's voice floats into the bedroom.

"Yeah, Mom. I think she'll be fine. She's back at work and everything."

Silence.

"Probably she will have to deal with it sooner or later."

Silence.

"Skye is just great. Her reading is getting so advanced. I mean, I was typing a pleading the other day and she was reading it out loud. Words like *defendant* and *corporation* and *regulations.* It's really amazing."

Silence.

Laughter. "I guess the apple doesn't fall too far from the tree. I'll have to tell Skye that one. Her class is still collecting those maxims. It drives me crazy some days. I mean, the kid knows every cliché in the English language."

Silence.

"Oh, work's fine. But there's a possibility that I might transfer next month to the law guardian unit. That means all my clients would be kids. I'd be the attorney for the kid in custody cases, or when the state is charging the parents with abuse or neglect. Or I'd represent kids who are being charged with being juvenile delinquents."

Silence.

"It's a state statute, Mom. The state funds it and our organization has one of the contracts. The children aren't necessarily poor, or from poor families, I mean. We even represent some kids of famous actors, moved up here from the city. In custody cases, I guess the state figures that all the adults have lawyers, someone should represent the child. And half the custody cases these days involve allegations of abuse . . . well, maybe not half, but a lot."

Silence.

"I don't know if I'd like it. But I'm ready for a change."

Silence.

"Love you, too, Mom. I'll let you know what happens. And I'll make sure to tell Skye your saying about the apple."

Silence.

Silence as Rachel comes into the bedroom, does not turn on the light, looks at her lover's closed eyes.

"Angie?" she whispers, but her voice is absorbed by the silence.

"Angie?" she whispers again. And later again. And later, without a whisper. But always the silence, even when she gets in between the cotton sheets and tells her lover that she loves her. Even when Rachel says: "I know you're not sleeping, Angie. I just wish you'd say something."

But to open her mouth, to open her eyes, feels impossible to Angie. Impossible in a world without Cheryl Martin. Impossible in a world with Rachel—Rachel, who tells her mother about a new job before she tells Angie; Rachel, whose new job is going to be defending children in abuse cases; Rachel, whose new job will mean Rachel will side with children against their lesbian parents; Rachel, who can only call Angie's name but cannot change anything; Rachel, whose fingers touch Angie's face, feeling for tears that will only arrive when Angie remembers how to fight.

Angie is pacing. It is Mother's Day. A capitalist invention, a conspiracy to make money. Otherwise May would be too boring, the sales too slow. Cards and flowers. Sent to Claire. And now the long-distance telephone call. The circuits are busy, children calling their mothers and the phone companies making money. When the phone finally rings, Claire does not answer. Sunday morning, Mother's Day and Claire does not answer. Like she said she would not. Said yesterday, said she is too depressed, even the Prozac does not help, said she does not feel like a mother, said a real daughter would be with her mother on Mother's Day, that single special day, said, Is that too much to ask? asking but not waiting for any answer.

Angie tries again and again. Knowing Claire is listening to the ring of the telephone. Hoping that the ring is comforting.

Angie waits for Skye. For Skye to kiss her, to say "Happy." To give her something she made in school. Something made from egg cartons and pipe cleaners, a bouquet of flowers. Something like the things Angie had made for Claire, things Claire had saved, probably still has. Things Angie had tired to shape during the spilled-paint terror of the school art period.

But Skye has no presents. Angie tries not to do anything that would induce guilt in her daughter. Perhaps arts and crafts are no longer devoted to mollifying parents. And perhaps parents who spend money to send their kids to expensive alternative schools do not require mollification. Or perhaps Skye could not do the project, some complicated weaving; or thought she should do two, one for each mother, and could not finish; or did not want to make anything for her mother and her other mother, either one, because she hated them both so much for taking her away from her real mother.

Angie dials Claire's number again. Again.

Angie calls Cheryl Martin's mother; hangs up when she answers.

✻　✻　✻

Angie is bleeding. It is the full moon. She searches for the Goddess Calendar in the bathroom on the wicker stand, tucked between catalogs and more catalogs. She pauses to pick up Generations: mail-order ecology, printed on recycled paper with soy ink. "Organically grown cotton cloth pads are more absorbent and comfortable than disposable menstrual pads . . . and better for the environment." She folds the catalog at that page, puts it back on the shelf. Finds the Goddess Calendar, its cover splotched with water stains.

Locates today, but it is not May. It is Uath, the sixth lunation, six out of thirteen. Thirteen full moons in a calendar year. So that one special month would have two full moons, the second moon the blue moon. Not this month.

This month has only one full moon, one circle. Surrounded by little astrological signs, recognizable as Aries—or is it Taurus?—a moon circle crowned with horns. And some other symbol that she thinks is Sagittarius. In the space that is not a square or a rectangle, but some sort of graphic womb, Angie writes her initial: A. Recording the start of her period, as if she has regular cycles, as if she has desires or fears about pregnancy, as if she still believes that menstruating during the full moon is cause for a ritual celebrating the goddess in all women.

Angie is sweating. It is Victoria Day. In Canada. At least according to the calendar in her Book. Victoria Day. In italics. Canada. In parenthesis. An entire country rendered optional by punctuation.

A fragment of geography captured in an accent. An echo of Claire, an echo down a deserted mineshaft. Catherine call-me-Cathy Chillicothe, is telling Angie about her daughter, Susannah, about her daughter's lover, Harriet, and about her daughter's child, dead.

"I read about the case." Angie feels the sweat dripping down her back, under her jacket, under her blouse, under her undershirt. She is back at work, back in the square womb of her office, looking at her appointment Book on her desk. Her eyes avoid Cathy Chillicothe's.

"None of it's true, what's being said."

"I don't doubt that."

"I know you can help. I know you are the one. I've been investigating. I heard one of your clients was on TV. There are a few people who are being kind. Most of them like rattlers, but a few people are being kind. And then I hear, never mind how, but I do hear that my mother and your mother are practically cousins, I know you are the one."

"I'm not a trial attorney." Angie does not add "anymore," does not dwell on the twinge of disappointment in her own voice.

"She ain't having no public defender."

"Public defenders are very good trial lawyers. Probably the best. You know, I was a public defender."

"In coal country?"

Angie shakes her head. No, she had to admit, not in coal country. No coal for years and years, really since World War II, but everyone still called it coal country. Probably because of the names of the towns: Anthracite City, Coaldale, Nanticoke, Slagville. Strip-mine country. Black-lung country.

"Then you tried cases? Murder cases?"

"No, no murder cases."

"A crime's a crime. Besides, she didn't do it. She wouldn't stuff no baby in a closet. It was like a little room, they had a crib in there and everything. Didn't suffocate it. Babies been dying for years. Years and no one cared. Her only crime is being a different kind of woman, like you. Hell, been your kind of women in those hills for years and years. You'd think it was something the newspapers just discovered, the way they go on and on."

"I just don't think I can do a trial."

"You're the only one we'll trust. I want you to take this." Cathy Chillicothe reaches into her knapsack. "It's what my daughter wrote. It proves it ain't her fault. It's her diary."

"I really can't—"

"If anyone did it, it's Harriet. Woman thinks she's some sort of beauty or something. But inside she's rotten to the core. You know what they say—"

"I really—"

"Skin deep, is what they say. And they're right."

"I—"

"But if you ask me, Harriet ain't really a beauty. You know what they say—"

"Eye of the beholder?" Angie is becoming comfortable, despite herself.

"Exactly." Cathy Chillicothe smiles, revealing a missing bicuspid. "Now my daughter, she's a beauty. Truly. Inside and out."

"I—"

"You got any kids? You must not." Cathy Chillicothe glances briefly at the poster-size photograph of Angie, Rachel, and Skye. "If you had a kid of your own you'd understand about flesh and blood."

"I'll take a look at it. See what kind of help we can get her." Angie forces a smile. Stands up.

"I got to catch the bus. I'll give you a call. You say hey to your mother from my mother. They was in school together, at least as far as they got!" She laughs, seemingly without embarrassment.


Angie is driving. It is another day in May. Just another day. The radio. The traffic. The trying-to-be-summer sun shafts over the river. Angie is in her car on the bridge. A standstill. Only the river rushes below the steel span, uninterrupted by the tons of metal suspended above.

Angie is thinking about Cheryl Martin, hanging. Thinking about Cathy Chillicothe, more or less the same age as Angie. Thinking about what she does not want to read: Susannah Chillicothe's diary, Kim's postcards, the opposition's brief to her motion for reconsideration in Sharon Delsarado's case, the book on grief that Rachel got her from the library, the newspaper articles on lesbians and murder that Walter has been clipping. Thinking about what she does not want to hear: Rachel talking about whether or not she should transfer to the law guardian unit, Rachel talking to her mother, Rachel calling her name as if she should answer to a name that might no longer belong to her, if it ever did.

Trying not to think. Not about Kim or Claire or Prozac.

The car is as anonymous as a womb. All that is missing is that salty fluid in which Angie could float, suspended and unborn, without desire or ambition. Unafraid of being drowned by Claire.

❖   ❖   ❖

Angie is leaning. It is Memorial Day. Once it meant something to her, the start of summer, now it only means the annual Triple-F picnic. Leaning against a tree, in some borough botanical garden. Holding a paper plate and talking to Ellen. Ellen, her soul-mate at Triple-F, straddling the border between friend and colleague. Ellen, who she has missed and missed. Ellen, who is suing doctors who thirty and forty years ago routinely sterilized poor women as a method of birth control: "It's hard to prove damages," Ellen says. "How do you talk about what your life would have been like if you had had more children? How do you get an expert to testify about the damages a woman suffers when she finds out she's been sterilized?"

Ellen changes the subject, indulging in gossip, even gossip about people who surround them. Safely innocuous in that absolutely private place possible only in public. Angie can see Chelsea and Chad, Coleman and Kaitlin, forming a quiet clot near another tree. Angie can see Rachel and Skye, playing Frisbee with Dorothy and Andrew. Angie laughs and touches Ellen's arm.

Their laughter draws Roger. Walter hovers at the edge.

"You're looking a lot better." Roger pushes between Ellen and Angie, punching Angie lightly on the arm and winking at Ellen.

Ellen grimaces.

"So are you," Angie answers. "How's Octavia?"

"I'm reconsidering my relationship to Octavia, actually. It's very stressful. Though of course I haven't been through what you have. At least my clients don't kill themselves."

"Maybe they would if they knew you were their attorney." Ellen arches her eyebrows at Roger.

"Ha!" Roger punches Ellen lightly on the arm, then turns to Angie. "You know, this place is like a dysfunctional family itself. Ellen, my sister here, treats me like shit."

"I thought *dysfunctional* meant everyone keeping a secret," Ellen says.

"You mean the way we all pretend Coleman doesn't have his hands down everyone's pants?"

"Down their pants?" Angie asks.

"Not all the way down," Roger laughs. "Just all over their asses."

"This conversations is depressing," Ellen announces.

"Not anymore. You girls got your way."

"What way?" Angie asks.

"Getting Coleman to resign," Roger explains. Ellen turns her head toward Chelsea and Coleman.

Walter breaks his silence with a shocked "Are you kidding?"

"No. All the senior attorneys went to Coleman to ask for his resignation."

"Were you there?" Angie turns to Ellen.

"Yes."

"Where was I?" Angie asks.

"Chelsea didn't think you should be involved." Ellen is apologetic.

"I wasn't that much of a basket case," Angie protests.

"It's not really that. It's just that she thought you'd take a position against this, since you thought the sexual harassment code would be used unfairly against lesbians and gay men."

"Coleman is not queer, at least from what I've seen. And my position was not against the code. I voted for it. I just made some observations, backed up by my read of the actual case law. I thought somebody would ask me. Or is Chelsea the expert on everything, including what I think?"

"Hey, don't get upset," Roger advises.

"I didn't want to agree," Ellen explains, "but I thought it was probably best to keep you out of all of it. You were a little upset about your client. And then there are all those rumors, about the intern thing. And you need some distance. I want you to be the new litigation director. A lot of people do."

Angie leans harder against the tree. No one speaks. They study their paper plates.

"So, are you going to do it?" Roger asks Angie.

"Do what?"

"Take the job."

"What job?"

"The director of litigation."

"Number one, no one has offered it to me," Angie says loudly. "And number two, who will take over my work? Or is that the point? So we can rid Triple-F of the killer dykes?"

"Don't be so sensitive, Angie. You are qualified, you know." Roger is whining. "You and Ellen have the most experience and the best reputations. And Ellen is Black."

"Oh, Jesus, Roger." Angie throws her paper plate on the ground.

"I'm just saying what everyone else is thinking. Triple-F—meaning the board of directors of Triple-F—meaning the *image* desired by the board of directors of Triple-F—is just not ready to have an African-American as litigation director. You know it and I know it."

Ellen is silent.

"And everyone is ready for a dyke?" Angie asks.

"No one can tell what you are. You look regular."

"Meaning white? Or meaning not like a dyke? Or both?"

"Meaning these days every professional woman looks like a lesbian. Don't be so sanctimonious. You're taking this the wrong way, Ange."

"How many times do I have to tell you, *Rog,* don't call me Ange?"

"Let's get out of here, Walter," Roger says, "these women are driving me crazy."

Left alone, Ellen and Angie each wait for the other one to speak.

One of them says she is sorry, and the other one says she is sorry, too.

"And what a sorry organization this is," one of them laughs.

"And what a sorry world," the other adds. And even though they both laugh again, each of them thinks about her clients.

JUNES

JUNES

**JUNES**

JUNES

JUNES

The greens compete with each other for attention. The house is cold, shadowed by the dense leaves. There is more sunlight on the wooden floors in winter, Angie notices now. Summer seems a damp hovel. Protected, too protected. It is June and the days follow one another too quickly, deadlines rolling like the summer clouds she sees only driving back and forth to work, when the sky is punctuated with a color somewhere between pink and yellow, glinting off the steel girders of a bridge.

The problem with June is that she had promised herself this would be her own deadline. The end of her exhaustion. Summer would be her rescue. She had promised Rachel. And she had promised Skye that she would go to the school play; that she would be home at noon for Skye's last week of half days; that she would get them bicycles and ride in the woods.

She would work in the garden.

A stand of tall trees like a blur at the edge of the backyard. Dominated by a pair of yellow poplars boasting their uniquely shaped leaves and tuliplike flowers. Angie is proud that she knows the name of the poplar, so she tells Skye again, as if it is an important lesson.

"How do you know that?" Skye asks.

"By the leaves. And now the flowers. Some people call it a tulip tree."

"But how do you know that's what people call it?"

"I read it in a tree guide."

"That new one Rachel bought?"

"Yes."

"Can I see it later?"

"Yes."

"Did you mark the page?"

"No."

"Then how will I find it?"

"You'll look. You can find it."

"How did you find it?"

"I looked."

"There's a picture?"

"A few."

"Have you ever heard anybody call it a pop-u-lar?"

"That's poplar. And no."

"I think it's pop-u-lar. Because it's a popular tree. Everybody likes a popular tree." Skye sings, off-key.

"No. Don't be a smarty. It's called poplar."

"Have you ever heard anyone say that?"

"No," Angie says without trying to remember.

"Then it might be pop-u-lar."

"It isn't."

"Could I call it that if I wanted?"

"I suppose. But you would be wrong."

"Not if everyone else does."

"It still would be wrong."

"Is it yellow popular because the flowers are yellow?"

"Poplar. Yes, I guess. Also because the leaves turn yellow in the fall. Do you remember last year?"

"No. We just moved here then. I wasn't paying attention to the trees."

"I wasn't either."

"I want to know all the names of the trees now."

"So do I. We'll learn. We'll use the guidebook."

"Why didn't you learn the names when you were a kid?" Skye is starting to ask both Angie and Rachel about their own lives as children, although she often acts bored if they answer.

"There weren't any trees when I was a kid," Angie laughs.

Skye groans, irritated at Angie's teasing. "Well," Skye suggests, "maybe we can ask someone."

"Maybe. But I don't know many people who know the names of trees." Angie is only half teasing now.

"There must not be too many." Skye is testing Angie.

"Actually, there are a lot of people who know the names of trees, Skye. It's just that I don't know many of them."

"Why not?"

"I don't know. I guess the people I know are better at knowing the names of books or opinions or courts or judges. People know all different kinds of things."

"I want to know everything."

"So do I." Angie agrees.

Skye slants her head in disbelief, as if considering whether or not to tell Angie that Angie's chance is gone.

"Help me with this ivy."

Angie rips the long thickened strands, moored to the ground by rather delicate looking roots. Remembering that she and Rachel had seriously considered naming Skye Ivy. Or possibly Ivey. Amid the pungent smell of uprooted vines, Angie is neither satisfied nor regretful that Skye is not named Ivey. All possible names had not been metaphors, but sounds. There had not been a rejection of the crawling clinging green in favor of the open expanse of blue. There had been a discussion of two syllables versus one syllable.

Angie is executing her plan to contain the ivy into a single space she has ringed with rocks and is calling a bed. She likes the way this sounds: ivy bed. It lends a certain order and allows her a momentary aristocratic pretense. She is a woman who has an ivy bed. She is not a dyke, not an attorney, not a daughter or a mother or even a troubled lover. She is simply a woman who gardens.

Although she knows that what she is really doing is resurrecting the gardens of the women who lived here before her. Women who did not work, or, as Angie has learned to say, women who did not work outside the home. Angie still believes that working inside one's own home is not exactly working, although she would not say that to anyone except Rachel. Rachel who would then tease her about her body sore from gardening—"If it's not real work then why does your back hurt?"—but would run some hot water in the tub and put in bath salts.

The resurrection is slow, slower than Angie thinks it should be. But there are a few rewards, little treasures amid the layers of wet decomposing leaves that lift like sheets of paper. A little succulent of some kind. Or a juniper spilling down a sheaf of rocks. Today she finds the sort of cache that sustains her commitment. An ethereal sprinkle. The color such a faint green it is almost white, almost blue. The texture such a soft tangle it is almost downy, almost a velveteen appliqué of itself. Angie uncovers it, carefully. Bends to smell it, as if its odor might be decipherable.

"Come look at this." Angie calls out to Skye, who is kicking a ball with Rachel, both of them bored with the garden.

"What is it?"

"A little plant. It's like a cute little fern. Only the color of a dusty miller."

"Oh! I love dusty miller," Skye says excitedly.

"And it's soft."

"As soft as you, baby?" Rachel says.

"Softer." Angie laughs.

"What's it called?"

"I don't know, Skye."

"We could look it up in the book."

"No, that's a tree book."

"This might be a tree. One of those tiny ones." Skye laughs.

"No, I don't think so."

"It could be," Skye insists.

"It isn't," Angie says. "It isn't."

"Well, we'll have to get a plant book," Rachel mollifies.

"Perennials," Angie says.

"Whatever."

"Although by the time I get to the rest of this, it won't matter because everything will be dead."

"I'll help you. Just give me a chance," Rachel says.

"I'll help too," Skye says, but she is already wandering away, throwing a stick up into the air.

"I'm not complaining. It just feels futile sometimes."

"It's supposed to be fun," Rachel says.

"I guess."

"Isn't it any fun at all?"

"Not when I look at the rest of this place and imagine all the little things being choked and know I should be inside working." Angie does not mention Susannah Chillicothe's notebook. Or the messages she should return from Cathy Chillicothe.

"Hey. This place did not get like this in a day and it won't be fixed in a day. There are three years of neglect in this yard. Three years of dead leaves. And you're tying to overcome it on weekends."

"I do a little when I get home some nights."

"It's hard to do after dark, Ange."

"Well, I'm trying."

"I'm not saying you aren't. I'm just saying don't expect too much."

"You always say that to me."

"And you never listen."

"If I would have listened to all the people who told me not to ex-pect too much I wouldn't be standing here with you, with our kid, and I wouldn't be able to afford any kind of house, let alone one with a wrecked garden."

"I'm not all those people."

"I know," Angie says.

"Okay. But it will get done. Maybe not today or tomorrow. But it will get done."

"If only we had a plan. I need a plan. I mean I'm doing one part and then doing another. Maybe I should go from left to right. Or top to bottom. What do you think?"

"I think I'm going inside to have another cup of coffee. Why don't you come with me? We could talk some more."

"About whether or not you're going to take the law guardian posi-tion?"

"That. Or other things. I'm glad we're able to carry on a conversa-tion again. Besides, I don't have to decide about the job until Septem-ber."

"And then you can start taking kids away from their mothers?"

Rachel sighs. "I know you're looking at it that way, but like I said, maybe I could help a few kids stay with their lesbian parents. I'll get to be a voice for the child. You know, maybe if I'd been the law guardian for your client—what's her name, in North Dakota?—the Bible-thumping husband would not have gotten custody and the kids could have stayed with their mother."

"They don't have law guardians in that state."

"That's my point."

"But you'd take a child from her mother, wouldn't you?"

"Yes. Yes, I would. But obviously not because the mother is a dyke. But if the mother was beating the kid, I would. Even if the mother was a dyke. Wouldn't you?"

Angie just looks at Rachel, at the rocks someone else had arranged in the garden, at the sunlight sifting through the new green leaves. Knowing she cannot admit that she might not be able to take a child— take a daughter—from her mother, even if the mother was abusing the child. What does that mean? she wonders. What could it mean if it was really true? True somewhere deep inside her, not a legal stance or polit-ical posturing, but true?

"Rachel . . ." Angie is still staring at Rachel, but she is struggling to focus, as if Rachel is very far away. Angie wants to bridge the space between them, but it is widening the way a river wears a gorge into a canyon and then into a softly spacious valley.

"Come inside. I'll make you a cup of coffee," Rachel says softly.

"I'll be there in a minute."

Angie stays outside, looking at the soft silvery stalks, watching them grow brighter in the day's last splash of sunlight.

Evangelina knows the name of her street: Poplar, and the number of her house: 21. But the way she finds the street when she walks home is by walking down Main Street until she gets to corner with the empty fac-tory, and the way she finds the house is by turning and following the factory wall until she gets to the first gray four-family house in a line of gray four-family houses. Her house is like a corner house, although instead of tree-lined avenues it is wedged into a thoroughfare of thick-walled factories.

Upstairs, Claire is washing dishes. From the kitchen sink, Claire can reach through the open window and touch the worn bricks of the factory wall. But Claire keeps the kitchen closed, so that the smells rising from the alleyway three stories below do not mix with the smell of the Ivory dish soap bubbles. "Men's piss," Claire says whenever she opens the window. Evangelina has seen the men slumping in the alleyway, so she does not doubt Claire, and does not doubt that men's urine smells different from women's.

And Claire keeps the kitchen window curtained. White lace café curtains, a ruffled valance over draped tiebacks. Curtains that Claire sewed. Claire washes the soot out of the curtains every other week by filling the bathtub with warm water and Ivory and a bit of bleach. Claire hangs the curtains out the window, on a line attached to a pulley on another factory wall. This other factory was once a warehouse and its walls are more cement than brick, and covered with ivy. A dark ivy with pointed leaves that Claire calls English ivy as if she knew what English ivy would look like; Claire and Evangelina both love it and can see from their bedroom window. A light ivy that Claire calls a weed or even poison ivy and warns Evangelina not to touch. As soon as the curtains are dry, Claire tells Evangelina to pull them inside. Evangelina reels them in, one by one, shaking the slight soot from their ruffles onto the men leaning against the ivy-covered walls. Then Claire sprinkles the curtains with water, rolls them into loose balls and puts them in the refrigerator, instructing Evangelina on her techniques for avoiding wrinkles and ensuring stiffness. "There is nothing like a crisp white curtain," Claire will say, again and again, later as she is ironing the ruffled lace on the ironing board spread across the apartment entrance like another barricade. "Nothing like it," Claire will say, as she is hanging the curtains in the window, as if such a precisely fussy frame could ameliorate the brick of the close wall.

Evangelina is sitting at the kitchen table, ignoring the curtain and the brick wall, reading a book, when Claire asks her to go to the store. Every day, since Claire decided Evangelina is old enough to cross Main

Street alone, Claire asks Evangelina to go to the store.

Sometimes Luke asks Evangelina to go to the store, but Luke only ever asks Evangelina to get cigarettes. Evangelina walks into the little store and stands on her toes at the counter, saying to the old man, "Pack of Kool Menthol, please."

"They're not for you, I hope," he teases, reaching up high to get a pack from a rack that faces him.

"No, for my father," she answers.

"Good girl," he says, and if there are men at the counter drinking coffee they look at her with appreciation. Good girl, maybe one will nod in agreement.

Evangelina always takes an extra book of matches. And on the walk home, she never turns right at the former factory, but runs a little farther down Main Street to squeeze her body into a place on the other side of the glass factory, into a gap between two endless brick walls. She lights the matches, one at a time. Watching each one burn, so close to her fingers, then throwing it on the shiny and sharp ground, crunching the last flame into the glass with her foot. Over and over, as if to prove she is not such a good girl.

Luke thanks her for the cigarettes.

"Good girl," he says, pulling out his Zippo lighter. "But don't ever smoke," he tells her. "It's a nasty habit."

If Claire can hear, Claire will agree. Claire smokes, but she never wants cigarettes from the store; Claire wants bread. Or milk. Or Kotex.

The Kotex are kept behind the counter. Facing the customers, but up high. The old man has to get out his little stepladder and climb up to get the package. He does not tease her, does not say, "They're not for you, I hope," does not say, "Good girl." And if there are men at the counter, they look away from her as she walks out the door, onto Main Street, directly to the turn at the glass factory and onto Poplar Street, rushing past the men in the alley and running up the stairs inside number 21. Thinking everyone can see what she carries in the thin paper bag.

Claire thanks her. Except when Evangelina lies and says the store did not have any. Except when Evangelina walks up and down Main Street instead of going into the store like a good girl.

"Someday you'll be a woman and you'll understand," Claire says.

Evangelina goes back to reading her book, imagining she is a man with a wolf in a wild place with trees where it is very clean. Imagining there is a place without café curtains, brick-walled factories, and piss-smelling alleys.

                                                            ■ ■ ■ ■ ■ ■ ■

At Grandmother's house, Hunter and Seven Hunter discuss their missing mother. Angie looks at the program: Act I, Scene 1. Angie looks for Skye amid the other children at Meadowlark School, excitedly serious about the Summer Solstice play. Angie pats Rachel's leg amid the other parents in the audience.

The Lords of Death prepare their tricks, but despite Grandmother's warnings, Hunter and Seven Hunter are unprepared and fail the tests. Take the wrong bridges to the wrong roads and answer the wrong names. Are put to death and their heads hung from the calabash tree.

Act I, Scene 3.

Skye as Quick, the daughter of the Lord of Death. Standing at the calabash tree, picking off the head that has screamed out to her, being entered by the Seed of Life.

Skye/Quick in the Overworld. Being mistreated by Grandmother. Being given impossible tasks. The little animals help her. Banished. Returns with her children, Hunter and Jaguar.

Intermission.

"This shit amazes me." Rachel whispers.

"It's the Popul Vuh. The Sacred Book of the Quiché Maya."

"Of course."

"At least, that's what the program says."

"I'm never sure this stuff is suitable for kids."

"Would you prefer 'Hansel and Gretel'? Where the witch gets killed?" Angie asks.

"I know you like this stuff. All this paganism. All these Solstice rituals. It is interesting, I suppose," Rachel concedes, "but it's still a little creepy to me. I guess I don't want to see some kid's head hanging from a tree."

"I know what you mean," Angie says.

Rachel pats Angie's knee.

Act II, Scene 1. Scene 2. Scene 3.

Hunter, Jaguar, Rat and Mosquito. The Lords of Death. The roads to the underworld. The names of the sacred. The tests passed. Greeting the dawn. Greeting the summer. Skye/Quick and Grandmother holding hands, kissing. The whole cast singing.

The parents applauding.

"You're Skye's, uh, parents, aren't you?"

Angie nods. Rachel studies the program.

"She looks so good in this play. Just perfect, with that little headband. Like a real Indian."

Angie tilts her head.

"I mean, like she could be Mayan. Like a little Mayan princess." Giggles.

Angie does not move.

"Where did you get her? Is she part Mexican or something?"

Angie does not answer.

"Am I being impolite? I'm sorry. It's just that she looks so cute. Of course, all the kids do. I just love children, don't you? I wish I could have more. I've even thought of adopting, some child less fortunate. From a disadvantaged country. I think what you have done is just so so brave. I don't know what your options were, under the circumstances and everything, but I admire it so so much. I just wish—"

But Angie is gone. Pulling Rachel toward the refreshments of apple juice and crackers. Toward the drama teacher, to congratulate her. Toward Skye, smiling in the twilight.

■  ■  ■  ■  ■  ■  ■

The Solstice. Summer. Full moon. There are chants, thick woods, and fires burning to keep away the insects. There are women. Thirteen women, including Angie. Facing west. Thirteen lesbians. Facing east. Thirteen glowing naked bodies. Facing north. Thirteen goddesses.

During the sex, the women gossip. Trade stories about some other coven. Banter with each other. Often the women smile, not only sexily, but slyly, somehow satisfied that people assume their spirituality is about weaving and granola. And here they all are, a bunch of dykes, fucking. Like the gay boys, only not in commercial bathhouses, and with people they know, even if Wildflower and Wolfdream are not the names on their drivers licenses.

Fucking. In the woods. With the woods. Rolling through the poison ivy. Menstrual blood like sap, smeared across each other, laughing and licking. It makes the ones who like it feel sinister and pagan. It makes the ones who do not like it gag.

Some women like to be tied to trees. Some like a thin branch slapped across their asses. Some like a well-handled wooden carving slipped inside them, again and again. Some like it near the stream so there is mud to smooth on each other. Some like it nearest the dawn when the first lights rise like a nightmare. Some like candle wax. And each of the women likes some of these things some of the time. More than any of them likes weaving or granola.

For Angie, Summer Solstice sex is always languid, more massage than fever. In the very season that makes the other women feel reckless and lustful, Angie is cool and distant. Women gravitate to her, as if for respite. In the celebration of summer, she is a strangely attractive center and a very marginal character, like the sun of some planet that no one inhabits.

She sits on the ground without ambition. Not thinking, except that maybe she could grow her hair long again. Not feeling like a child or a daughter or even a lesbian or a woman. Feeling like herself, only.

Two women approach Angie. She imagines herself as a bridge between their passions. She is strong and somehow metallic, while they are lush, yet rocky. But they take tender pleasures in comparison to Angie, who rolls from side to side like an earthquake and then splits the air with an after-orgasm cackle.

Later, she will smother her rashes with calamine lotion.

"Thanks for calling me back." Angie is finally speaking with Susannah Chillicothe's public defender, a woman named Elizabeth Walwyn whose voice is breathy and low—sexy almost.

"My client wants me to speak with you." Formal.

"I just want to offer my assistance." Angie assumes her friendly lilt.

"If you need some backup. I was a public defender myself." Angie pauses, allowing for an interruption, but none is forthcoming. "I've been looking at these cases across the country. It's almost becoming a trend."

"I heard you were an expert on lesbian legal issues." Elizabeth Walwyn's tone betrays nothing, not even modulation.

"Not an expert. There just aren't too many people working in this area. In the criminal area, I mean."

"We really don't see that her lesbianism has anything to do with the case."

Angie is not stunned, only disappointed. She always listens carefully to the way people say the word *lesbian*, listening for a hint, approval or hesitation or anger. Neutrality always gives her hope, usually false hope. Angie takes a breath and strives for a gentle tone. "Oh—I thought that the only witness against her is her lover, or I guess it's her ex-lover now."

"That doesn't make it a case about being a lesbian."

"I'm not saying the case is about being a lesbian. Although that can be a crime." Angie pauses again, although she does not expect an interruption. "I'm just saying that I'm sure her sexuality will affect the jury, and probably the judge as well. And I'd bet that her sexuality had an effect on the prosecutor, charging first-degree murder in a case like this."

"We just don't see her defense as involving, uh, sex, uh, her sexuality."

"I'm not saying it's her defense."

"I understand what you're saying. But you should understand me. This is not the big city. These people are different than you. You have no way of knowing."

"And you have no way of knowing what I know." Angie listens for traces of the attorney's accent. Notes the grammar slip: Different *from,* she mentally corrects. Hears the effort to pronounce every last syllable. Wonders what kind of woman public defender says the word "lesbian" as if it is the word "defendant," but stumbles over "sex."

"That may be true, but I'm her attorney. Until she can afford to get another one."

"I respect your position. But I'm just trying to offer some assistance. I'll send you some materials I have. And maybe we can talk again."

"That's possible. But I only wanted to have this conversation so that I could tell my client we had a consultation."


＊ ＊ ＊ ＊ ＊ ＊ ＊


Maybe she is. Maybe she is not. All clues skewed in the competition. Angie looks for her face in the bars at night, knowing she will not find her, not because she is definitely not a dyke, but because even if she is a dyke she is not a bar dyke. Not a social dyke. Not the kind of dyke who needs to be surrounded by dykes, to smell their sweat and see their laughter and anger, to touch and be touched. Not the kind of dyke that Angie is.

They smile at each other. In classrooms. In the library. But each of them smiles at all the other women also, because there are so few. So few. Sprinkled among the endless floor of men like little dots of paint that have flaked from the wall. Divided from each other by class and even color. Divided from each other by clothes: navy-blue suits or jeans or pantsuits. Divided between the women who will be in the women's study group and those who will not. Divided equally. Angie's study group has four other law students, all of them women. Not including the maybe–maybe-not woman. She says she does not want to join any study group, does not want to study in a group. The other four women disperse among the clusters of one hundred and seventy-three men.

All divisions, the ones of gender, of study habits, of dyke and class and clothes and even color, become subordinate to the official division. The posted list of students who made the dean's list. Seven students in a class of almost two hundred. Seven students; two women. Two women, and maybe two dykes.

Angie and the maybe–maybe-not woman go out for coffee. One of them is better at contracts. The other is better at criminal law. Angie no longer has time for the scheduled study-group meetings, which have become more frequent and more intense. The maybe–maybe-not woman invites Angie to study at her apartment.

"I work until three A.M.," Angie explains.

"I get up early." She smiles.

Their second semester arranges itself into a pattern. Contracts on Mondays and Thursdays. Criminal Law on Tuesdays and Fridays. Torts and Civil Procedure and Property on Wednesdays. It takes extended discussions of Section 2-206 of the Uniform Commercial Code and conspiracy theory before the maybe–maybe-not woman resolves all doubts.

⁂

"What's today's postcard?"

"Laurie Anderson."

"At least I know who that is."

"I never knew there were so many cards in that series until I started working for you. I mean, where does that woman get all these? She must have a wholesale connection."

"She thinks they're artsy." Angie expects to feel a twinge at her own disloyalty, but she does not. She rather likes it that Kim has been relegated to a joke, at least with Walter. It ameliorates some of her guilt at her failure of nerve. She does keep trying to get Kim to go out to lunch, but it never seems to work out. Maybe she should consider having their little talk somewhere else. But where? Her office? Kim's apartment?

"She thinks *you're* artsy. She's smitten." Walter's sarcasm is unrelentingly disapproving.

"She's a kid."

"She's got money enough for tons of postcards."

"I think she gets an allowance from her daddy." Angie says this more bitterly than she intends, but Walter does not mind.

Walter puts this postcard, with all the others, in a file he has labeled "Kim." "What's your favorite?"

"What?"

"What's your favorite postcard? I'm partial to the Patti Smith one myself." He holds it up for Angie to see the image of Patti Smith, white shirt and black suspenders. "It's from the Mapplethorpe exhibit."

Angie nods, recognizing the reiterated image, an album cover, and recovering her residual lust. She feels lonely remembering that Patti Smith album, remembering those clumsy ancestors of CDs.

"She was a good musician. I saw her in concert."

"Really?" Walter is genuinely surprised. "I didn't know she was in a band. She's pretty good-looking, though, don't you think, in that punky androgynous sort of way? Sort of looks like Rachel, not that Rachel's punked out or anything."

"Rachel?" Angie examines the postcard. "Well, maybe."


Angie retrieves the file labeled "Kim" when Walter leaves. Counts the postcards. Over twenty. Over thirty. Women. Women. Women in black and white, backlit and artificial. Posed. Hair across the face and black-gloved hands pushing up white breasts. Mouth open and nostrils wide. Jeans and a wide belt and head bent back so that Angie's neck aches just looking at the image of the woman she does not recognize. Even when she reads the names, Angie does not recognize the women. Does not recognize Michele and Julia and Melanie. Perhaps they are actresses, Angie thinks. Because she thinks she can pick out the musicians, spots Laurie Anderson, hugging her white violin. And she even identifies Madonna, although Angie turns the postcard from side to side, trying to decide whether the portrait should be vertical or horizontal.

But every postcard woman could be an exaggeration of some woman in her life—Jodie Foster as Kim, Patti Smith as Rachel. And even Annie Lennox as herself. And then those actresses, posed like Claire if Claire had been backlit by California instead of coal country.

And Madonna, some woman in a bar, vertical or horizontal. And all the ones she does not recognize, other women from other bars.

This is truly stupid, Angie thinks, looking at today's postcard, turning it over. The other side of Laurie Anderson's hug is stiff with slanted scribbles. One would think the girl would have better penmanship, Angie thinks. The letters and words crowd together, a little black forest, overgrown. Thick with vines: *if only, if only.* "If only you were here." "If only we could be together." "If only I didn't have to read these silly cases for school." "If only Daddy knew, he would . . ." Sticky with promises: *when, when, when.* "When we are together"; "When everything works out and we can"; "When I finally get on law review"; "When Skye gets to know me . . ."

This has gone beyond the truly stupid, Angie thinks. What has she been thinking? What did she think the postcards contained? Citations to cases? How could she be so naïve? Why hadn't Walter told her? She picks up the phone and dials Kim's number. Forget lunch. Forget being gracious over cappuccino. Leaves a message: "Please make an appointment to see me."


Kim is crying in Angie's office.

Angie is handing her a tissue, trying to be sympathetic and even supportive.

"My career is ruined."

"Your career is not ruined," Angie says. She is becoming impatient.

"It is."

"It isn't. Lots of perfectly fine attorneys were not on law review."

Kim's grades did not place her in the top ten percent of the class and she has not been invited to join law review at the end of her first year. Her disappointment has only been mitigated by the other option to "grading" on to law review: writing on. So she worked for four weeks on a casenote about some corporate liability case and submitted it for the writing competition. Waited for the results. Today the list was posted of writers who would be invited to join the law review. Kim's name is not on the list.

"You were on law review," Kim states.

"That's right. But it did not help me be a good attorney."

"You were an editor. *The* editor. There's a plaque right on the wall. So tell me it's not so important."

"I have nowhere else to put the plaques. And clients like them. But let me tell you, not one client has ever mentioned the law review plaque. Most of them like the community-service ones better. Or the one with the purple ribbon."

"But you were on law review. You made it."

"I did, Kim, but I'm telling you, it's not as big a deal as you're making it."

"It is a big deal. You can say that because you made it. You made it. You've never had to suffer."

"Suffer?" Angie stands up and walks behind her desk. "Suffer? You think you are suffering because you did not make law review?" Angie avoids contractions, as if she were delivering an oral argument, as if she were talking to someone else's father.

"Yes." Kim stares back at Angie.

"And you think I have never suffered because I made law review?"

"You were the editor!" Kim shouts.

"Get out of my office. Get out and do not ever come back." Angie's voice is so precise that the consonants bite.

"What?"

"You heard me. Get out. Now."

Kim stares at Angie.

"Get out. Get out."

Kim finally leaves. The tissue is crumpled in her fist.


All day Angie cannot believe it. That privileged twit. That ignorant brat. Sure, it's easy to lose perspective in painful situations, as Angie well knows, but that does not mean one should be stupid. To think she had not suffered because she had been on law review, had been an editor. As if this meant she had not been hungry. Had not stretched a package of ziti for a week. Had not worked in a bar her first year, adding a lawyer and two professors during her second. As if she had not cried on the floor of the law school library from exhaustion. As if she had not been hospitalized, twice, from exhaustion, from malnutrition.

As if she had not studied every morning after mixing drinks all night because she knew that if she didn't do well enough they would take away her scholarship, and if they took away her scholarship she would be mixing drinks until she was too old to be a desirable bartender; as if she had not worked because her scholarship did not cover her rent and food and even when she was made law review editor the school counted the stipend as part of her scholarship and she did not get any more money, not one cent more. As if she had not sent money home, to Claire.

Not suffered. Not been laughed at for her car, a Volkswagen with rust spots like small but growing animals. In the parking lot with the Volvos and Trans Ams. Not been intimidated because she had never heard the word *tort*, or *equity*, or *jurisprudence*. In classrooms with the children and grandchildren of judges and lawyers. Not been lonely because there were only ten women in her entire law school class. Ten, counting herself.

Ten, counting her lover. Her lover who never said she was her lover. Her lover, who let all the other editors on the law review call Angie "female faggot." Her lover, who never corrected them, never said the word *lesbian,* never claimed the word, never claimed Angie, never claimed anything except a casual friendship. Her lover, who graduated two places behind her. Her lover, who screamed at her that Angie was stupid: stupid for letting everyone know she was a dyke, stupid for taking a job as a public defender, stupid for hanging out with "lowlifes" at a bar. Her lover, the one who moved a walk-in closet filled with navy-blue suits into the corporate world. A banking attorney preaching Articles Three and Four of the Uniform Commercial Code. Not suffered.

Never suffered. Because every ambition could be reduced to a line on a resume: "Law Review, Editor."

J U L Y

J U L Y

**J U L Y**

J U L Y

J U L Y

Sweat from her forehead drips onto a page of her appointment Book, blurring an inked grid. Angie wants only to escape from this sweltering conference room full of people trying to agree on a date for the next meeting: "No, I have a conflict," someone says. On the twenty-fifth. The twenty-sixth. The twenty-seventh. Too many meetings, too many committees and organizations and worthwhile causes.

Her Book, her lovely Book, is a shambles. Post-it notes protrude all over, the sticky strips congested with other people's hair and lint from everything she wears. Announcements of future meetings and minutes from previous meetings. The Gay and Lesbian Section of the National Lawyers Guild. The Sexuality Subcommittee of the city bar. The Gay and Lesbian Task Force of the ACLU. The Governor's Advisory Board on Gay and Lesbian Issues. The Mayor's Working Group on Sexual Orientation. The Lawyer's Alliance for Reformation of New York Family Law. The Family Law Section of the American Bar Association, and the Public Interest Law Section, and the informal committee to lobby the Board of Governors for a Lesbian and Gay Section of the American Bar Association. As if fighting the good fight meant an organizational affiliation on a résumé, although she is still not sure she remembers how to fight. As if revolution could be accomplished with a fund-raiser; although she is not sure that what most of them want is revolution. Not any longer. Not since boards of directors replaced collectives, Robert's Rules of Order replaced consensus, and leather appointment books replaced leather jackets. Well, at least the letterhead is better now, she thinks.

Angie complains to her friend Vickie, as they ride down the elevator together. Vickie, a labor law attorney in a firm that represents only labor. Vickie, whom she does not see as often as she would like.

"I thought we'd at least have a summer recess."

"Not these days," Vickie sighs.

"Bring back the good old days!" Angie laughs. "When we could sit on the beach and drink frozen margaritas and look at women."

"I never had time to do that—and neither did you." Vickie shakes her head.

"Well, why don't I have the time now?"

"Hey, that's what you get for being such a muckety-muck these days." Vickie's soft tone makes the remark less cutting than it might otherwise sound.

"What about you?" Angie asks, defensively.

"I limit myself. One committee. I've got a life. Jesse will only be a kid once. And besides, I need to keep my eye on Laura."

Angie hopes Vickie is only teasing.

"Of course," Vickie continues, "I don't have to worry about you. I don't think you could schedule my Laura in. You're like lesbian-lawyer-of-the-month lately. How does it feel?"

"Exhausting. And sort of stupid. I mean, when I was winning cases, no one paid any attention to me. Just little lesbian mother cases, boring old custody. Lost a few, a couple of big ones"—Angie pauses, thinking of Sharon Delsarado—"but won quite a few. But now that I'm involved in high-profile stuff, now that *The Voice* did that exposé on my client who killed herself, it's like everyone suddenly noticed that I exist."

"Maybe all those past successes are just catching up. You've always had a pretty solid reputation."

"Maybe. But I really don't know how this happened to me, how my name got on all these letterhead lists of boards of directors. Maybe I'm just a good girl, a good girl who works hard. A good working-class girl." Angie looks at Vickie, who nods with recognition. "I feel like I always manage to be exploited. Always manage to justify my existence through work. You know, I used to think it was about being queer—you know, the super-dyke syndrome—but now that I'm in these organizations with all these other queers, it's still the same."

"But you know, being a lawyer is all about reputation. And you must get some perks. Some of those young things with lipstick throwing themselves at your feet."

They are standing outside the building now and Angie squints at Vickie, searching for her sunglasses and trying not to be paranoid.

"Not really."

"That's not what I hear."

"What do you hear? It's a big city, you can't hear much."

"Big city. Small community. What I hear is that every little law student wants to come to work at Triple-F for the summer with the great Angie Evans. At least, before they go to the law firms and make bigger bucks than either you or I ever will."

"Well, I hope some of them can cite-check." Angie sighs.

"They have other talents, I'm told."

"I'd rather have cite-checkers."

"I hope that's true."

"It is."

"Well, just be careful, girlfriend. You're getting too out-there not to be attacked."

"I'm pretty tough." Angie laughs.

"Not as tough as you think."

"I know. No one could be *that* tough."

Vickie is silent for a moment, then continues: "And, even if you were, which you are not, you aren't the only one involved. Rachel is tough, maybe even tougher than you if you want to know the truth, but she isn't all that tough either. And then there's Skye."

Angie is now the silent one.

"What you guys really need is a vacation," Vickie announces. "Hey, that would be just perfect."

"What?"

"You guys should take Marcia and Penney's place and come to P-Town with us. We rented a house right on the bay with them. Jesse would be ecstatic at spending two weeks with Skye."

"Why aren't Marcia and Penney going?" Angie assumes it must be financial. The last time she saw them, at the cheese-and-fruit spread during a reception for some lesbian and gay legal organization, they were chattering on and on about buying a co-op in the city.

"They broke up. Didn't you hear? Pretty nasty. Penney took up with some twenty-year-old she met at the park or something. I don't know all the details, but it seems pretty irrevocable. And they don't want to go on vacation together. Although—and you will not believe this—Penney said that maybe she and her new girlfriend would go. I had a hard time being civil. Though I've just heard Marcia is with some guy. Still, life is too short to take sides over breakups, but sometimes, it's difficult."

Angie agrees. "What's going to happen to the kid?"

"Erin? I don't know. I thought one of them would have called you by now."

"Hey, that's not my field."

"Unless Marcia murders Erin?"

"Thanks a lot."

"Hey, sorry. I guess that's not funny. But you probably know better than I do that these custody disputes between lesbians are the next booming business."

"Not a business I want. It used to be we just fought with men for the kids. Now we fight with each other. This is just too ugly."

"But let's get back to my proposal. It would be great to spend time with you guys. And it's a wonderful house. At least according to the travel agent. And reasonable, too. It's right on the bay."

"I'll talk to Rachel."

"Has she decided about that law guardian job? If she's going to take that, she'll need a vacation."

"I don't think she'll take it."

"Why not? It would be interesting. And a chance to do some good work. The legal issues are very hot right now, I hear. Although I can't imagine you'd be in favor of it. What would happen if you wound up on different sides?"

"That couldn't happen," Angie says definitely.

"Well, it might. Or maybe it might. Anyway, even if she stays with housing, she needs a vacation. Rachel will go. She's human about these things. She was up on the idea when we talked about it last winter. If you recall, you guys were our first choice for our sojourn."

"We were?"

"Yeah. But since you couldn't even manage to go skiing with us for a single afternoon, two weeks away from your desk seemed impossible."

"Well, I'm trying to change. Maybe getting away would do us all some good."

"Great. I'll call you tonight."


She tries to imagine it. Sandbars and sea and salt and lots of mostly naked women. Up the coast and onto the Cape. Hadn't she been there once? Or was it just that she knew so many dykes who had that it seemed as if she had.

But she cannot say the word *vacation.* Not to Rachel. Not in front of Skye. Not even in her own head. It is worse than any crime. It is like murdering her mother. When she calls Claire to tell her that she will be away, that she will be out of town, that she will telephone her, Angie does not say *vacation.*

To Rachel and Skye, to Vickie and Laura and Jesse, she jokes that she is "working in a different location." And she has more than a briefcase full of work. A draft of a brief. A few law review articles that Kim copied for her and she has been meaning to read. Another book on the fallacy of mother-child bonding. And Susannah Chillicothe's notebook.

But there is neither time nor space for work. Whenever she starts to talk about work, about the law or even gossip about some lawyer or judge whom Vickie and Laura and Rachel all know, someone changes the subject, usually Laura. To the tides, their schedule clipped from the newspaper and affixed to the refrigerator with a lighthouse magnet. To an art gallery, where a lithograph of a blue bay and a red-pink rowboat fades in the west window. To lobster, the best place somewhere down—or is it up?—the Cape on Route 6.

Angie and Rachel and Vickie and Laura sit on the deck, overlooking the bay, sipping coffee, watching the children. Skye and Jesse compete with each other, tousling their bodies for the adults' attention. Although they are physically quite different, they seem indistinct to Angie. No longer Skye, no longer Jesse, just children, almost generic. Children as only the children of the privileged are allowed to be children. Even if they are the children of privileged dykes.

"It's hard to believe that not so long ago these kids would have been working in mines and factories." Vickie shudders.

"Oh, I just love co-parenting with a labor attorney." Laura laughs.

"What's happening with your work on child migrant labor?" Angie asks. "Aren't you lobbying or something?"

"She's trying to have a vacation," Laura announces, moving to the lounge chair.

If Vickie were Angie's lover, Angie would cajole her into conversation. But Vickie is her friend. A friend she likes, likes better than Laura, who was once her lover, if having sex once with someone makes her one's lover. Sex when Laura was drunk, before Laura was in recovery. Sex when Angie was solitary, before Rachel and before Vickie, before Skye and Jesse. Angie cannot remember what sex was like with Laura, and she knows that Laura cannot remember; could not remember it the next morning. But everyone—Angie and Laura and Rachel and Vickie—remembers the fact of it; everyone except the children. And Laura and Angie are never alone together.

The dinners are fish. Smoke rises from the grill on the deck, swirling toward the Atlantic. Rachel and Vickie tend the grill. Laura supervises the sunburned children, cutting up tomatoes and lettuce for salad, arguing over the inclusion of olives. Angie makes dessert, a blueberry pie or a chocolate mousse cake. There is iced tea, not sweet enough for Angie. And coffee, always coffee.

After dinner, there are conversations that Angie always hopes will become more substantive. Tonight, repeating the pattern of the last few nights, the four women comment upon the children, complimenting each other's daughters. Laura and Vickie do not remark upon Skye's hissing speech or brittle hair. Rachel and Angie do not mention Jesse's awkward run or whining. Then the four adults talk about their mothers. Anecdotes punctuate the twilight. Even Angie has one, kept in reserve for such occasions. It seems to Angie that all lesbians—maybe all women—eventually talk about their mothers. Maybe they think this is a conversation about themselves, some deep part of themselves, but Angie knows it is not. Not about her, not about them.

It is the most superficial of conversations. Almost as bad as being with her colleagues from Triple-F, and again the danger in departing from the superficial is conflict. Now the still subterranean argument is over addictive behaviors: over alcoholism, over caffeine in the coffee, over co-dependency, over work. Laura's speech is infested with the homilies of the recovery movement: "One day at a time," "Love your inner child," "Each of us is special." Angie strains to bite her tongue, feeling the blood rush to her mouth as she strains toward an argument, feeling that silvery urge to fight coming back to her, like a long-lost lover. But there are no sparks of conflict to ignite Angie's fire, only Laura saying that there are support groups for workaholics, and laughing.

Along with Angie's fantasies of conversation, she had fantasies of nights out with Rachel. Shows starting at eleven, featuring lesbian comics. Stopping for a some icy tropical drink and to purchase a pair of original and unusual earrings. Walking home on the beach, kissing in the moonlight. Making love in their bed while Skye and Jesse sleep soundly in the middle bedroom, and Laura and Vickie curl around each other in the far bedroom. Staying home the next night, taking the kids out for pizza and saltwater taffy while Laura and Vickie go to dinner. Tucking the kids in to bed, leaving the outside light on for Laura and Vickie. And going out the next night, to a different show, a different jewelry store, a different bar, but the same walk home under a moon only slightly shifted.

But the nights out never seem to happen. Only the nights in. Only the nights when Angie looks at her briefcase, feeling mixed longing and dread at the thought of Susannah Chillicothe's notebook. Only the nights Angie and Rachel try to make love.

Rachel is sunburnt. Or Angie's legs ache from the dampness. Or their bodies do not seem to fit. Stroking without arching, stroking that tickles or irritates. Undecided desire. Undecidable.

In the mornings, they quarrel in their closed-door bedroom.

"You hate every minute of this, don't you?" Rachel accuses.

"I don't. Why do you think that?"

"You're gritting your teeth."

"I'm not."

"Let's not argue. What's wrong? Is being too close to Laura getting to you?"

"It's not Laura. Although I'm tired of the world revolving around her. Just because she doesn't want to go out. Just because she doesn't drink. Don't you think it would be nice to have a blender full of frozen margaritas out on the deck? Don't you think it would be civilized not to omit the sherry in the swordfish marinade? Don't you think they could go out, even once, not drinking, just *out,* so that we could go out and not feel guilty?" Even to herself, Angie sounds like an eight-year-old, whining and truculent.

"I didn't realize Laura's not drinking bothered you so much."

"It's not her not drinking. It's her constant patter about addictive behaviors and her self-righteous attitude. If I hear one more time about how we should all give up coffee—"

"You're just pissed off because she called you a workaholic." Rachel's bony knuckles cover her smile.

"Maybe I am. So what's wrong with that? If I wasn't—"

"What's wrong," Rachel interrupts, "is that you can't even enjoy a simple vacation."

"Maybe I'd enjoy it if I could have a fucking frozen margarita and sit on the deck and have a civilized conversation about something interesting. Or maybe I'd enjoy it if I could have a simple fuck from my girlfriend." Angie enjoys the harshness of her own voice.

"Spare me the Claire act," Rachel says, matching Angie's harshness.

"That's a shitty thing to say."

"It's meant to be. Because it's shitty that you're acting like your mother. You like to think you're so different from her, but you're just like her. Talk about addictive behaviors."

"I'll forget you said that," Angie declares, stretching on the bed.

Rachel sits on the bed, touching Angie's arm. "Look, I'm sorry."

"I'm sorry, too," Angie says.

"Is something else bothering you? This law guardian thing? I won't take the job if it's going to cause major problems with us. I mean, I'm not all that interested in it."

"It's not that."

"Do you think we depend on liquor that much?" Rachel is serious, concerned. "I mean, I never thought we drank that much. Do you think we can't have sex unless we have a drink?"

"Not really."

"Then what's the problem?"

"You tell me," Angie the eight-year-old demands.

"I don't know," Rachel admits.

"Me either." Angie knows it is not liquor or its lack. But maybe a drink is just a concrete solution to a problem Angie cannot name. Maybe a drink, or two, would blur the sharp edges of the wall in their bed.


At the bay, Angie and Vickie sit in the water and look for starfish with Jesse and Skye. Laura has a headache. Rachel is food shopping. The tide is going out.

Skye is aloof. As if proving her maturity to the younger Jesse, Skye wanders far into the low surf, turns to wave at Jesse. Skye, alone at the edge of the world, not in need of her mother, proud.

Jesse has not yet learned that pride. She clings to Vickie, climbing on her sandy lap. Sucking her thumb years after that echo of the breast should have receded. Jesse is a year younger than Skye—Angie always measures—but a year ago Skye had not clung. Or two years ago. Angie watches Jesse and Vickie, trying to decipher her own emotions, sifting the wet sand with her hands. Spotting something slightly shiny, she salvages it from the shimmering water as if it might be a mermaid. It is a skate egg sack abandoned by both mother fish and child fish, dulling rapidly toward ugliness in the brusque light. It is jealousy.

Angie blanches. Suddenly recalling Sappho's famous line about the squeamish not prodding the beach rubble, she resolves now—just as she had resolved when she first read that line in a college women's literature class—not to be among the squeamish. It was her personal proverb. So she turns the hardening egg sack over and over, inspecting it from various angles. She puts the tip of her tongue on it, half expecting the salt sweat of the baby Skye to come rushing into her mouth. Skye, who no longer cuddles. Salt, rubbing the thin cuts made with knives of comparison.

Instead, she is stung by Claire.

Angie's tongue probes. Claire: When? Where? Why? Claire a question, never asked. Claire. Claire. Claire. Vickie.

Vickie as her mother. Vickie applauding her, as Vickie applauds Jesse. Vickie wiping the sand from her bathing suit. Vickie picking her up when the water gets too cold. Vickie admiring the starfish, selected just for her. Vickie as her mother.

Angie gets up, walks toward the open seas in ankle-deep tides, toward Skye. Her mind spins with another course from college: "Theories of Women's Psychology." Freud and Havelock Ellis and some other German whom she cannot remember. Angie highlighting the references to lesbians, or to female inverts. Arrested development. Doomed to repetition of the originary bond: mother-infant. Seeking satisfaction with another mother, and then another. Never satisfied because the mother could never satisfy. Only a man could accomplish that. Only a man like the psychologist himself.

But Angie knows she is not attracted to Vickie. No bodily lurches, no liquid, no signs of sex. She walks back toward the beach, toward her friend. What she wants from Vickie is a friend, a friend who talks, laughs, and says something serious and intimate. Not a mother, not a lover, but a friend.

"Are you still writing poetry?" Angie asks Vickie.

Vickie shifts Jesse's weight on her lap. "Angie, I haven't written poetry since college." Vickie sounds embarrassed.

"Oh. Do you keep a journal?"

"Angie. Why do you ask?"

"I have this diary from a potential client."

"How did you get her diary?"

"Her mother gave it to me."

"You aren't going to read it, are you?"

"I don't know."

"Skye certainly turns brown in the sun. I wish Jesse tanned like that. Hell, I wish I did." Vickie snorts.

"Did you take many women's studies classes in college?" Angie attempts to resurrect the conversation.

"I think the kids are ready for dinner. I wonder if Rachel is back yet."


Without the anchor of work, Angie lists, adrift in other people's lives. Walking down Commercial Street, holding hands with Rachel, looking for earrings on a rainy day; Laura and Vickie bickering behind them.

Wrapping Rachel's jacket around Skye, searching the gray water for a fin on a whale-watching boat; Laura and Vickie and Jesse drinking hot chocolate at the snack bar. Sitting in traffic to drive to a marsh museum, like suburban couples, the kids in the back of the station wagon and the cooler full of peanut butter sandwiches.

"I just didn't realize they were so . . . so domestic," Angie complains, explains.

"Like we're not?" Rachel raises her eyebrows.

Angie goes for a walk. Every evening, down the street and around the corner, to a bank of phones near the Sand Bar Women's Hotel and Bed and Breakfast. To check her messages, hear voices full of requests that are explicit and somehow reassuring. Listen to Walter with his daily "Everything's fine, Angie." Listen to Roger: "If you're back yet, give me a call." Delete Kim: "I need to talk with you."

Telephone Claire.

"You get to go all over, with your trials and your little conferences."

"I really don't travel that much."

"That's the way it seems to you. I never go anywhere. Have I ever gone anywhere? Anywhere other than this hellhole? Never been."

"Are you going to the doctor?"

"You want to know if your mother is still taking them little capsules, don't you, Evangelina? So you'd have some reason I'm not just happy as a clam."

"I was just wonder—"

Claire interrupts: "I'm not. That Prozac stuff is dangerous. People killing themselves right and left. It's on TV every day. Every day and every night. And if I'm going to kill myself, I'm going to do it myself, not because of some medications."

Angie is silent. Attempts to eavesdrop on the conversation of the woman next to her. The woman is crying and has a beautiful tattoo of a butterfly on her shoulder blade.

"What's all that noise?"

"I said, I'm at a phone booth."

"Well, don't waste your money just checking to see if your mother is still alive. I'll talk to you sometime."

"I'll call you in a few days," Angie says to the air.

Says to the space evacuated by the woman who had been so close to her that Angie could smell her sweat, the woman with the tattoo on her shoulder. Angie notices that she is following the woman, not for any particular reason, but just to have something to do. She watches the woman, who goes into the bookstore and comes out with a lesbian novel that Angie has been wanting to read. She sees the woman cross the street, sit down at a table underneath a restaurant canopy, open the book. Sip the glass of water the waitress places in front of her, open the menu. Angie concludes that the woman is not waiting for anyone else, so she walks over to her, smiles. The woman smiles back. Invites her to sit down. Angie tries to talk with the woman about the book, but since neither of them has read it yet, it is not an easy conversation.

Angie orders a coffee and Kahlua. A coffee and vodka and Kahlua. A vodka. Listens to the woman, eating a Caesar salad, complain about her lover—her ex-lover, really, almost—the one she was telephoning. Angie tries not to give advice, tries not to ask questions about their joint assets, their joint debts, whether or not there are any children. Angie tries not to be a lawyer, tries to say the word *vacation,* tries to let the word "sex" float to the surface without being said.

When the check comes, the women split it. And Angie wishes the woman good luck with her relationship and tells the woman that perhaps she will see her around.

Around. Angie walks around and around. Until she is lost. Off the main street and lost. Wandering past the same group of women sitting on a porch, sliding long-necked bottles of beer from their tables to their lips, leaning toward the darkening sky. Angie tries to be casual, tries to pretend she is not lost, denying it to herself, even as she denies her denial.

When Rachel asks what took Angie so long, Angie says there was a line at the phones. "Every dyke in town is on the phone, calling her former lovers." Angie laughs, her voice loud in her own ears.

"That would be healthier," Rachel says simply, sharply.

Angie does not know the point of Rachel's comparison. Healthier than what? Checking her work messages? Telephoning Claire? Having a drink with a strange woman? And Angie does not ask.

Only takes a nap. Or pretends to. While Laura and Vickie and Rachel play a board game with the children in the living room. And Angie stretches across the bed, wanting Rachel.

The notebook is spiral. A design like feathers or marble printed on the cover. "Executive Document": The brand name proclaims itself, italicized in the lower righthand corner. "Wide-ruled. 500 pages." Advertisements, enticements, boasts. Angie cannot seem to open the cover.

Angie wishes for a catalog. Maybe two or three. Or something to read that is easy in its promises. "This little gadget will make life easier. Judge for yourself!" "Foot-loomed by peasants who share in the profits."

Wishes the little words did not bob on the blue lines underneath the white wide spaces.

> I bought the lace leotard because I thought Harriet would like it, but now I realize that was a big mistake. I shouldn't have gone to that underwear place and spent all this money, although she doesn't know how much money it was. She used to like almost everything I ever wore, but lately she acts like she doesn't want to touch me. She says now that she's annoyed at Desirée's crying. I have to remember to ask my mom how much I cried so I can tell whether Desirée really does cry a lot.

Angie closes the notebook. Opens it.

> Desirée lost another pound. The doctor says that's unusual. The nurse wrote down "failure to thrive." Harriet told me I'd better be careful, they're going to call the social workers and take little Desirée away. Said it happens all the time, especially to women like us. And I don't know if I have enough money to take her back to the doctor. I'm not going to the clinic. I've heard what they do to women there. Tie their tubes, for no reason.

Angie closes the notebook, but she can still see the small blue words, Bic pen words, dwarfed by the wide white rows. Angie closes her eyes, waiting for Rachel. But it is Laura who knocks on the door, waking her from a sleep she did not know she had entered, telling her that dinner was ready, asking her if she wants iced tea or coffee.

"Is that bookstore still open?" Angie directs her question to no one in particular.

"Everything's open pretty late."

"Just pretend you're in the city," Laura instructs.

"Anyone want to go with me?"

No one responds.

"Come on, Rachel. Let's walk down to the bookstore." Angie bites her lip to keep from adding, "And have a drink."

No one else urges Rachel to go. No one says that she will tuck Skye into bed if Skye will allow herself to be tucked. No one says anything.

"You go ahead, babe," Rachel finally responds. "I'll stay here and get Skye into bed."

"I could do it." Vickie's voice is flat.

"You don't need to do that," Rachel says politely. "But if you guys want to go out, I'll be happy to stay here with the kids."

"I'll stay, too." Angie offers. She thinks Vickie would like to go out, but watches her check with Laura and then defer.

"Some other night." Vickie sighs.

"I won't be long." Angie escapes.

The woman with the tattoo is not in the bookstore, although the novel that she bought is displayed prominently. Angie reads the back cover, thinking that Rachel would like it, decides to buy it for her. Then decides to try to find a book for Vickie and one for Laura, to come back bearing gifts. She should buy Vickie poetry, she thinks with nostalgia. And a mystery for Laura, or one of those sappy recovery books, she thinks without affection. She spends too long trying to choose, to select from the overcrowded shelves something that might placate. She grows bored with her project and settles on novels for each of them; at least then they can trade.

At the magazine rack in the back, she eyes the newsprint and stapled photocopied 'zines. She used to read this stuff religiously, was even on the edges of a collective once. She feels as if she is being welcomed back, so she scoops up everything that is not glossy, everything that does not have a half-naked and wholly erect man on the cover. This is her culture, after all, she reasons. The reason she does the work she does.

She takes care not to get lost this time. One straight street, what could be simpler? Still, the shop windows are seductive, especially on the side streets. A special purchase, a solution, a salve. The Universe of Shells. Trinkets from Around the World. Maritime Discount. Schooner's Reunion. The Shirt Shoppe. Each store has its own promises, luring Angie to its joys and disappointments. The shells are large, but too polished. The trinkets varied, but too expensive. The maritime equipment is cheap, but too technical. Schooner's well-lit but garish. The sayings on the shirts are witty, and Angie stretches her neck to read the ones pinned to the wall. "If you think I'm a bitch, You should meet my mother." Angie laughs, alone and loud, guilty. Backing out the door, away from the bold pink stitching on the polyester/cotton blend shirt, away from her realization that she had been looking for a present for Claire, away from any urge to purchase the shirt and put it under her bed at home, with her catalogs.

Back at the house on the bay, the children are sleeping and the adults are sitting on the deck, silent. Angie puts the novels on the table and each woman takes one to read, although none chooses the book that Angie selected for her. Rachel loops one leg over the arm of a chair in the living room, adjusting the lamp. Laura flops on the couch. Vickie goes to the bedroom.

Angie wanders back to her own bed, the bed she shares with Rachel, and spreads out the magazines. Flips through them, reading articles on rape and breast cancer and incest and a lesbian custody case decided months ago. Reading first the fiction, then, slowly, the poetry, and then the movie and book and theater reviews. Surveying the advertisements: therapists and therapists and therapists, jewelers, ritual healers, financial consultants and attorneys ("property and child custody agreements and mediation"). Studying the personals:

> Sensitive. Earthy. Drug and alcohol free. Wants same for conversation, moonlit walks, and sensual explorations. No bisexuals or dykes, please.
> Professional woman, straight-looking and acting, desires same for long-term discreet relationship.

> If you are an experienced lesbian who can treat a young woman right, I'd love to hear from you. I'm 21, attractive, green eyes and strawberry-blond hair, 5'5", and slender. I'm looking for that perfect someone to introduce me to the ways of Sappho.

"These are better than catalogs," Angie says out loud. But she is alone. And she falls asleep contemplating the ad copy she would write for herself. "Workaholic lesbian mother wants . . ."

"White workaholic lesbian mother and daughter, professional but from a working-class . . ."

"Fun-loving dyke in an open relationship . . ."

"Lonely lesbian lawyer who represents other lonely lesbians who have murdered their kids does not want same for a fucked-up relationship and maybe some sex if it isn't too inconvenient and we're both drunk enough."

AUGUSTS

AUGUSTS

**AUGUSTS**

AUGUSTS

AUGUSTS

There are many hollows in Angie's life, but there is a particular one kept vacant in anticipation of this moment. This ring of the telephone, the hesitation in the voice, the heat and cold rising to Angie's flesh, the bad news. A specific hollow.

Unfilled by lost cases and client suicides.

Undisturbed by Chelsea's call informing her that Kim has filed a sexual-harassment complaint against her under the Triple-F code as well as some new city regulations.

A hollow that is not the long thin crack reserved for Rachel or the spiral-shaped void for Skye, both for accidents, not inevitabilities. This hollow is a lifelong strip mine, deliberate and certain and singular. This hollow is Claire.

The call is from Luke. It comes while she is still awake, working, and not at 3 A.M., the way she always thought it would.

"She's in the hospital," Luke says.

Angie does not need to ask who "she" is. It can only be Claire.

"What happened?"

"Some stupid accident at work."

"How bad is she hurt?"

"I don't know."

"What hospital?"

"St. Joseph's."

"Well, I'll try to find out what happened. How did you hear?"

"She called me."

"Called you," Angie echoes. Meaning she could talk. Was conscious. Claire called. "I'll call you back."

Angie gets on the phone, calling information, then calling the hospital. "They cannot give out any information. No one can give out any information. No one knows anything. No one by that name has been admitted. No one can tell if anyone by that name is in the emergency room." Angie leafs through her Book, looking for contacts she could call at midnight for assistance with Claire. She cannot find anyone. She calls the airlines, checking flights. Calls Luke back.

"She called back. They're going to operate. Maybe tonight, but probably tomorrow."

"On what?"

"Her leg. Something fell on her."


Angie calls the hospital at six A.M.

"Is that you, Evangelina?"

"Yeah. How are you?"

"Just great."

"What's the doctor's name?"

"I don't know."

"When is surgery?"

"Today at twelve o'clock."

"What are they going to do?"

"Evangelina, I can't talk any more. I'm waiting for a call from the shop, see how any of this is going to be paid for. Call your father. That stupid bastard."

"I love you."

"Love you too, Evangelina."


At three o'clock in the afternoon—an hour for the operation, an hour for recovery, and an extra hour—Angie calls Claire's hospital room, expecting Luke's voice. No answer. At three-thirty. No answer. At three-forty-five. No answer. She calls the house, not expecting an answer but not knowing what else to do, surprised to hear Luke's voice.

"What's happening?" Angie modulates the panic in her voice.

"I'm waiting for her to call me."

"What?"

"She said she'd call me after the operation."

"You didn't go to the hospital?"

"I did. But she said there wasn't much I could do. Said she'd call me."

"After surgery?"

"It was supposed to start at noon. I thought she'd be in her room by now. I've been calling every fifteen minutes."

"Have you called the main number for the hospital?"

"Oh, they wouldn't tell me anything." Angie does not need to ask Luke if he tried. She recognizes the sigh of premature resignation.

"Let me try."

"It's long distance. You're going to run up your bill."

"I'll call you back."

Angie closes her office door, although if anyone can overhear it sounds like just another business call. That professional tone. Solicitous yet demanding. The floor nurse. The supervisor of the recovery room. No information on the patient's condition.

"I'll call back in ten minutes. I want the surgeon's name and phone number. I want the condition and location of the patient. I want anything else you can tell me about my mother. I'm calling long distance."

Angie keeps the office door closed. Pushes the Do Not Disturb button on her telephone. Watches the clock on her computer. Picks at the flesh on her knuckles.

"I just called." Angie is relieved to recognize the same voice through the telephone, through the hospital bureaucracy.

"Oh yes. She's fine. She just got out of surgery about ten minutes ago, which is why I did not know where she was. The surgeon came to the surgery waiting room but there was no one here. Are you her closest relative?"

"My father is there, but he must have become too anxious and left."

"Oh. I told the surgeon you called and he said to tell you it went well."

"What's the surgeon's name and number?"

"Dr. Peterman. 555-3992."

"First name?"

"Brad. Bradford actually."

Angie writes the name and number in her Book. Under today's date in her weekly calendar. Under the number of the hospital and the number of Claire's hospital room and direct-dial number.

"Thank you. You've been very helpful."

"Oh. You're welcome. I'm sure she'll be fine."

Angie calls the surgeon's office. Leaves her name and office telephone number. With a request that he get in touch with her.

Angie calls Luke.

"Thanks for doing that. I was beginning to go into a panic."

"That's okay."

"No, I do appreciate you doing this for me. I guess you really do care about her."

"I love you, too." Angie emphasizes both "you" and "too."

"I love you, too." Luke echoes, without emphasis.

"It's just a bunch of broken bones, no big deal. I'm not going to die or anything."

"How are you feeling?"

"Fine. You should have seen the woman who came for me, from the rescue squad. I mean, I was in pain but not blind. I couldn't tell whether she was a guy or not. She looked just like a guy. I mean, really. She got near me and if I would have been able to stand, I would have run. I mean, you probably know her, she must be a lesbian. She was huge. But very nice. A nice girl."

"I'm glad she was nice."

"Very nice. Came to see me this afternoon. She had to drop someone else off here at the hospital, so she thought she'd stop by. Wasn't that nice?"

"Real nice."

"I asked her if she knew you, but she said no."

The plaques in Angie's office startle her. She is disoriented to be here after talking to Claire, after talking to Luke. She goes down the hall for a late-afternoon cup of coffee, hoping to relax. Finds Walter in Roger's office, the two of them in a serious conversation.

"Join us, Ange, we're talking Foucault." Roger strokes his beard.

"I haven't heard he said much about women," Angie says flatly, reaching for the coffee pot.

"The depth of your knowledge constantly amazes me," Roger says.

"Bug off, Roger. I'm having a rough day."

"Sorry," Roger says, thinking of Kim's complaint. "Her father talked her into it, you know. I don't know how that girl constructed such a fantasy—and you know most of us believe it's her fantasy—but she must have told dear old Dad that she wanted to be a lesbian or something and he put some pressure on her."

Walter glares at Roger. Then Walter sing-songs: "Hell hath no fury . . ."

"I'm sure it will all blow over," Roger adds, asking, "what are you working on now?"

"A few briefs in custody cases. But I'm also monitoring this murder charge, Chillicothe."

"Is that the dead baby in the closet?" Roger asks.

"Ah, the closet," Walter puts in. "The defining symbol of queer culture in this century, and increasingly the defining symbol of all culture."

"Spare me the Foucault." But Angie cannot resist giggling at Walter's pretentious parody.

"It's not Foucault. Just my professor," Walter corrects.

"Don't tell me they're teaching symbols of culture in paralegal school?"

"Of course not, at least not until it makes it into the Uniform System of Citation. I'm taking a course, Queer Theory. At the New School."

"Good for you," Angie says.

"It sounds simply fascinating." Roger strokes his beard again. "Maybe I'll take a course."

"Or you could just pay for Walter's next course, and he could tell you about it."

"You are so crude, Angie."

"Cruel or crude?" she asks.

"Both," Roger says, but he laughs.


Angie on the phone. Claire, not recovering. Claire, with a fever. Luke, crying. The surgeon, not returning Angie's phone calls.

Angie on the phone. Susannah Chillicothe, not being offered a plea bargain. Susannah Chillicothe, awaiting trial in county jail. Cathy Chillicothe, crying. The defense attorney, not returning Angie's phone calls.

Angie on the plane. To Claire. Reading Susannah Chillicothe's notebook.

> I could hear little Desirée in her crib screaming. I bought a pair of black underpants that I thought Harriet would like. Harriet said I had to quit my job on the construction crew because too many men looked at me. Desirée does not want to eat. I felt so ugly when I was pregnant, until I met Harriet and she showed what love was. I want to go over to my mom's house, but I never have time. I'm trying to love Desirée, but it's so hard, she cries all the time.

Angie renting a car; red is the only color available. "Harriet said I looked sexy in red." Angie driving. "I love to drive with Harriet, Desirée in the backseat." Looking for the hospital; it's not where she thought it would be. "I called the doctor, but he said just take her to the emergency room if it got any worse." And nicer than she thought, like new. "I wish Harriet liked my mom more." The fifth floor is quiet. "My mom is going to make me some more baby mobiles, from old bleach containers like she saw in a book." Claire, sleeping, tied to the bed.

Only twenty miles from Susannah Chillicothe's residence at the county jail. Twenty miles, without traffic. Twenty miles without a span of suspension bridge. Unless one counts the conveyors across the strip mines, which no one does.

＊　＊　＊

"Evangelina? Evangelina?" Tears explode across Claire's face. "They have me locked up here. It's a prison."

"It's a hospital. It's all right. It's a hospital. And they just have to find out what's wrong."

"What did I do wrong?"

"You didn't do anything wrong. I think you're just having a reaction to the surgery."

"I should never have let those men inside me. Those men with their dirty, dirty hands."

"It's going to be fine."

"Where's Luke?"

"He's home, probably cleaning the house." Angie adds the last part because she thinks it sounds like it might be true, sounds better than "lying on the couch."

"What a waste of a man. I mean, I've needed him here. I need someone to brush my hair. Can you brush my hair, Evangelina? Can you? Do you think he can come to this prison and get me out? He's afraid, ain't he? I should never have married a man that saw his own father shot dead. Shot singing union songs. Luke comes from stupid stock, and now scared stock. That man just can't do a damn thing."

"He called me."

"Well, at least he did one thing right."

The nurse's aide interrupts to take Claire's vital signs.

"She still have a fever?" Angie wonders if Claire can understand her, wonders why she is speaking as if Claire is not in the room.

"It's down to one hundred and two."

"Untie her."

"She keeps ripping out her IV tubes and trying to walk down the hall."

"I'll stay here with her."

"All night?"

"All night."

"I'll bring you a blanket."

Sundown syndrome. The fluorescent lights seek to regulate time, but patients hospitalized this long inevitably succumb to it. At least according to the supervising nurse in whose office Angie is now sipping coffee. No one seems to know what is wrong with Claire, why she screams, why she refuses to eat, why what they term routine surgery has rendered her condition near critical. They think it is the blood clots. A complication from the surgery. Angie imagines all of Claire's blood clotting uncontrollably, not only near the site of the surgery, the incisions and sutures, but in her blood vessels, in her heart, in her brain. One IV is blood thinner, heparin. The other is nutrition. The nurse is brisk, but sympathetic.

By midnight, all the rapists and cannibals and police officers who people Claire's hospital world are sleeping. Tired from harassing Claire and being banished by Angie. "I've spent my whole life being so afraid," Claire says. And Angie knows that this is not a part of Claire's delusion.


Luke comes in the morning, before work.

"You need to stay with her."

"I have to work."

"You have to stay with her. That's more important."

"Are you telling me what to do?"

"Yes. Yes. I am. But I'm also asking."

"Well then, I reckon I'll have to stay."

"Don't let them tie her to the bed."

"I won't."

"I'll be back. I'm going to try to find out a few things, take a nap. Then I'll be back."

"Don't worry. I'll be fine. I'll just watch television."


Claire's house is silent. Angie dials the rotary phone, looking at the cross-stitch *Home Is Where the Heart Is.* Looking at the photograph of herself, a little angelic girl with a mane of curls and expectant eyes. Why does Claire keep these things, on the wall, over her bed? Information. Doctor Bradford Peterman. Leaves a message at his office. Dials Rachel. Talks. Dials Walter. Asks questions. Dials Cathy Chillicothe. The trial starts Monday.

"There won't be a jury."

"Why not?" Angie is incredulous.

"I think Sunny's lawyer said they shouldn't have one."

"They waived a jury trial?"

"I just know there won't be a jury and it's Sunny's lawyer's idea."

"Then the trial will start first thing in the morning?"

"She said I could be there if I wanted."

"Do you know their first witness?"

"No. I'm not sure of any of this. I really think you should call the attorney."

"She's not taking my calls."

"Maybe she's just nervous before the trial."

"Did you see Susannah . . . Sunny? Have you told her the situation with my mother? I did want to get over to the jail to see her, but I'm not sure I can."

"Sunny's an understanding girl. And I hope your mother is feeling better."

"Not yet. But she will be," Angie vows. "And I'll be there when the trial starts."

"You will? I would really like that. I'm sure Sunny and her lawyer would too."


Angie washes her face in the hospital restroom, with water hot enough to dissolve her lethargy. She wanders the halls, looking for a nurse who can help her decipher the medical scribbles in Claire's chart, who can help her navigate the hospital's lulling labyrinth. Looking for a dyke. There has to be a dyke in this hospital, she thinks, there just has to be.

The doctor is cordial, but only because Angie has made it an implicit demand. Introducing herself, shaking his hand, treating him like a colleague, like an opposing attorney. Claire is screaming that she is in prison. The doctor is shaking his head.

"Let's go in the hall and talk," she says to the doctor.

"Fine," he says.

Questions. Some answers. Drugs like heparin and coumadin to dissolve the clots. Caution, care. On blood thinners, she could bleed to death from a minor cut. No discernible sources of infection.

"We're doing everything we can, but she's a difficult case. She wasn't in very good shape when she was admitted."

"She's had a hard life," Angie admits.

"She smokes, doesn't she?"

"Some. But I meant working. She's worked hard all her life."

"Cigarettes really destroy one's health."

"Perhaps. But she's probably breathed more coal dust than cigarette smoke. Besides, the problem's not her lungs, is it?"

"No, we've X-rayed those. But I've ordered respiratory therapy and treatments just in case. She's horizontal so much her lungs could collapse."

Angie is looking at the surgeon's hands. So clean and white, with nails that shine. "I want to be consulted on all treatments," she says to his hands.

"Your mother has been giving consent."

"She also thinks she's in prison."

"Some disorientation is normal."

"This much? If that's your standard, then every informed consent given by a patient in this hospital is a problem."

The doctor straightens his back. "Didn't your father say you were a lawyer? From New York City?"

Angie nods noncommittally. Not New York City, not really. Not Manhattan. No, somewhere else. She practices in a mundane brick building in a neighborhood of reasonable rents. She lives in a wood-floored house surrounded by trees. She tries to preserve these facts about herself, but only for herself. She knows New York City sounds the most impressive.

"And what kind of law do you practice?" the surgeon presses.

Angie could say family law, criminal law, civil rights, lesbian rights, and each of these is accurate, deployed for various effects. And Angie could say trusts and estates, or probate, which would be incorrect, but usefully deflective. But Angie has never before said what she says now, to her mother's doctor in the hall outside her mother's room, while her mother screams from her hospital bed.

"Medical malpractice," Angie says. And she runs her right hand roughly through her needing-a-haircut hair so that her head tilts back. And her laugh is almost a cackle.

The moment Angie spots Susannah, she ceases her resistance to thinking of her as Sunny. Standing at the defendant's table, next to her attorney, Sunny is tall and vigorous, even after several months in the county jail. Angie tries to suppress two smiles: the reflexive smile that taunts her mouth whenever she sees an attractive dyke, and the sardonic smile that flattens her face whenever she is amused at her own delusions. Sunny is a solid woman with curly hair and tight skin, a tomboy heartthrob, looking like she belongs on a softball field on a brilliant spring afternoon. Confronted with Sunny in the flesh, Angie realizes she had assumed that Susannah would be pock-marked and pitiful, slight and stooped, with the sharp features of a rodent, and particularly darting eyes. Angie has difficulty reconciling Sunny with the timid mother and insecure lover in the pages of the spiral notebook.

"Opening statements?" The few people in the courtroom have barely seated themselves before the judge invites counsel to speak. "Judge Parsons," his nameplate reads.

"Waived."

"Waived."

First the prosecutor, then defense counsel. Angie angles herself on the bench to try to see their faces, but their backs are straight and unyielding.

"First witness."

"The state calls Harriet Sanford."

"I can't believe this," Angie whispers. Cathy Chillicothe shrugs a question, but the courtroom is too quiet for Angie to elaborate. Besides, she thinks, perhaps there is some reason for the prosecution calling the main witness, the defendant's ex-lover, first, before testimony establishing the death of the child victim. Just as there must be a reason for the empty courtroom, empty of supporters or spectators or the press. Harriet Sanford's footsteps echo as she approaches the witness stand.

She swears to tell the truth, so help her God. She smiles at the prosecutor, a smile that has benefited from fluoride in the water but not orthodontics. Angie thinks she looks ordinary, almost too ordinary to be natural.

She answers the precise questions, precisely. Her voice is measured, practiced. "My roommate." "Her baby." "Crying." "A closet." "I said we should." "I was worried."

. "Now, did you and your roommate have an unusual relationship?"

"Yes. Yes, we did."

"And what was the nature of that relationship?"

"We were romantically involved."

"Does that include sexually involved?"

"Yes, it did."

"Are you a lesbian, Ms. Sanford?"

"No. No, I am not, Ms. Heeley."

Angie suppresses a groan. Such a practiced direct examination. The lack of tension in their voices, their references to each by their last names, the satisfied looks on their faces. Any jury would be suspicious, but there is no jury.

"How did you come to have a sexual involvement with the defendant?"

"My boyfriend had just broken up with me. And Susannah Chillicothe befriended me. Because I was lonely, she was able to persuade me to be romantic."

Cathy Chillicothe cannot suppress her groan. Angie gives her a pat, but, looking at Sunny Chillicothe, she thinks that Sunny could persuade anyone to be romantic.

"And what did you do when the defendant told you the baby had stopped breathing in her crib?"

"I told her to call the rescue squad."

"Did she do so?"

"In a minute or two, she did."

"What did she do in the meantime?"

"She just stood there, looking at her baby."

"Your witness."

Direct is over in less than an hour.

"Cross-examination," Judge Parsons announces.

"A few questions." Elizabeth Walwyn walks to the podium. She seems short and a little unsure in her pumps. She straightens her skirt, looks at her legal pad, introduces herself to the witness.

Elizabeth Walwyn's first few questions all begin the same way.

"Did I understand you to say . . . ?" This or that. A good judge would instruct defense counsel that the witness has no knowledge of what counsel understands. Judge Parsons looks too bored to be a good judge.

"Why didn't you call the rescue squad yourself?" Elizabeth Walwyn asks the major witness against her client. Angie cringes. Perhaps this is the million-dollar question, but every law student who has passed Evidence knows that a lawyer does not ask "why" on cross-examination.

"She told me not to."

"Did you think the baby was going to die?"

"I did."

"But you didn't call for help because she told you not to, is that what I understood you to say?"

"Yes, ma'am."

"And why did you listen to what she said if you thought the baby was going to die?"

"Because I was afraid." Harriet Sanford lowers her head.

"Afraid?"

"Afraid. Afraid of her." Harriet Sanford nods toward the defendant, her former lover, Sunny Chillicothe. Angie strains to see who is the object of Harriet's attempt at eye contact.

"Why were you afraid? Afraid of her?" Elizabeth Walwyn tilts her head to the side. Angie's fist comes down on her own thigh. Cathy Chillicothe pats Angie's other leg, near the knee.

"Because she said that if I called the police or rescue she would tell my mother that I was a lesbian." Harriet Sanford's voice is flat. Angie notes the absence of emotion, but cannot decide what it means.

"You would let a child die because you didn't want your mother to know that you were involved in a lesbian relationship?" Elizabeth Walwyn raises her voice a pitch.

"Of course." Harriet Sanford announces. As if she has just been asked whether she would carry an umbrella when it is raining. Wouldn't everybody? Wouldn't you?

"And is that why you told the police later that the baby had been lost—or kidnaped—when the baby was actually in the closet?"

"Yes, ma'am."

"Because you were afraid?"

"Yes, ma'am."

"Because the defendant threatened to reveal your sexual relationship to your mother?"

"Yes. Yes, ma'am."

"No further questions." Elizabeth Walwyn announces, looking around the near empty courtroom. As if she has just noticed that the rain has stopped.

Angie's fist comes down on her leg again. "That incompetent bitch." Cathy Chillicothe is too worried about her daughter to comfort Angie.

"No redirect." The prosecutor, Mary Heeley, stands, then smooths her skirt under her ass as she sits back down in the wooden chair at the counsel table.

"Court is in recess until further notice." Judge Parsons wipes his glasses on his robe.

" 'Further notice'?" Angie's whispered question is swallowed by the clerk's "All rise."

After the judge departs, Angie strides over to Sunny Chillicothe before she can be handcuffed and escorted out of the courtroom. Introduces herself to the clerk, to the guard, to Sunny. Says she is a lawyer, although not in this state. Shakes hands with the clerk, with the guard. Smiles at Sunny. Sunny smiles back as she is being taken to spend another night in the county jail.

Angie then walks between the counsel tables, turning first to the prosecutor because she thinks this conversation will be briefer. It is brief, although the interaction with both attorneys is astoundingly short. Angie, in professional mode, introduces herself, shakes hands. Tells the prosecutor, "I am very interested in this case, as are many people." Tells the defense attorney, "Let me know if there's anything I can do to help, I'm in the area for a while." Is welcomed by terse nods from both attorneys as they gather up their papers and yellow legal pads. Angie knows they each have cause to be suspicious of her: out-of-town lawyer, New York lawyer, lesbian lawyer, some radical who does not appreciate how things are done in this heterosexual enclave. Angie retreats to the back of the courtroom, stands next to Cathy Chillicothe, and watches the attorneys.

"Talk to me, Cathy," Angie says, "but I'm not listening to you."

"Excuse me?" Cathy Chillicothe is polite.

"I want it to seem like we are having a very important conversation," Angie whispers.

"Oh. Well, what did you think of today?" Cathy Chillicothe stalls, then follows Angie's gaze to the prosecutor. "I think that Harriet is just a liar, a terrible liar. . . ."

Angie watches the attorneys. Watches each one not glance in the direction of the other. Watches each one not approach the other. Watches the defense attorney not ask those mundane questions of court etiquette: How many more witnesses? What day do you think the state's case will conclude? Watches them not resort to the familiarity of attorneys who work in the same courthouse, now that the judge is gone, now that any clients are absent, now that there is no reason not to. Angie stands at the door, as each attorney leaves the courtroom, watching each one. Notices that Elizabeth Walwyn has a run in her stocking. Notices that Mary Heeley does not. Notices that they wear the same shade of stocking; Angie would guess Suntan, according to the Hosiery Wholesalers catalog that she remembers looking at when she was home, so long ago.


Angie senses it. Senses the impossibility of it; the possibilities of it. Somewhere between a hunch and an articulable suspicion, it follows her as she follows the lawyers outside of the courtroom. In the courthouse hallway, dim with afternoon dirt, she turns to Cathy Chillicothe.

"Tell me everything you know about the prosecutor."

"Nothing."

"You must know something. Know her mother? Know her family? If she has a husband? If she's from around here?"

"I don't really run in the circles to know lawyers," Cathy Chillicothe explains.

"You know my mother," Angie cajoles.

"I suppose. Though it's my mother that knows your mother," Cathy Chillicothe corrects, implicitly emphasizing the closeness of her own age and Angie's.

"Don't you know any Heeleys?"

"Maybe. Let me think. Rich people, maybe mine owners. I don't recall."

"Could you try to find out? And ask your daughter if she knows Mary Heeley."

"Sunny? How would Sunny know her?" Cathy Chillicothe pauses. "Oh."

"Are you going to see her this evening? I've got to get back to the hospital. But if you could talk to Sunny about it, it might be helpful."

Angie and Cathy Chillicothe look at each other for a long moment, an admission of the possibility of attraction between them, a realization that any trace of attraction is absent. They are just too different, just too similar.

Lawyers exist on reputation. Her friend Vickie had said so, just last month. And Abraham Lincoln had said it, just last century: "A lawyer's reputation is his stock in trade."

Lesbians subsist on gossip. Vickie had proven that too, telling her that everyone knew about Kim, even before Kim had filed the complaint. And probably some famous lesbian had noted it, someone like Gertrude Stein or Natalie Barney or maybe even Sappho.

Reputation and gossip. The tools of her trade as a lesbian lawyer. A few well-placed telephone calls could access a world of information, or at least rumors. But before Angie reaches for the address section of her appointment Book and pulls out her AT&T long distance card, she knows she must narrow her search. Like a good legal researcher, a good appellate attorney, Angie goes to the nearest law library.

The county law library is in the courthouse, behind a door guarded by a woman law librarian who does not return Angie's smile. No, Angie answers, she does not have a state bar card or proof of county residence, but she is a lawyer. Yes, she answers, from New York. Yes, she answers, observing the Susannah Chillicothe case. Yes, she agrees, it is a shame about that poor little dead baby.

The librarian agrees to allow Angie to look at the lawyers' directory. University of West Virginia College of Law. Good, Angie thinks, small school. Undergraduate at a private women's college. Year of birth, the same as Angie's. No organizations listed. Angie flips the pages, carefully, under the obvious observation of the law librarian. Interesting, Angie thinks, both of them in the same law school, graduation date two years apart. Different undergraduate colleges, this one a state school. No organizations listed. "Thank you so much," Angie says to the law librarian, who smiles, albeit slightly.

Then asks if the library has law reviews.

"Of course," the librarian answers, smugly satisfied.

The white covers of the *West Virginia Law Review* are soiled, slightly browned, and unbound into hardcover volumes. Like most law reviews, struggling for a niche, there is a yearly special issue. "The National Coal Issue," blue lettering, fading on even the most current copy. This summer the articles address prosecutions of mine companies for violations of the Clean Water Act ("a defense perspective"), the Mine Act's application to non-employee union representatives' access to mine workers ("a misinterpretation"), an economic analysis of externalities in coal production ("a simple cost-benefit exercise"), and a state statute requiring law officials to be "neutral" in "labor disputes" ("a critique"). And after the biographical asterisk: "The author represents the mining industry in litigation pertaining to the the subject areas discussed; however, the views expressed in this article are the author's own and do not necessarily reflect the views of his client." Angie sighs, quickly stifling it so that the law librarian will not hear.

The summers before, ten years ago, twenty years ago, the articles are almost always the same, in slant if not in subject. But Angie is not reading the table of contents any longer, but the lists of board members, editors. Looking among all the men's names—James, Robert, Paul, Edmund, Christopher, Gerald, David, Joseph, Patrick, Matthew—she finds only one of the names that interest her. Staff. Never an editor. And the other name is absent entirely.

"Did you find what you needed?" the law librarian asks, almost helpfully.

"Yes," Angie says. But she does not know why she needed it, why she wanted to know. Only knows that she feels some shallow advantage. Only thanks the law librarian, sincerely.

\* \* \*

During the twenty-minute drive through the August-green hills, marveling at the lack of traffic, the lack of toll booths and bridges, she is so confident that she is almost exceeding the speed limit in her red rental car. Angie hums along with the radio, an old Rolling Stones song, which follows her into Claire's hospital room. Claire hovers between sleep and consciousness, an IV in each arm. Angie talks to Claire, talks to the nurses, tries to decipher Claire's thickening chart. She brushes Claire's hair, Claire's teeth. Goes down the hall, to use the telephone. Dials Luke. Dials the surgeon's office, the consulting doctors' offices. Leaves messages. Comes back to Claire's room.

Twilight is a blur, like the blurs of Angie's life. Time collapses and contracts and dilates and explodes. Windows. Mirrors. Streets. Looking out. Peering in. Hallways. Staring down. Waiting for the telephone. To use it, to ring. Waiting for the doctor to call. Waiting for Claire. All night. Half sleeping in the chair, waiting for Claire's moan, Claire's scream. Waiting for Claire's fever to break. Waiting for the nurse. Waiting for answers. Waiting for the morning.

⬛ ⬛ ⬛ ⬛ ⬛ ⬛ ⬛

Evangelina is waiting to arrive. Evangelina is singing in the backseat of the two-tone blue Hudson she loves so much, with the wire coming out of the back of the driver's seat. The car floating down the road like a little whale on its way to the beach. Early, early in the morning, so they can stay all day. Sun and swimming, Evangelina and Luke in the waves while Claire shakes the sand off the blanket. Then, change out of their wet bathing suits in the car. Evangelina in white shorts with sand scratching in her underpants and a pastel-striped top, sewn by Claire, that irritates her sunburn. They go to the boardwalk, like a carnival. Let Evangelina choose a ride, buy her tickets for whatever ride she wants. Luke urges the roller coaster. Claire suggests the twirling teacups. Evangelina chooses—predictably—the House of a Million Mirrors.

"How boring." Claire sighs.

Luke buys three tickets, a bargain compared to the teacup's five and the roller coaster's seven. Still, he wishes the kid were more adventurous.

"How boring." Claire sighs again, as Evangelina walks up the wooden ramp, already fascinated.

In the maze, confronted with multiple images of herself blocking her own way, Evangelina's heart rushes blood wildly through her body. Her reflections are not distortions—she hated the funhouse mirrors the one time she went with her cousin Carol at a carnival—but accurate reproductions. She feels her way through the labyrinth of dangerous glass, taking care not to damage any of her appearances. She does not want to smash, or even smudge, the glass; she does not want to bruise, or even bump, the flesh. What she wants is to find the secret path, the most logical escape, and take all of her bodies with her into a future.

      ■ ■ ■ ■ ■ ■ ■

Evangelina is waiting in the principal's office. It is the first day of school and she is already in trouble. It is the first day of school and Claire cried all morning, releasing her only child to compulsory kindergarten. It is the first day of school and the August heat still vibrates in the deathly ill hills of coal country.

"She punched that boy right in the face," the principal tells Claire. "That kind of conduct cannot be condoned."

Evangelina does not know what *condoned* means, but she thinks it sounds serious. She looks at her knee socks, new for today, still proud that they are not ankle socks. She is pulling at the band of the sock when she hears Claire's shrill reply.

"You'd better keep that boy away from my daughter."

At home, Evangelina starts to cry and says she is sorry.

Claire whirls around. "Don't you dare say you're sorry. You have to learn to fight back. Don't be running scared like your father. When anyone hits you, you fight back. Do you understand?" Claire is screaming now, "Do you understand?"

Evangelina nods quickly, her head bouncing on her neck like the boy's did when she punched him. She cannot tell her mother that the boy did not hit her, but only hurt her in some wild way she cannot explain. Only sat next to her and smelled like grocery-store soap and put his arm around her like he knew her. So she punched him. Her fist catching the tip of his nose and his lip. Not much blood, but lots of excitement. Evangelina did not expect that much excitement.

"No," Claire is screaming, "It isn't wrong to fight back. If you don't fight, they'll take everything that's yours. Don't forget that. Just don't forget."

Evangelina is waiting for Claire to finish. She is sitting on the floor, between Claire's legs, which hang down from the chair. The chair has an aqua slipcover with deeper aqua piping, ripped at the armrests and the pleats at the bottom torn. Evangelina is pretending to watch television, *Disney's Wide World of Color* or *Lassie* or *The Patty Duke Show*. Claire is coiling strands of Evangelina's hair, piercing the pincurls with bobby pins. Their bodies are close, close. Evangelina closes her eyes as her mother nears the nape of her neck. Claire's fingers twist the hair, never pulling too tightly, never hurting Evangelina. When Claire is finished, she squeezes Evangelina's shoulders and kisses her pincurled head.

"Time for bed."

Evangelina sings: "When cousins . . . are two of a kind."

"I hate that show," Claire says.

"They're really twins, you know," Evangelina explains.

"They're really the same person," Claire explains.

"They can't be."

"It's done with mirrors," Claire explains.

"Really?"

"I think so." Claire's voice edges with doubt.

"Can I read?"

"Tomorrow is a school day."

"I don't want to go to school."

"Already? It's only the first week. You used to like school."

"It makes me nervous."

"Nervous? You sound like an old lady."

"It does," Evangelina protests.

"Okay, then. Stay home. But make sure you dust. And I'll put out something for supper. And don't leave the house."

"Okay."

"And don't open the door for anybody."

"I won't."

"Good night."

"Good night. I love you, Mommy."

"I love you too, my little Evangelina. Don't forget not to open the door."

"I won't."

◼ ◼ ◼ ◼ ◼ ◼

Angie lets the nurse's aide bathe Claire and goes down the hall to the little foyer she is beginning to think of as a second office. Gets out a piece of graph paper from the pad in her appointment Book, dials Rachel. The first person on her mental list. Leaves a message. Not a message about what she wants to know, but a message that says good luck; a message prompted by the receptionist reminding Angie that Rachel is "in trial" today. Angie wishes she could remember Rachel's schedule, wishes Rachel had voice mail so she could tell Rachel she loves her, wishes Rachel was holding her and kissing her, now, right now. Angie's love for Rachel is purest when she misses Rachel. It is love uncomplicated by the wrong dishtowel folded the wrong way, the jacket sliding off the back of the couch, the negotiations for dinner in harried tones, the unrequited lust or annoying attempt at seduction. It is love without the trivial. Absence makes . . ., Angie cannot help but think, as she dials their home number and leaves a message on the answering machine: "I love you. I love you. I always realize how much I love you when we are apart."

Then Angie throws herself into the net of lesbian lawyers. She is constrained only by her long-distance credit card limit and some residual reserve about who she feels entitled to intrude upon. She feels no need to be careful, does not care who knows that she is asking: What do you know, and do you know anyone who might know? She leaves explicit messages, checks her own voice mail. It is too early for replies, but soon. Soon.

There's got to be a dyke in this hospital. Someone she can trust. Someone she can cajole into assisting her read the chart, read the X-ray reports, tell her the side effects of the medications. There must be someone here, someone who is her own kind. Her own kind within her own kind.

"The CAT scan reveals some inflammation, a rather low-level regional pelvic infection."

"What could cause that?" Angie is asking the technician. Not a dyke technician, but a woman from New York. Angie has come to the point at St. Joseph's Hospital when she will bond with anyone about virtually anything.

"Probably not that ancient tubal ligation, if that's what you mean," the technician says quickly, or perhaps just at a normal New York pace. "Although," she adds, almost interrupting herself, "I suppose that it is possible that after the procedure someone might develop PID—pelvic inflammatory disease—but it seems highly unlikely."

"Is that what she has? PID?"

"I do not diagnose," the woman says, rotely.

"Can you tell how old that tubal ligation is?"

"Not from the CAT scan image. But I bet I could figure it out."

"How?"

"It's your mother, right?" Angie nods. "And you look to be between thirty and forty, and say your mother gave birth between the ages of fifteen and twenty, that many years ago. And say she wasn't a Catholic and didn't give birth at St. Joseph's—am I right so far?" Angie nods again. "But in a public hospital. And say maybe she didn't look old enough to be married or wasn't married. Then she would have had a routine tubal ligation."

"You mean an involuntary sterilization?" Angie does not know why she sounds so shocked. Ellen and Angie have talked so many times about this. Ellen has practiced oral arguments, with Angie playing the role of the judge. Ellen had written briefs and Angie had edited them, giving Ellen feedback the way Ellen always gave Angie feedback. Ellen has had hundreds of cases. But, Angie thinks, none of Ellen's cases is Claire, none of Ellen's cases is Angie's mother.

"It depends on what you think of as involuntary."

"I've seen what passes for consent these days, I can just imagine. . . ."

"I heard it was very poor down here in those days. I don't think you should judge so harshly." The technician sounds officious, suddenly.


"It doesn't sound very ethical," Rachel says.

Angie twists the phone receiver cord around her hand. She is at the pay phone, down the hall from her mother's room, in the familiar foyer. Angie dislikes the wallpaper, green and pink, but at least the phone is Touch-Tone.

"Me or them?"

"Neither. How's your mother?"

"I'm really not sure." The uncertainty in her own voice surprises Angie. Confidence. Control. Calculation. These are the effects for which she calibrates. "How's Skye?"

"Enjoying summer camp. This day-camp idea is really working out. Although she doesn't like the swimming days. She wants to play tennis with one of the counselors."

"And how are you?"

"I miss you, Angie. I really miss you."

"I miss you too. But I'll be home soon. No matter what happens here, I'll be home soon."

"You sound so worried. Take it easy, baby. You know what they say? 'It's always darkest . . .' "

"I suppose." Angie is unconvinced.

She hangs up, checks her Voicemail. Again. Not yet, not yet. Maybe she should not rely on the phone so much, she thinks. Dialing Rachel back again, just to hear her voice, again, and ask about Skye, again.

And to tell Rachel that it isn't always darkest before the dawn. It is actually darkest just when one expects that it would be darkest: in the middle of the night. Everything is gradual, incremental.

Everything except bad luck. No, bad luck is sudden. One minute Claire is standing up at work, laughing even, and the next minute she is on the floor being crushed by a machine. One day Angie is congratulating herself on an accomplished oral argument, a mature decision about a misguided legal intern, a sensible vacation; and then the next thing that happens is an opinion that judges her a deviant animal, a sex harassment claim against her, and a fight with Rachel after following some strange woman around town.

Disaster is instant. She could be driving across a bridge one moment, and then something like an earthquake could plunge her into the flooded strip mine below.

Rachel does not answer the phone.

The bar is in the same place, with a different name. A few video games by the pool table now. And a mirror behind the bottles, reflecting an expectation of tranquility.

Angie knows the woman she is looking for at the bar, just not who she is. Knows the woman will be a little set apart, a little too well-dressed, a little self-conscious. She will drink wine, white. Or seltzer. She will be in the bar early and leave before midnight.

When Angie discovers her, she asks the bartender to send her a drink. Chablis. Angie violates bar etiquette by not approaching the woman. Finally, the woman comes over to Angie.

White skin, pale, milky. Red hair, not flaming but not auburn. A librarian for the county school system. Angie judges her perfect.

Angie tells the woman she is an investigative reporter. The woman starts to feel important. Angie mentions the Chillicothe case. The woman nods gravely. Angie wonders aloud about the prosecutor. The woman shows her overbite. Angie says she thinks there is something funny about that defense attorney, too, but she just can't figure it out. The woman ushers her to a corner table. The woman tells her everything she knows and a few things that she does not.

*　*　*

"This is too crazy," Angie says to Margot, a suggested source from two Voicemail messages. A friend of a friend of a friend. And Rachel's girlfriend for a few months in college, although Rachel did not suggest her and Angie did not remember her. The relationship is tenuous, a winter-holiday-card-with-child-photograph exchange-basis, but amiable. They consider each other contacts.

"I'm looking for someone who went to law school at West Virginia. Didn't you? I—"

"I certainly did. I practically integrated the place single-handed. They were buying minorities that year," Margot remembers, "and I was selling. They were giving scholarships in order to keep their federal funding and they needed Blacks and women."

"Hey, two for the price of one," Angie acknowledges.

"Some things never change. It's still the same in academia." Angie remembers that Margot is some sort of academic adviser at a University of California law school. L.A. or Berkeley, Angie did not recognize one of those new area codes as she dialed the number.

"But now it's three for the price of one. Aren't they counting sexual orientation these days in California?"

"Dream on, Angie. I still have college kids cornering me at recruitment fairs asking me whether they should be out on their applications. And law students looking for jobs? You'd think the only existential crisis they'd ever faced is whether or not to be out on their résumé or in the interview."

"That's sort of what I'm calling you about," Angie admits.

"It's too late for you." Margot laughs. "I think everyone knows you're queer. I even saw you quoted in a newspaper out here, about some lesbian mother—a custody case, maybe, but it seems like there was something about murder. I forget, it was a while back. I meant to send it to you. I think I saved it."

"I'd like to see it. But I'm actually wondering whether you know if Mary Heeley is queer. White woman, our age, went to your law school."

"As a three-dollar bill. She was a class ahead of me. Rich girl—family owned some mines, although not in West Virginia. Perhaps Pennsylvania? Could be Kentucky? I was never good with that geography, it all looked like a pit to me. Anyway, old Mary Heeley acted like she was slumming by going to a state school. Actually, I always thought it was odd she was there."

"Did you know Elizabeth Walwyn?"

"Sure did. Lizzy, she wanted everybody to call her. But no one did. I tried, but it always made me think of Lizzie Borden. She was a year behind me. A little less pretentious than Mary; came from less money, or maybe no money."

"I assume she's a lesbian."

"You must know if you're asking." Margot notes. "And you must have already figured out they were lovers. Might still be. Although there was a bit of a scandal during law school."

"A scandal?"

"I'm not sure what it was. Very hush-hush, but you know us scullery-maid scholarship students toiling in the dean's office." Angie giggles with affinity. "Anyway," Margot continues, "there was some scandal about their affair. With the families. They're cousins or something, you know. It was really one of those hillbilly gothics of incest and smoldering sexual passions."

"Interesting. And you think they might still be lovers?"

"As a matter of fact"—Margot pauses for effect—"I saw them out here a year ago, or maybe two. But it was definitely June, during the Gay Pride festivities, when every closet case comes to the West Coast to be queer on vacation. Not at the parade or anything, but on the street. They acted like they didn't recognize me."

"Were they holding hands or anything?" Angie asks hopefully.

"Not that I remember. I probably would have remembered that. No, I think they were just together."

"That's helpful," Angie says summarily.

"Now that I've told you everything I know, why don't you tell me what this is all about?"

"Sure. I'm observing a case in which Mary Heeley is the prosecutor and Elizabeth Walwyn is the public defender."

"That doesn't sound very ethical—if they're still involved, that is."

"What if they're not still involved, but the case involves a lesbian relationship?"

"That's a closer question," Margot says thoughtfully. "It's probably not an ethics violation, but it's certainly interesting."

"It *is* interesting, isn't it?"

Margot is thinking of people she can telephone; at least one of her former law school classmates would appreciate this tidbit. "Anyway," she says hastily, "say hello to Rachel and give that kid a kiss from me."

"You do the same."

"And Angie, I really didn't mean anything about the hillbilly quip."

"No problem. Thanks for all the information."


"I have to go," Claire mumbles.

"You're not going anywhere right now." Angie attempts a soothing but strict tone.

"Not anywhere. Bathroom." Claire says.

"You want the bedpan?"

"No, bathroom."

"Let me call the nurse." Angie rings the buzzer. No reply. Rings it again. Goes out into the hall, the wide empty after-midnight hall. Forest-green flooring stretches under the fluorescent lights. Looks right, looks left. Looking for a nurse, a nurse's aide, someone. The station is empty.

Back in the room, Claire is leaning over the bed's side bar, looking like she is going to vomit. Angie holds a plastic tub under her face, but Claire shakes her head. Angie's words rush around Claire: "What do you want?" "What do you want?" But Claire, who has wanted so much for so long, who has poured her diluted desires into Angie as if Angie could contain them, is silent now. Until a scream starts at the back of her throat and projects itself out of her mouth, filling the room and then funnelling into the hall. Angie expects a nurse to come rushing in, but the doorway remains hollow. Angie is still watching the door when Claire falls backward, into the bed. Ripping the IV needle out of her arm. Angie almost falls over herself, trying to grab the IV, grab Claire's arm, the doctors' warnings screaming in her head, blending with Claire's screams as the thinned blood streams from Claire's arm. Spurting, almost, like water from a summer fire hydrant in the city.

Then Angie is yelling: "Help!" Pushing the nurse's call button and winding a blanket around Claire's arm. The blood surges out of the tiny hole no longer stopped by the IV needle. Claire twists to cover the place with her other hand, ripping the IV out of the other arm.

When the nurse's aide enters, Angie is holding each of Claire's arms, screaming for help. Blood is splattered on Angie's face, Angie's arms, Angie's hands, and Angie's shirt. Claire is white, white under blots of red.

It takes two nurses, two nurse's aides, and a woman from House-keeping to restore order. The small IV wounds are stanched with gauze, Claire wiped down, the bed linens changed, the floor mopped. Angie tucks Claire in to the white sheets, smooths her hair. Then she goes to the public bathroom in the pink-and-green foyer, near the telephone that has become her lifeline, her own IV. At least she feels competent on the telephone. At least that is something she knows how to do. Angie washes; she is astonished at how much of Claire's blood comes off with simple soap and water. And how much does not.

Back in Claire's room, she crawls into the ugly green armchair that has become her bed. She is still freckled with blood, and her shirt looks as if she has hemorrhaged from the chest. But she falls asleep, listening to Claire sleep the sleep of the bone-tired.

Walking to the car, the red rental car, the morning sun glaring its celebration of summer, Angie looks back at the hospital, back at the window she knows is Claire's room, hoping that if the same thing happens this morning, Luke will be able to handle it. Feeling as if she is still covered in her mother's blood, as if she will never not be covered in her mother's thin blood.


"Mary Heeley?" Angie walks toward the prosecutor as she leaves her office, on her way downstairs to the courtroom.

"If you don't mind, I'm on my way to trial."

"I believe we need to talk."

"You might believe we should, but it's what I believe that's important, don't you agree?"

"Actually, I don't agree." Angie says. "But Margot Young certainly described you accurately."

"I don't know any Margaret Young."

"It's Margot. You might remember that she went to law school with you."

"She was one of many."

"One of the many who know about you and Lizzy Walwyn."

"I don't know what you mean."

"The sexual relationship between the two of you."

"Just because you have bad blood, Ms. Evans, it doesn't mean everyone else does."

"Bad blood? That's a unique way of phrasing it. Is that what your daddy said to you when he found out about your little affair in law school? I assume the family relation is through your mother's side."

"I really don't know what you're talking about. Or what you want." Mary Heeley starts to walk down the hallway. Angie can see a splotch forming on her neck, like a hickey.

"Then let me tell you what I want. I want you to *nol-pros* Chillicothe."

"Drop the charges against Susannah Chillicothe? You've got to be joking."

"I think there are experts who will testify to some congenital problems with the baby. Sudden infant death syndrome can be confused with intentional—"

"May I remind you that you are not Ms. Chillicothe's attorney?"

"If we don't reach some sort of understanding, I will be."

"If you think that Judge Parsons will let Walwyn withdraw, so that we can all be dazzled by some New York lawyer—"

"He will if he thinks the prosecutor and the defense attorney are in bed together. Literally."

"You really do have bad blood. No one would believe that."

Angie watches the splotch sprawl across Mary Heeley's neck. Angie feels an adrenaline tingle in her own fingers.

"No one has to believe it. Not—as you prosecutors have to prove—beyond a reasonable doubt. They only have to suspect it. Really, they only have to gossip about it." Angie waits for the splotch to get bigger, but instead it turns a deeper color, almost purpling. "It would make a very compelling motion to disqualify counsel, both counsel, in this unusual case. Judge Parsons would most likely hold a hearing, it would all be so interesting."

"Judge Parsons would never order a hearing."

"Then some other judge would. On a collateral attack of the conviction for ineffective assistance of counsel. I think it's very difficult for a defense attorney to be effective when she's fucking the prosecutor; seems like a conflict of interest to me. It would be a very interesting hearing. There could be witnesses from your law school days, maybe even some records from the dean's office. And maybe someone could subpoena some travel records; there must be a few trips together. Maybe during Gay Pride month, maybe to the West Coast somewhere? And I think I know an investigative reporter at *The Village Voice* who would just love this story—you know *The Voice,* don't you? She could write a steamy small-town exposé of closeted power dykes trying to railroad a lesbian from the wrong side of the tracks."

"I think I need to remind you that extortion and obstruction of justice are crimes in this state." Mary Heeley's entire neck is magenta.

"So is sodomy." Angie's laugh has become an actual cackle, filling the hallway, following Mary Heeley to the courtroom.

The psychiatrist has a slow voice; the combination of southern breeding and professional training makes every vowel long.

"Dr. Peterman ordered a consultation."

Angie is not surprised. She has learned a great deal by reading the notes in Claire's burgeoning file. She's been expecting him, knowing his name but not what he looks like. She tries to remember each doctor's face.

"I'll have to refuse that," she says. He is tall. And maybe a few years older than Luke, with sophisticated silver hair.

"I don't believe you understand. It might be necessary. Psychiatry might have something to offer her. During an extended hospitalization, patients disorient."

"I realize that. So I'm working on trying to get her out of the hospital."

"We're thinking of institutionalizing her."

"In what type of institution?" Angie wants information, so she postpones her outrage.

"A long-term care facility. Preferably with a psychiatric wing."

"What makes you think she needs long-term care?"

"I know it is difficult when our parents age, but that means we must each make difficult decisions."

"My mother is younger than you are, Doctor. I am not institutionalizing her."

"Should I report to worker's compensation that you have refused my consultation?"

"I cannot decide what you should do, but I am refusing your examination of my mother."

Both Angie and the psychiatrist run their fingers through their respective heads of similarly short hair without giving the impression of being mirror images.

"Ah," he finally says. "You're the New York City medical-malpractice attorney, aren't you?"

"Is there only one?" Angie asks lightly.

"You're a very disarming and charming young lady," the psychiatrist says.

Angie is silent. Her usual retort when called young, or charming, or a lady—"Most dykes are"—remains unsaid. But the psychiatrist does not credit her self-restraint. "Despite," he continues, "your hostility. Although I suppose that one must employ certain aggressive strategies to be a successful big-city attorney? You must have learned a great deal in New York."

"Maybe that's not where I learned to be aggressive." Angie smiles. "Maybe that's where I learned to be so charming."


"Time served." Angie is sitting in the courthouse snack bar with Mary Heeley and Elizabeth Walwyn.

"Just a casual meeting," Elizabeth Walwyn had suggested, but now she is mumbling, "This is ridiculous."

"Don't you think one should drive a hard bargain on behalf of one's client?" Angie says. What she wants to say is "Whose side are you on, anyway?" but she thinks there is no answer, thinks there are no sides, because they are sitting in a circle, crowded at a little table. Because Sunny Chillicothe sits in jail while her former lover is on the other side, testifying against her. While the dead baby is dead. Why isn't it simple anymore? she wants to ask, why isn't it us versus them anymore? Why are all the lesbians on different sides? And why does everyone here remind me of someone else, and even worse, remind me of me? Angie wants to ask, but she is in the courthouse, even if it is only the snack bar, and she has been trained not to ask any question to which she does not know the answer. She did very well in her evidence class during law school.

"I think"—Elizabeth Walwyn is steady—"that one should be—"

"Don't even bother attempting to be rational with this woman," Mary Heeley interjects.

"That's what I was going to say," Elizabeth says. "Rational. Reasonable."

"Different people have different ideas of rationality," Angie says.

"Obviously." Mary Heeley punctuates her statement with a snort.

"Do you want to know what I don't understand?" Elizabeth Walwyn, the defense counsel, glares at Angie. "I don't understand why we are having this conversation. I don't understand why some lawyer from New York is so interested in all of this. And I don't understand why some lesbian lawyer is spending her time blackmailing people she thinks might be lesbian. Do you think you're the only one who can investigate?" Elizabeth turns to Angie. "I checked up on you. You're supposed to be so progressive, so liberal, so *radical*. Do you think threatening to ruin people's lives by exposing their relationship is liberal? It's not."

"It's not my fault that you think such 'exposure' would ruin your lives."

"Of course it isn't. You left here. You cut off your hair and got the hell out of Dodge." Elizabeth's voice does not waver. "Well, some of us have to live here. Some of us have to stay."

Angie looks at Elizabeth Walwyn, public defender, and fights against identifying with her. Tries to distance herself from Elizabeth Walwyn's failure, her failure to become Lizzy, to become someone different. Tries not to see Evangelina in Elizabeth Walwyn's confused face.

"Some of us don't have a trust fund." Angie sips her coffee.

"That's not the point," Mary Heeley interjects. She is very good at refocusing attention on herself, away from her lover.

"It is to me"—Angie looks at Mary Heeley—"and maybe to your girlfriend."

"When are you going to mention that it's a trust fund full of blood money, gotten from the exploitation of those poor unfortunate miners? I'm just waiting until the violins get here," Mary Heeley mocks.

"I don't need violins. I'm not interested in how that money got to be in any trust fund. I'm only interested in how badly you two want to keep it. Time served?"


"Stop all the medications," Angie orders the doctor.

"Does your father agree? He's her next of kin, you know."

"I have a medical power of attorney."

"Signed when?"

"Signed the day I arrived. I'd estimate that you and the other doctors as well as the hospital have obtained six or seven signed consent forms from her since then. So I hardly think you can attack this one."

"I didn't say I thought it should be attacked. I just believe that the cessation of medications would be unwise at this point."

"And I believe she's overmedicated. She's on a million pills a day. Xanax. Coumadin. Demerol. She had morphine yesterday—"

"That was an oversight," he admits, "which caused no problems."

"—iron. Calcium. Magnesium. Stool softeners. Estrogen. Heparin in the IV. One day you put cold packs on her, the next day heat packs. One day it's blood clots, the next day it's her hormones. She's had so many X rays and CAT scans she glows. She came in with a broken leg and now she has dementia."

"She is in serious condition."

"But you don't know what's wrong, do you?"

"It's complicated. I have had to call in many specialists for consultations."

"Why don't you try to explain it to me?"

"There's no precise diagnosis."

"Then I want the medications stopped."

"You'll be responsible."

"I already am." Angie asserts. And walks back into Claire's room.

SEPTEMBER

SEPTEMBER

**SEPTEMBER**

SEPTEMBER

SEPTEMBER

The woods coagulate toward autumn. The colors thicken, redden. September is a scab waiting to be scratched by the first chill. The relief of blood running down the dry flesh of the hills. The river huddles against the Palisades like a dull knife. The valley seems poised to die, or at least be imprisoned for another winter, as Angie drives on the highway in her little car, her not-red not-rental car, carefully on every bridge.

The afternoon is all autumn light. In her house of wood, in the woods. A soft sort of sparkle, as if the sky were water and every surface a clean window. Angie's hand makes a shadow as she writes. With her ink pen, only slightly clogging as she makes notes for her résumé.

Until Rachel and Skye return from the grocery store.

"I just can't believe all this," Rachel is saying. Later, in the kitchen with the last lights already dissipated into the dark trees, the two women sit at the kitchen table with their after-dinner decaf, talking. "Wasn't there a chief assistant in the Public Defender's Office? Or even in the District Attorney's Office?"

"Mary Heeley is the chief assistant," Angie sighs. "Besides, no one was really watching the prosecution. That was the part that amazed me. I mean, the courtroom was empty. And the defense attorney, Walwyn, was getting a damn good deal for her client, so who was going to criticize her? Two years, double credit for time served in the county jail, and good time at two and a half days' credit instead of one and a half is a pretty good deal, don't you think?"

"For murder? I'll say!"

"She pleaded to involuntary manslaughter. It really was, you know. No intent. Just neglect."

"Even the cover-up? Telling the cops the baby was lost," Rachel's bony fingers make quote marks in the air, "or kidnapped," Rachel repeats the gesture, "seems pretty intentional to me."

"It's intent to do the crime that matters. She wasn't charged with being an accessory after the fact."

"Legal technicalities!" Rachel laughs with lawyerly camaraderie, as if she is kidding with a colleague instead of talking with her lover. But as she licks her upper lip, her tongue reaching almost to its nuance of dark down, Angie senses an invitation to retrace the path of Rachel's tongue with her own. They stare at each other for a while.

Rachel breaks the mood: "So, when will she be out?"

"If she doesn't start a riot in jail, she'll be out by Halloween."

"You're really pretty proud of yourself, aren't you?" Rachel smiles.

"I guess I am. Is that so bad?"

"No. No, it's really not. I guess I'm proud of you, too."

"I'm so glad to be home, you don't know."

"I think I do."

"And I'm glad that we're connected again." Angie stares again at the soft shadow of her lover's sultry mustache, wants to touch it, kiss it.

"Too bad you can't take any credit. I mean, you can't even put it on your résumé, can you?"

"What would I say? I don't think I can add this to the list under 'Important Litigation.' 'The procurement of a plea bargain from murder to involuntary manslaughter in the case of a lesbian mother. The unique strategy in this case was the delicately employed threat to reveal the attorneys' sexuality as well as their mutual sexual relationship.'" Angie laughs, but only slightly. "No, I don't think that sounds like attractive professional experience."

"So what will What's-Her-Name—Sunny?—do when she gets out of jail?"

"I've got no idea. Probably go back with her girlfriend."

"The one who testified against her?" Rachel gasps. "I hope you're joking."

"That's what her mother sort of hinted. But I didn't pursue it. I just can't get involved in my clients' personal lives."

"People can be very stupid." Rachel shakes her head.

"Do you really think that some things are absolutely unforgivable?" Angie asks, risking a question when she does not know Rachel's answer.

"Would you go back with your lover if she testified against you in your murder trial?" Rachel answers with her own question.

"If it was you?" Angie volleys back.

"If it was anyone," Rachel says flatly.

"I think"—Angie tries to choose her words carefully—"that there is such a thing as true love. And maybe circumstances twist it. Or maybe the person does not always honor it. Or maybe a person makes mistakes."

"But just answer me this," Rachel asks, "how could she ever trust her again?"

"I have to admit, I don't know. I just don't know."

Rachel seems satisfied with Angie's answer, but still the cup twists in Rachel's hands.

The two women do not look at each other's eyes, each other's faces.

Skye interrupts the long silence: "Wouldn't you love me no matter what I did?"

"Little pitchers." Rachel laughs, startled by Skye's forgotten presence in the room.

"Little pitchers?" Skye asks.

"There's an expression you don't know?" Angie teases. " 'Little pitchers have big ears.' It means we didn't know you were listening."

"But I've been sitting here. Drinking my milk. Just like you said."

"I know. But we were talking adult talk."

"You didn't tell me not to listen." Skye pouts.

"I know. But when you listen to adults' conversations," Angie says, "you should just listen. And not ask questions too much. Maybe later, but not then. Because sometimes adults are talking in a way kids don't really understand."

"But I do understand. I know about trials and testifying and all that stuff. And about these cases when the kids get taken away from their mothers. Or mothers murder their kids. Just shoot them right in the head! Or beat them to death! You talk about it all the time. And I've been to court a million times!" Skye is both bragging and anxious.

"That's true. But you still shouldn't interrupt like that. It's just rude." Angie's voice is even. "But if something does bother you, or you want to know more, you should talk to us. One of us or both of us. And you know, no one is going to take you away. And nothing bad is ever going to happen to you."

"I know that," Skye says matter-of-factly. "Especially if one of my mothers is the person who decides whether kids can stay with their mothers."

"Skye . . ." Rachel scolds.

"B-but," Skye stutters, "but that's the new job you're going to have, isn't it?"

"No, that is *not* the new job I would have. And it's looking more and more like I'm not going to take it. It isn't worth the hassles." Rachel sounds as if she is the one who is pouting now.

"That's not a very good basis for a decision," Angie says.

"Maybe not. Or maybe it no longer sounds as interesting as it once did."

"I think we should talk more about this."

"What's to talk about?"

"We used to talk about everything." Angie reaches for Rachel's hand. "And I don't think we should feel pressured about work by anyone else, even people we love."

"Why not? I mean, isn't it a valid consideration that every time the law guardianship possibility comes up you cringe? And now Skye is talking about it like I'll be deciding which mothers deserve their children."

"Skye, I think it's time for your bath."

"Can I read in the tub?" Skye presses her advantage.

"Yes." Angie says. "But not a library book." She waits for Skye to leave, then looks long at Rachel. "I'm not saying it's not a factor. I'm just saying it's not a real basis to make a decision. You're right, I'm not crazy about it. But I'm trying to be rational. To think this through. I mean, I wouldn't want to base my decision on whether to leave Triple-F and do trial defense on what other people thought."

"Oh, and now I'm 'other people'?"

"No. You know what I mean. I wouldn't have wanted to base my decision about doing some of these murder cases in the first place on the fact that they might make you squeamish."

"You never asked me," Rachel says flatly.

"I guess not." Angie shakes her head.

"You know, you never asked me. Never asked me what I thought. Never explained to me why you were representing dykes who killed their own kids. Never told me what that had to do with Skye."

"Skye? It's got nothing—nothing to do with Skye."

"But think of how she must feel."

"I'm not sure I ever really thought of that."

"Or of me?"

"Sure, I thought of you, Rachel. I mean, I guess I thought you agreed with me, politically and everything. I mean, that every lesbian deserves a defense."

"That's rhetoric, Angie. I'm talking about our lives."

"So am I. It's not just rhetoric to me."

"I know it's not. That's why I'm trying to figure out what it is, what it really is."

"Oh. Like it's some psychological secret? Why can't it be about politics? About how no one seems to notice that men murder children all the time? And how dykes lose their kids all the time? About gender? Sexuality? And oh yes, class. Let's not forget how the poor dykes are the ones who get screwed the most."

"You forgot race," Rachel says, almost sarcastically.

"I did not forget race." Angie replies. "And I don't know why you're being so . . . so . . . Oh, I don't know . . . so negative!"

"Negative?"

"It was the only word I could think of." Angie suddenly laughs.

"It's kind of harsh, don't you think?" Rachel laughs, too.

Skye comes back into the kitchen, as if drawn by her mothers' laughter, to stand between Angie and Rachel, announcing that she is hungry. Somehow managing to sit on both—and neither—of their laps. Angie strokes Skye's wet hair, which seems almost shiny in the glare of the kitchen light.

"Did your mother call you today?" Rachel changes the subject, consciously.

"Yes." Angie is still stroking Skye's hair. "She seems a bit better every day. She's still using the walker to walk, but she can get up and around. She's eating. And she seems happy to be home."

"Happy?"

"Maybe not happy"—Angie half laughs the admission—"but happier than in the hospital. And Luke seems to be taking care of her. So that's pretty good. She has a nurse coming in just a few days starting next week, instead of every day. So it seems like things are getting better."

"And worker's comp is paying for all this?"

"Unbelievably, no problems. She's getting weekly checks, too."

"You must have intimidated the hell out of everyone. I guess you're pretty proud of yourself on that one, too."

"I suppose," Angie allows.

"I just hope your mother appreciates it," Rachel says.

"Me too," Skye agrees enthusiastically. But when Rachel and Angie both look at Skye, the child realizes her transgression. "Oops. Sorry," Skye mumbles. And the two adults stifle their smiles.

"Isn't it time for bed?" Angie finally says.

"What pajamas should I wear?" Skye asks.

"Which ones do you want to wear?" Angie asks.

"Which ones do you like best?" Skye answers, asking.

"Since no one but me"—Rachel stands up—"seems to be able to do anything except ask questions, I'll decide. Skye, put on the pajamas with the blue moons. Get into bed."

"Can I read?" Skye asks.

"What would you like to read?" Angie smirks at Skye. Skye smirks back.

"One book," Rachel declares. "The book you brought home from the school library. Now, get to bed."

Angie is looking at Rachel's back as Rachel stands in front of the closet, taking off her shirt and hanging it up. Angie loves women's backs, or maybe it is only Rachel's back she loves. Has loved Rachel's back since that precise moment in the woods, since that image occupied her mind. Angie wants to think about this, does not want to think about this.

Angie moves toward Rachel, pushing against that smooth back, pushing against the jeans, putting her head on that bare solid back. Nuzzling, like a horse or some sort of animal hoping for a hint or memory. Angie's arms drift around Rachel's ribs, sliding up to the breasts, hands like broken cups separating the soft flesh from the rest of the world. Rachel shifts. An arch of the back. A lean forward into the hands. Nipples dancing.

"We have to talk." The voice is sturdy, strong, sullen.

Angie is surprised, surprised to recognize her own voice erupting from her own body.

Rachel turns around, walks away from the closet, back toward the bed. "I'm not sure I want to."

"Not about work. There are certain . . ." Angie struggles, wishing Rachel would turn back around so Angie could stare at her back instead of having the eyes of Rachel's breasts stare back at Angie. "Certain . . . things . . . things we should talk about."

"I think I already know more . . . *things* . . . than I want to." Rachel's tone is measured.

"I thought so. So, I think maybe we should talk about . . . about those things. About it, it's nothing, really. Sort of clear the air."

"Why? So you can feel better?" Rachel pulls on her nightshirt, covering both sets of accusing eyes for a moment. "So you can make excuses? So you can confess? Maybe I'm not interested."

"I—"

"I'm not interested." Rachel puts up her hand as if to stop traffic.

"Not interested?"

"That's right. Not interested in what you have to say about things. Things I might have heard." Rachel's voice rises in pitch. "I don't want lies and I don't think I want the truth."

"What do you want?" Angie whispers.

"I want a life. I want to be a good mother to Skye and I want her to have another parent, another mother. I want a lover, a good lover. Someone who understands I have a life, a damn job too." Rachel is hoarse, but not crying.

"I want to be that lover, Rachel. I really do."

"Someone who doesn't run away. Into work or . . . or wherever."

"I want that, too. I do."

"Maybe. Maybe. But I really don't think you know what you want."

"Maybe I don't, don't know what I want. But I know I want you. You and Skye."

"Well, then, start acting like it, goddamm it."

"I intend to. I—"

"How?" Rachel challenges.

"I'm not sure."

"Well, you'd better figure it out pretty fast. You can't lapse into that comfortable emotional state of being a child."

"A child?" Angie struggles to keep talking, to keep listening.

"What book did you say I could read?" Skye yells from her bedroom.

"Any one you want," Rachel calls back, climbing into bed, centered in her own side of the bed, leaving Angie room to come closer, or not.


It is blue and thick and plastic, with white lettering: SAVE OUR VALLEY. Such a simple command, brimming with its implicit and smug promise: Just place newspapers in this bin instead of in the garbage, and the entire river and valley will be safe, safe from pollution, from radioactive waste, from guilt. It is a promise in which Skye believes. She would no more throw a newspaper in the garbage can than she would murder her mothers. At Meadowlark School, the children have a class in "environmental awareness."

"Get that bin," Angie tells Skye. Angie always remembers the bin as green, is always slightly surprised when Skye brings it from the garage and it is still blue. And today, as on every Saturday that she and Sky fill the bin, Angie thinks the plastic should be green. And, just as she does every time she fills the bin, she thinks that she always thinks the bin should be green, and she wonders why she has to think this again and again and again. Even as she is comforted by her own predictability, she chafes.

"Have you started studying repeating decimals yet?" Angie asks Skye, who is carrying the bin.

"No, what are those?"

"Never mind. Put the bin near the door."

Today, as on every Saturday, as she does every time Angie and Skye do the newspaper recycling, Skye puts the bin in the middle of the floor. Not near the door. And today, as on every Saturday, as she does every time Angie and Skye do the recycling, Angie says, "I said, Near the door. Not,"—Angie pauses—"in the middle of the wooden floor."

But today something is different. Not what Angie says or what Skye does or even that the bin has become green instead of blue. What is different is that Angie is filling the bin with catalogs instead of newspapers. She pulls them from wooden shelves and wicker baskets and under the bed and in the bathroom. She stacks them in the bin, neatly tying them with string, resisting the temptation to leaf through *Approaching Spring* or *Summer's Best* or *Homes for the Holidays* or *Colors of Autumn.*

"Do you think the truck will take these?" Skye asks.

"They'd better," Angie answers.

Not so easily disposed of is Angie's residual belief that the right shower curtain would be an accomplishment. Not too expensive, not too simple. Yet not cheap or elaborate. Some sheet of material that will never mold, never tear at the hook holes, never look dirty or boring.

Maybe a rug. A new rug for her office. A tangible demonstration of change. Like that rug she saw in the catalog, months ago, thought about ordering even as she put the catalog in the bin this morning. But, as it was with Kim, it is not as if Angie articulates a desire and then searches for satisfaction. She did not know she wanted a rug before the seduction, before the description: "rich saturated color of ink blue"; "hand-woven coir made from the outer fibers of coconut husks, soaked in water, then woven into cords and hand loomed"; "tactile, tough-wearing and soil-resistant." And on sale. In that catalog. One of the catalogs in the green—or blue—bin now outside.

She could go outside, get the bin, search for the catalog. But the pages, she thinks, are not enough this Saturday. She wants to feel. Sand-washed silk. Weathered leather. Denim subjected to acid and stone. Distressed wood. Hand-painted porcelain.

She does not go to Fifth Avenue. Or to the Village. Or even to Fourteenth Street. She collects Rachel and Skye and drives deep into the highways of suburban New Jersey. A mall. Or more precisely, a mall annex, where discount stores preside over huge parking lots.

The heavy doors open with promises.

"Remember where we came in," Angie commands.

"Near the 'Celebrate the Sales' sign," Skye announces.

"No, something more distinctive. Those signs will be all over."

"How about the mannequins without any heads," Rachel suggests.

"Rachelllll . . ." Skye elongates her sigh. She has been practicing expressions of exasperation with her parents. Saying their names with operatic breaths.

"Okay." Rachel laughs. "By the socks."

"The socks," Skye repeats and repeats, half serious with the task of memorization necessary to prevent hours of circling dark parking lots until the last car is left.

Angie inhales the reassuring smells of department-store circulated air. Tinged with perfumes from labyrinths staffed by white women with white hair and white coats, ready to make over any woman who approaches the shimmering counters less than resolutely. They navigate through the cosmetics, avoiding the young women dressed like gypsies who give away samples from wicker baskets tied with rags. From department to department, from store to store the trio parade, checking prices, styles, colors. Touching metals, materials. Judging patterns. Looking for sales, markdowns.

In her head instead of her Book, there is a list of what she wants. A rug for her office. An outfit for an interview, just in case. And clothes for Skye, and maybe one of those closet organizers so that her clothes do not slip off the hangers and collect on the floor. A briefcase for Rachel, tanned leather. Cereal bowls that will not crack the first time one is dropped, but that are not plastic.

The credit cards nestle in Angie's Book. Encased in plastic protectors, three per sheet of six-hole punched sheets. Security. Two Visa. One American Express. A few department stores, including Sears, the only card Claire has. Maybe she will buy a present for Claire. Something blue or green. Something new and beautiful. Something.


It is not true that Angie is always reading in *The Times* or *The Voice*— or always hearing on her car radio—about some lesbian losing her kids in a custody battle with her husband or mother. And it is not true that

Angie is always reading or hearing about some mother who has murdered her children, without mention of the word *lesbian* but it hangs between the lines or in the breathy silences. Of course it is not true; only seems that way. Only seems as if what she has been doing for years is suddenly newsworthy, and more real because it is newsworthy.

Her Voicemail messages are from people she does not know. Some reporter wants a quote. Some law student somewhere in some state like Idaho or Iowa wants to talk to her about coming to speak to some local group. Some professor in some province in Canada wants to ask her some questions for some law review article she is writing. Some attorney wants a reference list. Some mother wants assistance on her case and then some other mother wants to talk about her case.

"All hell broke loose while you were gone," Walter complains. "I've felt like a clearinghouse."

"Thanks for taking care of everything. I . . . I bought you something."

"You did? From there?"

"No. I never went anyplace other than the hospital or the courthouse while I was away. But I just saw this coffee mug shopping the other night and I thought you might like it."

"Thanks. I won't tell anyone that you're so sweet." Walter does not laugh. "Especially if you become litigation director."

"Oh, that's all off." Angie sighs.

"That's not what I heard. I heard you're back at the top of the list."

"Don't tell me *you* took Kim up on her offer?"

"Which one?"

"The one on that last postcard. Saying that we should meet for coffee—espresso, I think—and talk things over. Hinting that if I leave Rachel she'll drop the charges against me. And the two of us—she and I, that is—can live happily ever after."

"Oh. *That* postcard. The one with the creepy Lolita. I hope you put it in a Ziploc bag to save as evidence in your sexual-harassment trial," Walter teases.

"I suppose," Angie says noncommittally, thinking of the postcard in her desk drawer. Its relentless ability to unsettle her. Not just Kim's words, their adolescent desperation, the little hearts instead of dots in "Kim," and in "happily." But the image, the photograph, the girl. The child with long curly hair and mascaraed lashes, with naked shoulders and a sensuously serious mouth, looking part Shirley Temple doll and part prostitute. An adult's vision of innocence, off-center against the black background. Angie keeps putting the postcard away, but she still sees herself at Skye's age, in the photograph that is still on Claire's wall. Angie keeps taking the postcard out of her desk drawer, hating the model, hating the photographer, hating the girl's mother for allowing whatever is being allowed. Her reaction is more visceral than she usually allows herself; she struggles to suppress it in the presence of Walter.

"But wait until you hear this. I got all the scoop from an attorneys' meeting last week." Walter's voice is a stage whisper.

"You're going to the attorneys' meetings?"

"Of course not! I'm just a lowly paralegal, remember? But I do have my sources. Anyway, it was suggested that you apologize to the board of directors for your little indiscretion with that little Jodie Foster clone, the vampire intern—"

"Apologize? To the board of directors? Only two people deserve an apology. And they're not on the board of directors."

"Two?" Walter asks. "Well, let's see. One has got to be that sultry, simmering beauty at home. Even I am not going to try to find out what's happened there. I'm better off not knowing *some* things."

"That's what *she* said," Angie admits. "It's funny. I thought I was the one who practiced denial."

"Hey, we all do. Though most of us just indulge occasionally, to keep our sanity. With you, it's high art, or an addiction. But I want to know who gets apology number two. Not me, I hope."

"The kid," Angie declares, as if it is obvious.

"Well, sure. But isn't she a little too young to realize all the ramifications when things like that happen?"

"That's the point."

"Well, if you want my advice—which you're going to get anyway—just don't try to apologize. I mean, you'll just confuse the kid. And she's just too young to know she's better off not knowing." Walter laughs at his own observation. "And knowing Skye, she'll ask a bunch of questions."

"Skye? I'm not talking about Skye. I'm talking about Kim."

"That bitch?" Walter is incredulous.

"She's just a kid."

"She's probably the same age as me."

"Probably," Angie admits. "But we all have our ambitions."

"And you were her ambition?" Walter puts his hand on his hip.

"Only part of it."

"That's ridiculous." Walter is definite, defiant almost.

"How quickly they forget." Angie is condescending, but also angry. "Don't you remember wanting to be something other than the lackey receptionist? I know you know that bloody taste of ambition, of wanting to be something more. A paralegal, sure. But then there's your classes on Foucault, so that you can have your pretentious discussions with Roger. So you can't really blame someone for trying to get what they want."

"I can," Walter proclaims. "And I can blame them for what they want. I mean, why can't she want to do well in school, or something?"

"She wanted that, too."

"Not enough to work hard."

"Well, I'm not sure about that."

"Well, I am." Walter shakes his head in disgust.

"Whatever. I shouldn't have exploited her ambitions."

"What ambitions? The girl has no ambitions. She's just a rich little daddy's girl looking for a sugar mama. And would you please stop comparing me to her? Don't insult me. I didn't try to fuck you—or Coleman—to get what I wanted." Walter is self-righteous. "And I really don't see why you're so hell-bent on defending some little rich bitch. She really doesn't fit your underdog pattern, does she?"

Angie shakes her head. Their anger dissipates into the silence.

"Sorry, Angie," Walter apologizes. "It's just that I never could figure out why you even gave her the time of day, let alone got involved as much as you did."

"I guess I can't figure it out myself," Angie admits.

"Well, don't spend too much energy on it. Just stop thinking she's like you were. She's not. And the whole thing is just water under the bridge, as they say. Just forget her, and her twisted ambitions. Let's talk about your ambitions. I'm still hoping they include litigation director."

"I don't know."

"Well, let me just tell you that no one really wants you to apologize. It's just a matter of thinking about Triple-F's public image. You know, is the future for families going to be run by dykes?"

"I'm not sure I want the job." Angie looks at the ceiling.

"People will get over the dyke thing, Angie."

"No, it's not really that. And I don't know how I could take it when they won't even consider Ellen. I'm sure she'd be better at it than me."

"Maybe you two could do it together. Like co–litigation directors? Each keep your own caseloads?"

"That's actually a good suggestion. But I'm not sure I want to run an organization, including this one. Hell, I'm not even sure I want to be in this organization."

"You're burnt out." Walter shakes his head sympathetically.

"Maybe. Or maybe I'm bored. Just bored with the meetings and with acting like an expert. Maybe I'll enter the fray again, go back to being a trial attorney. You know, I think that's what I want. What I've missed. Maybe I just want to get back and fight the way I know how, instead of all these committees and conference calls. I think I do my best work when all the odds are against me."

"That," Walter declares, "is absolutely crazy."

"What's crazy?" Roger interrupts, pushing through the doorway. He looks larger to Angie.

"Speak of the devil." Walter laughs.

"You were talking about me?" Roger asks.

"No, just about someone crazy."

"Oh, I'm so glad you're back, Angie. I've missed your supportive sisterhood," Roger says sarcastically. "Who would have ever thought you'd pull a Foucault?"

"Resisting the system from within?"

"No, spending August with your mother." Roger slaps his thigh.

"Could you call Octavia? I think I'd rather talk to her."

"Alas, Octavia is no more."

"Oh, shit."

"Yes. I've exiled my woman within. Given her back to the mothers who put her within me. She was just a phase."

"That's what they say about being a dyke." Angie snickers.

"Oh, Angie. I can only hope you'll be able to understand. I've got to connect to my wild man. He's the one who's been denied to me, to all modern men."

"You mean you've decided you're queer?" Angie teases.

Walter winces.

"Not every same-sex connection is sexual, Ange."

"Why not?" Angie feigns surprise.

"It's male energy. Male bonding. Men are being denied each other."

"It sounds sad."

"Of course, we can't expect your sympathy. Women, however well-intentioned, just cannot understand our pain. Yes, you have suffered as well by being a woman. But trying to subdue us, to stifle our masculinity, to deny us our wild man, has caused us great harm. As little boys, our mothers terrorize us."

"It's always the mother's fault?"

"In a conspiracy with other women. Mothers refuse to nurture the possibilities of wild man. If only I'd had another mother."

"Roger, everybody in the world thinks that."

"But for men, Angie. For men, the consequences have been devastating."

"Roger, are you saying you're pussy-whipped?"

"You are so crude."

"And cruel." Angie laughs.


"You're home early," Rachel announces, but she seems pleased.

"It's my new leaf." Angie winks, putting her briefcase on the chair.

"We have to collect leafs for school," Skye says, stirring the tomato sauce.

"That's *leaves*. V. You do? Again this year?"

"It's very popular," Skye explains. "But we're doing a whole motif on this valley."

"Motif?"

"Yes." Skye sounds exasperated. "Like theme."

"Turn over a new leaf. That's another expression for your class collection."

"That was last year." Skye attempts to sound even more exasperated. "I don't need any more expressions."

"Oh. What's after the leaves?"

"I think agriculture. You know, like growing things, like our garden."

"We do have a few tomatoes left. You should bring them in before they freeze."

"The early settlers, the white ones from Europe, they thought tomatoes were poison," Skye says authoritatively.

"Then how did they have pasta?" Angie asks.

Skye considers this a moment before she answers. "They probably preferred a cream sauce."

"Go get the tomatoes, will you?" Angie points outside. Turning to kiss Rachel. "How did she get to be such a precocious child?"

"She's always been this way. You've just been too busy . . . with *things* . . . to notice."

"Ouch," Angie tries to joke, tries to finish the kiss.


"Turn over," Angie whispers. "Let me hold you."

"I am turned over."

"A little more? Just a little?"

"I don't know if I'm ready for this," Rachel says.

"I just want to hold you."

"Is it always what you want that matters?"

Angie does not answer.

Rachel does not speak.

The bed stiffens with their silence. The night is long, long. Finally, they sleep the sleep of habit, deep and dark, rolling to the crevice in the middle of their bed, to each other. And when they wake up, they are holding each other, shaped together by some law of nature that regulates their bodies at rest.

Their sex then, in that morning, is simple, soft. Perhaps not as passionate as it could be, given the tense interlude, given the lapses of attention, given the way Rachel starts to stroke Angie's night-spiked hair. Perhaps not enough to compensate for everything that has happened, and everything that has not. But perhaps enough to start.

*    *    *

Begin again. Turn time backward and inside out and rearrange the grids that navigate their lives. The light in the woods when Rachel took off her shirt, turning her back to Angie. Turn back, turn back. But not too far back.

It is a slow slide to a complicated night. And then another. Sex is no longer simple, no longer soft. Passion overwhelms, is overwhelmed. Bit breast, scratched ass. Whispers inside/outside heads.

"Tell me you're a whore."

"I'm a whore."

"Tell me you're a dyke."

"I'm a dyke."

"Whose dyke?"

"Yours."

"And who else's?"

"No one's."

"Are you sure?"

"I'm sure."

"Tell me what you want."

"Fuck me."

"And what else?"

"To fuck you."

"How?"

"To hurt you."

"Like you did before?"

"Yes."

"You want to hurt me?"

"No. Yes."

"Fuck me."

"Hurt me. Don't hurt me."

Then no words. Only sounds. Then no sound, just sensation. Something like water running from Angie's cunt. Maybe blood, maybe piss. Her thighs are soaked. She does not even care if the one-hundred-percent-Supima-cotton-sheets are ruined.


Angie is in a meeting with Chelsea and Roger and Terry, discussing possible futures for Futures for Families, half listening to Roger paraphrase Foucault's theories of resistance yet again. Chelsea keeps catching Angie's gaze, as if to prompt Angie to quell Roger. But Angie remains silent, even when Roger veers toward the salacious rumors regarding Foucault's sexual practices. Chelsea notices—and she is not the only one who does—Angie's recent reticence in Roger's company. Some people attribute it to Roger's rejuvenated masculinity; others to Angie's possible promotion. A few others know or guess: Angie is simply embarrassed. Irrevocably embarrassed.

Embarrassed that Roger was the one who Coleman appointed to do the internal investigation of Kim's complaint. Embarrassed that Roger "interviewed" Kim over an expensive dinner at an Italian restaurant, complete with a bottle of Beaujolais, and said who-knows-what. Embarrassed that Roger conveyed Kim's offer to drop her complaints, including the one filed with the city, in exchange for the postcards Kim had sent. Embarrassed that Roger had possessed that Ziploc bag of postcards; had probably peered through the plastic at Kim's signature with its casual heart; had possibly read Kim's protestations of love.

And embarrassed most of all that Roger had asked her "Why?"— that question which a good attorney never asks on cross-examination— and that she had not made a courtroom joke out of it, objecting to the question as irrelevant. Embarrassed that she had answered, and answered truthfully: "Just repeating old patterns I thought I had escaped."

Embarrassed because Roger had nodded knowingly. Although what Roger thought he knew was that the patterns had been fashioned by Angie. And what Angie knew, finally, was that the patterns were older and more intimate than that.

The only shred of self-respect Angie feels as if she retained was that she did not tell Roger about Claire. At least she did not do that. She may have cried. She may have thanked him, genuinely grateful. She may have let him closer to her than she ever intended, but at least she did not tell him about Claire.

Still, sitting next to him, she is contrite. It is as if she had had sex with Roger, instead of with Kim. It is as if Rachel had been right, after all.

Chelsea, having giving up hope that Angie will take control, is attempting to focus the conversation on Triple-F rather than Foucault.

Roger resists. Terry gets up for another cup of coffee, and when he sits back down Angie spots Walter at the door, motioning her to come outside the conference room.

"You've got a collect call through the main number. From Sharon Delsarado."

"Tell her I'll call her back," Angie says, not really wanting to be screamed at by another former client, another case in which she gets all the blame although she did not do the trial, only the appeals. Angie still shudders when she thinks about that North—or South?—Dakota Supreme Court opinion.

"You won't be able to. She says she's just been arrested. She's calling you. I guess you're her one phone call."

Angie runs to the nearest phone, in Roger's office, Walter following.

"Sharon?"

"Yes. I need a lawyer. I'm in trouble."

"Have you been charged?"

"Yes. Murder. I—"

"Murder? Okay. Don't say another word. Don't talk to anyone. Don't talk to any cop, any prisoner, *anyone*. Do you hear me?"

"Yes. But—"

"No. Listen to me, Sharon. This is very important. Don't talk to anyone. Don't say a word about whatever might have happened or what you think might have happened. Not one word."

"What should I do?"

"Just keep quiet. Let me find out the charges. And then we'll talk about who should represent you."

"I want a woman," Sharon says.

"We'll find someone. Just remember: Don't say a word."

"Can't you come? What about you?"

"You need someone right away. To do the arraignment. I'll find someone. Meanwhile, I'll talk to the public defender's office. Just remember, don't say anything. Do not say one thing."

"I won't," Sharon Delsarado says, sobbing.

"Promise me."

"Promise?"

"Yes. If you want me to help you, to defend you, you have to promise not to discuss the charges. The only thing you can say to any-one is 'Not guilty.' Understand?"

"Okay."

Angie looks at the phone after she hangs it up.

"I heard you say murder. Did she kill her kids?" Walter looks slightly pale.

"I don't know who the victim is."

"I hope it's the husband," Walter says. "I just hope it's the husband."

"Me too," Angie says, doubtfully. "But it doesn't matter who it is." She starts walking to her office to get Delsarado's old file. "I'm going to do that trial. All I need is local counsel to back me up and I can do that trial." Angie is talking to herself out loud now, "Damn it, I'm going to go to South Dakota and do that trial!"

"It's North Dakota," Walter says, following her.

"Wherever." Angie is dismissive.

"You have to know where you're going before you get there."

"No, I don't really have to know what a bunch of idiots decided to put on a map, in between all those little lines."

"That's very Dylanesque."

"What?"

"You know, 'You don't need a weatherman . . .' I figured you'd be a Bob Dylan aficionado. You seem like the rock poet type. Probably even had long hair."

"Actually, I preferred the Stones."

"Really? Aren't they a bit sexist and violent?"

"I guess," Angie says defensively, suppressing thoughts of Rachel. "But they did some great ballads, you know."

"Name two," Walter challenges.

"Well, let's see . . ."

"Can't think even of one, can you?"

"There's 'Angie,' " Angie says, slightly embarrassed.

"Never heard of it." Walter shakes his head, as if Angie is teasing him.

"It was popular once. Maybe before you were born?" Angie re-gains her composure. "Anyway, I'll agree with you and Dylan on this one. Don't need a mapmaker to know where something is."

"It helps if you're going to make plane reservations," Walter explains.

"I was going to ask *you* to call the travel agent," Angie says, and almost does not laugh.

Walter shakes his head.

"I was even going to ask you to come out there with me, be support during the trial."

Walter looks at Angie, amazed and trying not to be flattered.

OCTOBERS

OCTOBERS

**OCTOBERS**

OCTOBERS

OCTOBERS

Maybe she should stop resisting. The possibility of a car phone seems attractive at this moment, sitting in traffic trying to get off one bridge and onto the highways that will take her to another bridge, over the river and into the valley and home. She could return business calls; she could call home to say she is on her way. As it is, she has opened her Book and placed it on the passenger seat, looking at the Voicemail messages noted in her own rebellious handwriting on the white paper with its thwarted blue-lined grids. Looking at the list of potential local counsel for Sharon Delsarado, a list with too many names crossed off. Turning the pages to the official calendars. Looking at the month of October, which has too many days and too few, which has Columbus Day and Halloween and two full moons. Turning the pages to the back cover, its slit stuffed with Kim's last postcard, a letter from Sunny Chillicothe, a prescription to fill for Claire, a crumpled yellow credit card receipt from flowers sent to Cheryl Martin's funeral, the program from Skye's Summer Solstice play, and a piece of blue paper with the dimensions of a photograph she wants to frame for Rachel.

Bored with her Book and tucked between two trucks, her vision blocked forward and backward, Angie is looking at the driver in the next car, who is looking at a catalog, propped on top of a newspaper folded expertly over the steering wheel. Listening to the radio, pushing buttons for fragments of news and weather together on the hour, golden oldies and modern rock, a long interview with the rumored-to-be-lesbian author of a book Angie would read if she had the time, and always the commercials, advertisements for things she does not want and a few things that she does. Smelling the gasoline, seeping in through her car's smudged metal and fiberglass, mixed with the damp air and molecules of fallen leaves and some particles of mold from a relic of a refrigerator someone discarded on the highway. Motionless. Then a little movement forward. Then her foot on the clutch again, feeling numb. The cars from the left lane edge to the right and the cars from the right lane edge to the left. The cars in the middle lane diverge on both sides. Angie, as is her habit, remains in the slow lane, almost patient, between the two trucks.

What Ellen and some of her other co-workers with long commutes call the Zen of traffic has its own miracles. Like a river suddenly undammed or a clot abruptly dissolved, the cars begin to flow. Wild with gratitude, drivers speed to compensate for lost time.

Angie does not speed, but she does turn up the volume on the radio, hoping for some driving music. She wants something predictable and safe, but brisk. She wants some postmodern rock, searing music with words that have not become the clichés of a generation, perhaps several generations; some music without words. She is relegated to listening to some old song she recognizes and then another, in a rock block of songs that no longer make her cry. She even sings her own name loud; her imperfect tonalities ricochet in the little car, absorbed by Mick Jagger's redigitalized voice. "Ain't it good to be alive?" She estimates she will be home in another half hour. One more bridge and then a few exists and then Rachel and Skye.

Almost the bridge. The ramp is concrete.

Suspended over water. The bridge barriers are steel.

Her foot. The brake—or is it the clutch?

Her first thought is an earthquake; the geographies of east and west coasts conflate.

Her best thoughts are ambitious, as her best thoughts have always been. Small ambitions, things to list in her Book, things that could be accomplished and crossed off with satisfaction: Find co-counsel; call the travel agent; write a recommendation letter for Walter; call Roger about the litigation director search; call Sunny Chillicothe's mother; read the appellate brief in that new case from Oklahoma or Idaho; make pumpkin bread with Skye; take Rachel out to a fabulous dinner, just the two of them. But bigger ambitions also, the ones that surface rarely and never become part of any list of things to do: Love more, and love less.

Work harder, and work less. Free the lesbians; free the children; free the mothers; save the world.

Her last thought is of Claire. How angry she will be that Angie's mouth is filling with some slightly salty liquid, distending with blood and water.

■ ■ ■ ■ ■ ■ ■

"Are you dead?" Evangelina heard her mother ask. Evangelina did not answer, but stayed motionless in her huddle at the bottom of the stairs. Evangelina did not know if she could move her mouth to answer—even if she wanted to—because her lips felt bigger than her whole head and her teeth felt like they were growing in her throat. Maybe her hair could answer, her hair still in her mother's hands, maybe there still, when her mother had pushed Evangelina down, down the stairs almost out into the alley that smelled of men's piss. Maybe her doll could answer, the one she had clutched to her as if it were a baby and she was its mother—or maybe it was the mother and she was the baby—but now it poked its plastic fingers into her face. But Evangelina did not hear any answer, not from her hair and not from the doll and not from her own voice; she only heard her mother's voice, again and again, calling "Evangelina, Evangelina."

She knew she should answer her mother, knew she would get in trouble if she did not answer. But she did not know if she wanted to answer, wanted to say anything ever again, anything to her mother or to anyone else, especially to anyone who had heard her mother screaming those things at her, those words *dyke* and *whore*—what did they mean?—or to anyone who had heard her screaming for help and had not answered. Had not answered her.

■ ■ ■ ■ ■ ■ ■

"Angie," she said in answer to the woman's question. But the name still felt strange in her own mouth, as strange as sucking the cigarette that the woman gave her, as strange as sharing a joint and then blowing the smoke into each other's mouth, accommodating a kiss.

Angie kissed with her eyes open. Inspected the woman's apartment, its shower in the living room without a shower curtain, only a moldy hose running from a faucet. There were no sheets on the bed; there was no bed, only a mat on the concrete floor. There were no books in this room; no light through the bricked windows.

"Close your eyes," the woman said.

"You kiss like a dream. A bad dream," the woman slurred.

And then the woman wanted more than kisses. And maybe Angie wanted more too, but she did not know how to say what she wanted, did not even know how to think it.

But Angie never thought it was this: the woman and the cigarette and skin curling around red ash tip. Angie's flesh; the woman's cigarette. Angie's ass; the woman's laugh. Angie's thigh; the woman's tongue licking the singed circles.

Angie knew in this moment that she did not know what she wanted, but that it could not be this.

That there must be more than this, some way to feel wanted in the world other than being pain at the end of someone else's pain, some way to have some beauty, some way to work herself out of these shallow but persistent strip mines.

⁜ ⁜ ⁜ ⁜ ⁜ ⁜ ⁜

Her face pressed into the linoleum floor of the law review office, Angie felt herself get up and walk out and leave her body, that cave of hunger and exhaustion, stretched out for the woman who was her lover and was not her lover to find. Panic was calmed, the emergency vehicles called, the smelling salts stuffed up the nostrils, the body lifted into the ambulance, removed from the campus. Transported to the hospital, made to sign forms and authorizations; student insurance checked and rechecked; and then strapped into a bed. And then punctured with fluids, green and salty.

Discussion at the law school swirled in predictable patterns. Explanations: drugs, or maybe stress, attributed to her success in law school or her failure in some secret and "unconventional" love. Envy vanquished or envy redeemed: hugging the knowledge that number one in her class and editor of law review was not invulnerable. Speculations: She would take an academic leave; she would quit forever; she would come back and act as if nothing had happened.

And although many students and a few faculty members expressed concern and took up a collection for a cliché of flowers, only Mr. Frame, the law school bursar, wanted the best for Angie and knew that she should have it. Knew that she would have it. Bet his one good leg on it. Took the dean out to lunch to discuss Angie. Telephoned the physician, telephoned the hospital administration, telephoned the insurance company. Impersonated her father, made official inquiries on behalf of the school, even said he was her lawyer. And maybe even prayed, for good measure.

In the hospital, Angie came back, as if from a great distance, as if she had been away for days or weeks or some time that made no sense on a calendar from some place that was not on any map. And somehow it seemed safe again to want what she wanted and to want it with such overwhelming power.

Some strange power transfixed Angie while she was driving on the highway, more exhausted than she had ever been. Driving home to Rachel, with their baby in the car. Their baby, this baby. Suddenly, as if there was a great fissure in the terrain of time, her life sharply divided between the time before the baby and the time after.

Before the baby, Rachel had a smile only for Angie; they had laughed and made love whenever they wanted. Before the baby they talked about whether class politics were viable; now they talked about baby shit and maybe what color it was. Before the baby, Angie could work until midnight and sleep until court; now the baby cried at whatever time the baby wanted to cry.

And other things had changed. For one thing, no one thought

Angie was a dyke anymore, as if she had proven she was not, could not be, just because she had a maroon-and-pink diaper bag hanging off one shoulder balanced by a wet-faced teething creature on her hip. And for another thing, people were always touching her now, touching her baby and touching her body. And telling her what to do, ugly strangers telling her she should have more clothes on her baby, or less. And treating her like she was no longer a lawyer, just a mother, just a know-nothing mother.

How had this happened? Although she could retrace her steps, could explain how she had this child, this baby only several months old, this thing that could not walk or talk or desire anything but her, she did not know how it had happened. The baby, breathy in the car seat next to her, had stolen all the power Angie had worked so hard to acquire. This baby had changed Angie's life, perhaps irrevocably.

Or maybe not irrevocably. There was still one power that Angie had; she could forget the baby. Pretend none of it had ever happened. Leave the baby by the side of the highway or under a bridge or at the door of a hospital emergency room. Tell Rachel she did not know what had happened, how whatever had happened had happened. Tell her a strange woman who looked a lot like the baby's real mother would have looked came with a gun and told her she'd shoot the baby in the head if she did not give her the baby, so of course, she gave the baby to this woman. She would tell Rachel that. And maybe the police, if they investigated. And then she would say she was too traumatized to ever talk about it again.

And maybe no one would ever know.

But before she knew it, she was home.

❊ ❊ ❊ ❊ ❊ ❊ ❊

"Come back. Come back."

"Just talk to her. That's fine. You think they can't hear you when they're like this, but she can hear you." The nurse, a dyke, says to another dyke, as they flank another dyke's body. There are tubes down a throat. There are uniforms. There are hands clenched into fists, opening with great difficulty, smoothing down damp spikes of hair.

In the waiting room, there is a map of the county, including the river, including the bridge. An emergency worker points to it, tracing something blue with her finger, tracing something black. The police officer makes a red mark with a pencil.

In the waiting room, there are two clocks, on opposite walls. Round as two moons, white and scarred with symbols. People in the waiting room watch the clocks for clues. As if the long black lines can be dialed to the future. Or dialed back, past the past.

In the waiting room, there is a child, not crying. Her hair is wild. She sits close to friends of her mothers, who are sipping coffee. "I could use a fucking drink," one of them says.

"A crisis is no excuse," the other repeats rotely.

There are explanations and fragments of conversations. A tractor-trailer. The bridge. The guardrail must have been inadequately repaired. The same place that truck skidded off during the summer. The woman driving the tractor-trailer, the one who looks like a dyke, is going to survive. The other one? The one in that little car in front of the truck? The one that also looks like she might be a dyke? What's the name? With that short, short hair? No one wants to say.

■ ■ ■ ■ ■ ■ ■

Roger will say, "And she was always such careful driver. Ange was too careful, if you ask me."

"Fuck you, Rog," Walter will say.

■ ■ ■ ■ ■ ■ ■

Claire will say, "My Evangelina. My Evangelina. My little girl. My Evangelina. A mother gives her whole life, for something like this to happen?" Claire's words will be barely intelligible, compressed by the weight of her screams which will continue until her mouth is parched.

There are times when there is nothing to say.

Not the way the leaves turn to blood and dive deep into the mud, not the way the bare branches lash bare skin, not the first buds that terrorize with their vulnerability or the last leaves that shatter their promises of immortality.

Nothing to say. Not even the names of the lovers who guard this place, this place that is always full and green, always barren and flat, always a memory and a future. This exploited site, this strip mine, this empty river. The place that she could never name, the place she could never survive. The place where women comb their hair and cut it off and scratch beautiful incisions into each other's scalps.

She has said this place is sex. Has called this place Claire. Has called this place Rachel, Skye. Has called this place mother, work, daughter.

She has said this place is a time. A time in her life. Her life.

Has hated it so much.

Has tried to love.

In the Emergency Room, the nurse is professional. She has entries to make for her chart.

"Do you know what day it is?" The nurse bends close to the body, looks at her watch. "What month?"

Silence.

*Not oriented as to time.*

"Do you know where you are, dear?"

Silence.

*Not oriented as to place.*

Rachel is whispering, leaning into her lover. "What do you want, baby. Just talk to me baby, please. Please. You want to say something?"

Angie's mouth seems to move.

"What is it? What do you want?" Rachel's tone suddenly coveys an odd rationality. It is as if she expects Angie to sit up and request a glass of water. Or perhaps a Coke.

"Just tell me what you want."

．．．．．．．

Evangelina wanted so much. And wanted it more than anything. And worked so hard, against all those impossible odds, to get it. And when she got it, she still worked hard, as if she could give it to other people. Or at least give other people a chance to get what they wanted, more than anything.

Angie still wants so much. But more than anything, she still wants it. The "it" she has never been able to name. That "it" others call love. Not love as redemption from the past or love as protection from the future. But love as incessantly present.

．．．．．．．

When the first coughs shudder across Angie's chest, Rachel grabs one of her lover's hands and someone else grabs the other, both of them staring into Angie's face as she opens her eyes, sees two lesbian angels, and wonders if she is alive.

"Baby." Rachel cries.

"Do you know where you are?" the nurse asks.

Angie just stares.

*Not oriented as to place.*

"You're in the hospital," Rachel whispers. "You're going to be fine."

Angie just stares, unblinking. Not squeezing Rachel's hand back when Rachel squeezes.

"Do you know what happened? What day it is?" the nurse intrudes.

Angie closes her eyes.

*Not oriented as to time.*

"It's October, baby," Rachel bends her head close to Angie's body, blocking the nurse. "You were on your way home from work. It's going to be okay."

· · · · · · ·

Skye will be in the tropics when it happens. Skye will be surrounded by people who look like she does; people who speak a language Skye is still learning.

She will not be looking for her mother. A few people will assume that must be her motive for joining the program and coming here; Skye will even believe it herself for a few moments. It makes some sense; searching for her origins. But then she will rehearse the reasons which led her to this place and this time: the war and the ways she could be both unobtrusive and useful. And she will recall her mothers, Angie and Rachel, who taught her the significance of work, and so much else. She will wonder: Why would she need another mother, when she already had two?

She will not be looking to become a mother. A few people will assume that must be her motive for coming here; Skye will not believe that herself, not even for a few moments. It made no sense; go back and find a husband? She will insist upon the events which led her to this place and this time: the love and the ways she could be both careless and carefree. And she will think often of her lovers, Akia and Domingo, who taught her the costs of love, and so much else. She will wonder: Why should she need birth control with one and not the other?

When the pains start to tear through her, more sudden and more extreme than she anticipated, she will stand up. She will think only of water. Not drinking it, but being drunk by it. She will want water as she has never wanted anything else. Anything else.

Her baby will be born near the river. Skye will be streaming wet, slightly salty, and somewhat muddy, from her plunge. The stars will shift in the October sky. The midwife, arriving to sever the cord, will look deep into Skye's dark eyes. Together, they will choose a name for the child.

Rachel will call this the "terrible year." She will say it with a certain trepidation at first, as if invoking the memory will renew its pain. But soon it will become obvious that such a phrase is an accomplishment. A talisman of perspective, of distance. The ability to refer to the past means that the past is behind one.

They will take a trip; as long as October and as far as the other coast. On motorcycles. Used German ones, bought from some dykes. And classic black leather jackets, worn softer than any attorney's appointment book, bought from a factory outlet store.

They will ride. Through Indiana. Through Dakota, North and South. Through coal country and silver country, where the mines fill with water whenever it floods. Through the hills and the deserts.

They will make love. Tired and still vibrating from the road. Sometimes before they have showered. And sometimes after. And sometimes both.

They will buy scenic postcards mass-produced from color photographs. Devil's Tower. The Great Salt Lake. Seals at Monterey. The Petrified Forest. An Idaho Potato. They will send them to their offices. To Skye in Central America. To Claire. To each other.

Angie will navigate. She will know exactly where they are and where they have been and when they should arrive at where they are going. She will keep the maps in her knapsack and consult them religiously. She will be tracing her finger along a dotted route one night in a bar when a woman she will think she recognizes will approach. The battered jukebox will be playing an old Stones song, asking "Ain't it good to be alive?" Angie will hum.

"Do you know your name?" the nurse asks.

"Tell this woman your name," Rachel coaxes.

Angie opens her mouth, her teeth bent with blood, bubbles of polluted river water still on her tongue. And she answers the nurse's question with a name. And then another name.

The nurse looks at Rachel as if for an explanation. Rachel mouths the word "mother" to the nurse.

Angie struggles to open her mouth again. The names spill out. Syllables slurred with river water.

Rachel nods to the nurse, as if to tell her that maybe the answers are right, or at least not as wrong as the nurse might assume.

Her mother. What her mother named her. Her daughter. What she almost named her. Her client, a mother who may have murdered her child. Her client's mother, the one who supported her, and another client's mother, the one who cursed her and called her names.

The nurse is persistent in her quest to document coherence. "Do you know what year it is, dear? Do you know where you are?"

Angie's swollen lips recede from her broken teeth. She swallows, struggling against the eddies of blood.

"Here." She says finally. "Now."

## ACKNOWLEDGMENTS

I have been fortunate to receive both support and critique from many intelligent sources, including: my editor, Keith Kahla, my agent, Laurie Liss, Victoria Brownworth, Joyce McConnell, Marge Piercy, Sima Rabinowitz, S. E. Valentine.

LOCAL
AUTHOR

## DATE DUE

| | | | |
|---|---|---|---|
| | | | |
| | | | |
| | | | |
| | | | |
| | | | |
| | | | |
| | | | |
| | | | |
| | | | |
| | | | |
| | | | |
| | | | |
| | | | |

JUL  - '00

DCB